Destiny's Gold

Captain Jane Thorn Series: Book One

Pamela Grimm

Published in Australia in 2018 by SisterShip Press Pty Ltd

Part of SisterShip Magazine, NSW, Australia
www.sistershippress.com

Printed and bound in Australia by SisterShip Press Pty Ltd

National Library of Australia data:

SisterShip Press Pty Ltd, 2018, Destiny's Gold

ISBN: 978-0-6484283-3-6

Also available as an ebook, ISBN: 978-0-6484283-2-9

In collaboration with SisterShip Magazine

www.sistershippress.com
www.sistershipmagazine.com

For my mother,
who inspires me every day
to steer my own ship on the grand ocean of life.

CONTENTS

I
First Day Muster

New York Harbor
May, 1820

"We're going to have trouble with that one, Captain."

Captain Thorn turned to look at the man in question. Tall and broad-shouldered, he seemed healthy and strong enough. With the jaunty air of the seasoned sailor, he was tossing water barrels to one of the ship's boys, who rolled them down the ramp into the hold.

"Seems hardy enough, Mister Galsworthy. Where's the trouble lie?"

"I don't like the look of him Captain. Especially when ye came on deck this morning and he seemed right put out that the rumors were true."

Galsworthy twisted his cap in his hands as he muttered the last bit. He never liked reminding the captain that the master of the schooner *Destiny* was gossiped about in every east coast port from Maine to New York.

"The rumor that we're sailing short-handed to Cuba? Or that I really do wear a skirt under my greatcoat?"

"Yes ma'am. The, well, the skirt thing, if you don't mind my saying," Galsworthy choked out. Sometimes he thought it would all be easier if she would just pretend to be a man, the way so many seafaring women did.

"Well, he won't be the first son of a sea cook to swallow his opinions for the sake of a generous pay packet."

Jane Thorn, master of the schooner *Destiny* out of New York, found that muster week helped reveal the weaknesses in the new crew. Insubordination, laziness, ineptitude, the three deadly sins of the sailor, reared their heads quickly when recruits were put through their paces the first week aboard. Men who had looked strong and hearty on the dock, and came with good references, showed their true mettle once aboard and sent aloft to repair the rigging.

Under the watchful eye of Second Mate Galsworthy, the men had been rousted out of their hammocks at dawn to start preparing the *Destiny* for departure. During the next seven days, they would either come together as a crew, or be put ashore to find another berth. Captain Thorn didn't much care which as long as the men who made up the final roll were competent, loyal, hardworking; and of course, willing to serve under a woman. The days spent in port preparing for the voyage gave her a chance to find out which of the new hands would be able to accept her as captain, and which would never be able to bring themselves to bow to her command.

Turning to face Galsworthy, she asked, "What is it about him that gives you pause?"

"When he got a good look at ye, he curled his lip and whispered to that fella in the red shirt over there. I suspect Seaman Fairchild has little respect for a captain who pisses settin' down. Ma'am."

Fighting to keep her laughter under control, the captain looked out over the crew hard at work stowing provisions for the coming voyage. The *Destiny* had arrived at her home berth on New York's East River in April expecting to change out the coastal crew for a new set of hands more experienced in the sailing routes between Europe and the United States. She had taken on a ballast load of logwood a week ago, and would be ready to head for the sugar plantations of Cuba as soon as she was fully crewed and her shipping orders had arrived. She was making good use of the interval to effect a number of minor repairs to the spars and rails caused by a storm that caught them as they were making a run for home earlier in the month. Squalls in the north Atlantic didn't usually cause trouble in April, but it seemed like the trade winds had moved up early this year. Jane hoped that wasn't a harbinger of things to come, or the trip up the Atlantic current on the way to St. Petersburg would be more exciting than usual.

"Well, let us see what he's got to say for himself. Bring him to my quarters."

Jane was glad to go below and escape the turmoil of the deck. Once at sea, the *Destiny* settled into a quiet routine of watch rotations and sightings. But here in port, the sheer amount of work to be done in a very few days meant the ship was teeming with port officials, delivery men, shop runners, lawyers, insurance brokers, and all of their various assistants, clerks, and other hangers-on. Seeing to the cargo and preparing for departure was the responsibility of the first mate, but Jane found it helpful to set foot aboard from time to time as the work progressed. The chaos, though, was enough to drive a sane woman mad.

In the saloon, which served as the navigation station as well as the officers' mess, Jane found First Mate Dawkins hard at work on the ship's manifest. Bent over the table, Dawkins was running his hands through his graying hair as he scratched away at the numbers. With his long legs folded under the carved table and his hair standing on end, he reminded Jane of the gray herons who populated the marshes along the Hudson. He looked up distractedly as she closed the door and turned up the lantern that hung from a bracket above.

"Leave it for now, Mister Dawkins. I've got a seaman to interview. And better have the cash box handy. I don't think he's staying."

"Aye, ma'am. Which one is it?"

"Fairchild. I know you thought he might be worth a trial, but it seems his attitude may be lacking in proper deference to the captain. Unless that landshark Sculley can find a replacement, I am afraid we shall still be down a sailor for the coastal leg, and I had hoped to beat the weather around Hatteras."

Crawling the docks of ports large and small, landsharks scoured the coasts seeking mariners to sign aboard their clients' ships. Jane had lost many a good man to the enticing offers held out by Sculley and his ilk, and was no fan of the system. But times were changing and her family had to change with them or lose their business. Sculley had helped fill out her crew for this voyage, but had come up one man short in the end. As a result, Dawkins had been happy to consider the employment of seaman Fairchild when he had appeared at the *Destiny's* side the evening before, asking to see the first mate. Dawkins had taken a long, hard look at Fairchild's papers and credentials, and the letter of recommendation he carried from an old acquaintance of the captain's, before deciding to give him a chance. Like the other new recruits, Dawkins had hired him for one week to help prepare the vessel for departure. Should Fairchild prove to be a competent hand, he would sign articles for the voyage with the rest of the men at the end of the week. However, if things went as Jane suspected in the next few minutes, they would soon be short one more able seaman with little time to find a replacement.

A sharp knock on the door brought the second mate into the cabin with Fairchild hard at his heels. Jane could see the insolent laughter in the sailor's eyes as he straightened up to his full six-foot height and affected something like a half-salute in her direction. Curious to find out just how much cockiness he thought he could get away with, she waited calmly until he pulled his eyes off the floor and tried staring her down. A lot of cockiness, apparently.

"Fairchild, is it?"

"Yes sir. Ma'am. Sir."

"You may call me ma'am. If I remember correctly, you came to us with a strong letter of recommendation from Captain Jamison of the *Betsy Lee*. William and I have been friends since childhood, and he knows my preferences in men."

Fairchild had obviously interpreted her reference to "men" on a more personal level, as witnessed by the smirk that ghosted around the corners of his mouth.

"What I mean to say, is that Captain Jamison is well aware of my demands for competence and loyalty, and a positive attitude with regard to the unconventional nature of the officers aboard this vessel. Perhaps you can enlighten me as to why he might have considered you suitable to my command, Fairchild."

"I had the pleasure of serving under Captain Jamison during

his last run from Montreal. He spoke kindly of my skills as helmsman during the voyage, and he hoped that I might be of able service aboard the *Destiny*, sir. Ma'am."

"I see. I understand from Mister Galsworthy that you had some comments this morning at muster. Perhaps we could prevail upon you to share those thoughts with us."

Appearing to consider his options, Fairchild looked around the cabin at the assembled officers. As rumor had it, the captain did indeed wear a skirt under her greatcoat, which along with her fine features and an auburn plait cascading nearly to her waist, made it clear that the master of the *Destiny* was without doubt a woman. But her erect stature and firm brow bespoke a determined captain who had the clear loyalty of the mates who were regarding Fairchild now with unconcealed hostility.

"Ma'am, I was remarking on the general seaworthiness of this fine vessel. And our great fortune to sail with her..."

"Enough! Mister Dawkins, pay the man off and see him ashore."

Jane's patience had run out. Like many others before him, Fairchild thought that a woman would countenance insubordination because she had few choices in crew. He was wrong. Her reputation as a skilled navigator and steady master in the coastal trade meant that many experienced mariners were willing to put aside their prejudices and sign on to sail aboard the *Destiny*.

Reaching into the cashbox, Dawkins extracted a week's wages for an able seaman and handed the coins to Fairchild with a sigh. The captain's penchant for fair play meant that the promise of a cash bonus for the muster week would be honored. Even for a worthless wharf rat who had worked less than a day.

"Shift yer legs, man," Galsworthy growled as he opened the cabin door.

Bending his head to pass through it, Fairchild took the opportunity to scan the captain from head to toe. With a wide grin, he winked at her, and was gone.

II

Anchors Aweigh

The morning breeze cut sharply across the flats of the New Jersey marshlands to the west as Jane stood on the quarterdeck listening to Mister Dawkins direct the men. All hands had been called above at two bells of the morning watch to prepare for weighing anchor. With any luck, they would catch a northerly coming down the Hudson as they rode the morning tide out of the harbor. The bustling port in the East River had come alive early as other captains sought to make the most of the strong spring current, and Jane wanted to be well out of the channel before the larger ships began the complicated process of getting under way. At 350 tons and 130 feet on deck, the *Destiny* was not a small schooner, but she was dwarfed by many of the tall brigs and frigates that cluttered the waterfront and river. The last thing she wanted was for one of them to come crashing aboard.

"Prepare to hoist the jib!" Dawkins' bellow cut across the sounds of the busy port. As they were planning to catch the early ebb at the front of the pack, he was pushing the men to run from task to task.

An hour earlier, the harbor pilot had come aboard and was now standing forward of the helm. The Thorns had nurtured their contacts with the Sandy Hook pilots over the years, and a message to them the evening before asking for an early departure had been met with a promise of one of their best men joining them in ample time to catch the outgoing tide. Mister Soames' yawl had appeared in due course out of the morning mists and he had been hoisted over the side along with his latest apprentice.

"Heave short!" The foredeck crew rammed home the capstan bars and prepared to pull the *Destiny* downriver until she floated over her port bow anchor. As soon as the tide turned, they would heave the anchor and set sail on a broad reach with the wind on the starboard quarter. It was a tricky maneuver in tight quarters, but would give them a jump on the larger vessels if they could pull it off.

Perched on the near end of the *Destiny's* eighteen-foot jib boom, Galsworthy peered down at the anchor chain, waiting for it to draw slack.

"Heave ho!" came the call, and the men bent their backs to the work, pushing the bars around the capstan as one of the hands led them in a rousing chorus of *Maid of Amsterdam*.

"Anchors aweigh!" rang out as the flukes cleared the bottom and the *Destiny* began to move with the outgoing tide.

"Hoist the jib! Helm to windward!" The orders were coming fast as Jane watched her crew move nimbly to execute Mister Dawkins' commands. Over the past week, these seven sailors had come together under the firm hand of the chief, and Jane felt a shiver of pride and anticipation as the sails filled and they began the long tack down the harbor and out into the Atlantic.

What had started as a trying few days with the dismissal of the insufferable Fairchild had not improved as the time in port wore on. While at the dock, the crew had moved swiftly to stow casks of fresh water, sea bread, salt beef, cheese, and butter in the hold, and to load crates of fresh vegetables and fruits into the galley. The men were glad to see that they would eat well during the ten-day run to Cuba. Three days of hard toil had seen the vessel provisioned for departure earlier than anticipated, and Jane and the crew were eager to get underway.

Then, on the fourth day, she received word from Messrs. Bernard & Banks, the cargo brokers, that a special consignment of luxury textiles from the new mills in Lowell was on its way from Boston. The New England mills were turning out products to rival the best that England or France had to offer, and they hoped to expand their markets abroad. The schooner was to wait at anchor until it arrived, delaying their departure for another three days. Impatient to be off on the first long voyage entrusted to her by the family shipping firm, the young captain had used the time to check and recheck her navigation plan for the trip. She also pestered her officers with questions about the fitness of the crew, the status of several minor rigging repairs, the condition of the ballast and cargo, and a dozen other matters.

Eventually, an exasperated Mister Dawkins asked if there were perhaps any final arrangements to be made at the shipping office prior to their departure. Not one to ignore a hint, Jane turned her attention toward home and made use of her final days in port to visit with friends and family. The following days spent ensconced in the elegance of her uncle's home waiting for the merchant house's final direction for the cargo were a torture for Jane. While the sumptuous house was a second home for her, it now felt like a gilded cage. Long evenings in the bosom of her family were delightful, but her mind was already in the middle of the north Atlantic.

When the final orders were at last delivered to her on May the seventh, Jane was dismayed to learn that the *Destiny* would pick up a smaller load of sugar in Havana than anticipated. The trade route from Cuba to Russia and back to New York had recently opened to American vessels, and Thorn Shipping and Cargo Company was determined to win a substantial portion of the business. Sailing for the Baltic with a partially filled hold would make the trip more costly and profits leaner.

Bursting into her uncle's den waving the orders above her head, Jane demanded, "Can they do that? Just cut my load at the last hour? Surely they knew we were offering favorable terms because they would stand for the whole cargo!"

Josias Thorn, long accustomed to his outspoken niece, smiled at her from behind his desk as he reached out to take the offending papers from her.

It had taken some doing to talk Jane's father, Richard, into sending his younger daughter on this transatlantic run, but she had proven her mettle in the coastal trade. At nearly twenty-four, Jane had been working the family's fleet of sloops on the Hudson River, and up and down the eastern seaboard, for ten years. The hardy men she sailed with had taught her well, shaping her into an able sailor and captain.

With their recent purchase of four sturdy schooners, Thorn Shipping was branching out into international waters, carrying cargo from abroad to the growing domestic markets. When they sought captains for their new fleet, Jane had put herself forward.

"I have as much time on deck as any of those other masters," she pointed out at the company meeting. "And besides, it will be good for the firm to have one of the family in command."

Josias' brother had finally come around when the other family members, including Jane's elder sister Prudence, could see no objection to her taking on the schooner. He made only one stipulation before allowing her to spread her wings and take on the challenge of the Atlantic trade, however.

"You've got to take Galsworthy with you. Ezra will see you right, and keep you out of trouble while you learn the way. He's had the teaching of you all these years, and it will be good to have a familiar face aboard."

"Aye, that it will," Josias agreed. "And I am thinking of sending Dawkins along as chief to show you the ropes. He's sailed that route for a dog's age and can help you keep the course."

Opening the orders, Josias now read quickly through the cargo manifest. Jane was right; those bastards Bernard & Banks had shorted them on the tonnage. The only way he could see to make up the difference and preserve the financial success of the trip was to carry sugar on their own and sell it at market price in St. Petersburg. They would have to extend their credit with the bank in Havana to do it, but he couldn't see any other solution at such short notice.

"You shall just have to buy on our behalf and do your best at the other end. It may delay you a couple of days in the Baltic, but there you have it. Sorry, Jinks, but that's the way of it sometimes."

Watching the shore slide past as they finally left the dock, Jane shifted her thoughts away from the close-knit family she was leaving behind for six months. It was time to turn her mind to the coming voyage and the need to make it a success. As she looked out over the bow from her place on the quarter deck she suddenly noticed an odd movement out of the corner of her eye. Waiting another few seconds to be sure, she shouted to the pilot, who was now standing at the foremast.

"Mister Soames, is that vessel adrift?"

Soames peered over the starboard rail and then bolted aft, calling to Griggs at the helm, "Hard over! Hard over! She's heading straight for us!"

Before the *Destiny* could turn away, the wayward sloop, unmanned and unmoored, crashed into the starboard bow, sending a shudder through her and tossing men to the deck.

"Bear away! Bear away!" Back on his feet, Soames was lurching again toward the helm while Galsworthy mustered the men at the rail with spars to push off the intruder. Long minutes later, they had drifted away from danger without evident damage to the *Destiny's* hull. The crew, though, had not fared as well, with several men complaining of bumps and bruises. One sailor, a salty fellow named Tyne off the Grand Banks fishing fleet, had been thrown against the capstan and appeared to have broken a rib or two.

"Mister Dawkins, give the order to heave to and drop anchor. We shall get this man ashore and assess the damage." Jane knew that the captain's first duty was to the souls aboard, and she would lose another day in harbor rather than endanger a single man. Within minutes, the bow anchors had been dropped with a splash and the small boat launched to take the injured man ashore along with Galsworthy, Soames and the apprentice.

Later that morning, the second mate returned to the *Destiny* without the wounded sailor.

"Bad news, ma'am. Doc says Tyne's punctured a lung as well as broke a couple 'a ribs. He's off the muster and we're down another man."

Now, this was bad news indeed. Her skeleton crew of eight was reduced to six and they needed to fill at least one of the two empty berths before the schooner left port.

"Mister Dawkins, pray take Mister Galsworthy with you and see if you can scare up a man or two at the hiring hall. I should like to make the morning tide tomorrow, if you please." Resigning herself to another day in New York, Jane turned and went below to go over her plotted course one more time.

The *Destiny's* voyage would start with the run down the eastern seaboard to Cuba. Mostly within a few miles of the coast, the trip would eventually take them off Cape Hatteras and out around the barrier islands where the shifting sands of the Diamond Shoals, along with the low-lying islands, made for a treacherous passage. Just six weeks earlier, the *Islington* had been blown ashore and wrecked on the cape. All aboard had survived, but it was a sobering reminder that trying to dodge the currents along the coast was a perilous business.

Adding to Jane's worry about the weather was the knowledge that the yellow fever season in Cuba was beginning to advance. Already subject to being detained for quarantine at the toll station in Elsinore, reports of a major pestilence in the West Indies would encourage the health authorities in Denmark to delay their passage into the Baltic by many weeks, and each day of delay increased the cost of crew and provisions. It was imperative that their voyage be prosecuted with all possible dispatch. Jane knew that her reputation as a successful master in the transatlantic trade was riding on her ability to make this voyage pay off handsomely, and she was determined to see it through and sail home in glory.

It had just gone eight bells on the afternoon watch when Jane climbed back onto the deck to clear her head. Looking to the west, she saw the *Destiny's* skiff headed out from shore with the sturdy second mate at the oars. A lifetime aboard the trading fleet had turned Galsworthy into a compact sailor, half a head shorter than Jane but all tattoo-covered brawn. With long, efficient strokes, he moved the small craft swiftly along. Dawkins in the stern was helping steer around the many river obstacles, shouting out in his clipped Yankee accent.

"Avast there! Ye'll have our heads off if ye' don't come to starboard and quick!"

Squinting to catch sight of the third man in the bow, Jane gasped. No, it couldn't be. The closer the boat drew, however, the clearer it became that the single seaman her damnable officers had managed to round up in all of the great wide city of New York, was none other than that confounded scallywag Fairchild.

III

Back Aboard

"Explain yourselves, gentlemen," Jane demanded.

Dawkins and Galsworthy had left the returning recruit to cool his heels on the deck and followed their captain below. Jane was careful not to display signs of disagreement among the officers in front of the crew, but she set a swift pace to her cabin once her mates had climbed back aboard the *Destiny*.

"Are you set to tell me that there were no other seamen in the whole of New York who were willing and able to sign on? And what godforsaken hole did you dig him out of? Did you think to speak with me before bringing that grinning bastard back aboard?" For the love of God, what were you thinking?"

Jane's tirade lost some of its menace given that it was delivered in a loud whisper, albeit with much gesturing and waving about of arms. Her two mates, standing awkwardly just inside the closed saloon door, exchanged glances while waiting for her to run out of steam. Eventually, Dawkins laid Fairchild's articles on the mess table and drew himself up.

"This had better be good," Jane crossed her arms and looked directly at them.

"Yes ma'am, we did consider your feelings in the matter before bringing the man," Dawkins said. "The long and short of it is that we could not find another suitable man in the hiring halls. Unless you were looking for someone with a peg leg or half an arm, there was not a hale and hearty sailor in the pitiful bunch on offer. Galsworthy and I had given up our quest and were headed back to the *Destiny* when Fairchild accosted us outside the tavern. Turns out he had not found a new berth and heard we were looking. He wondered if we would plead his case with ye. Those articles there are not signed, and won't be until ye give the say-so. Ma'am."

The silence that followed this explanation stretched uncomfortably long while Jane pondered her next move.

"If I might, ma'am?"

"Yes, Mister Galsworthy?"

"His transgression was of the milder sort, and he is willing to apologize to ya' and beg yer pardon," Galsworthy said.

"Did he say that himself?" Jane was skeptical.

"He did indeed, and was right gentlemanly about it, ma'am."

Jane paused a moment to consider. "All right. Fetch him below, but don't let him think I am mollified because I most surely am not."

A moment later, a knock on the saloon door announced the return of the second mate with a hangdog Fairchild in tow. Lest he consider her an easy mark, Jane stood squarely with her arms crossed and a frown fixed firmly to her brow.

"Here we are again, Mister Fairchild. My mates tell me that I ought to listen to your tale before throwing you off my vessel again. So, have at it."

Keeping his eyes firmly glued to the floor this time, Fairchild cleared his throat and spoke quietly. "My sincere apology ma'am for my unwitting remarks and disrespectful attitude the other morning. I would be most grateful if you would consider me a changed man and your most loyal servant. Ma'am."

The captain didn't believe it for a minute, and she could tell that neither of her mates were swayed in his favor either. However, she was dangerously short-handed at this point, and the journey to Havana would take just over a week. If he proved more trouble than he was worth, they could put Fairchild ashore in Cuba and find another man.

"I shall make a bargain with you, Mister Fairchild. I shall take you on for the passage to Havana, and if you prove your mettle, mind your tone with the crew, and show yourself an able sailor, we can then see what is what when we arrive. Fair enough?" Jane's stern tone didn't seem to make the man cower, but neither did he show any of his earlier cockiness. This might work if Galsworthy kept an eye on him.

"I am most grateful, ma'am." With that, Fairchild signed his name to the articles lying on the desk and left the cabin with a short salute. Galsworthy followed him out the door with a nod to Jane and a somber look upon his broad face.

As he filed the signed articles among the crew's papers, Dawkins watched Jane pace the cabin. Clearly, the corner she felt herself backed into was chafing at her. He would never undermine her authority by questioning her actions or offering an opinion, even if he agreed with her. Not only was he bound by law not to usurp her right as master of the vessel to assert her will, but he had been tasked by her uncle to help her without stepping on her toes. This decision to sign the troublesome Fairchild was hers and hers alone. May she not live to regret it.

Later that night, Jane found herself pulling those same articles out of the filing chest along with Fairchild's sea papers. Alan, he was called, and he hailed from Ottawa of all places. What was a Canadian doing seeking a billet on an American vessel? It had been a short five years since the peace with Britain had been ratified after the border skirmishes in the north, and pro-British feeling still ran high in the Tory provinces along the border. Surely he could have found a place on one of the many ships flying the Union Jack as they plied up and down the American coast.

Shaking her head, Jane replaced the papers and climbed into her berth. As she blew out the lantern hanging above her on the bulkhead, she could hear the tread of the watch pacing the deck above. In the morning, they would make another attempt to leave the port of New York and head south. She hoped there were no more delays in store, and no more troublesome sailors to think about as she fell asleep.

IV

Making Southing

Tuesday, May 9, 1820   Passed Sandy Hook at noon. Pilot left us. Winds moderate NW Sandy Hook. SSW about 2 miles from which I take my departure. Lat. (chart) 40° 30'N Long. (chart) 74° 00'W. One man injured and sent ashore during dep.

The following morning saw the captain at the rail as the pilot arrived and once again the crew executed the familiar drill to get under way. The breeze had freshened over the last twenty-four hours, blowing steadily from the north, so picking up a starboard tack and slipping through the channel was a simple matter.

By midmorning, they were out in the bay and making the most of the *Destiny's* sleek hull and generous canvas to pull away from the trading fleet leaving the harbor on the early tide. When they passed the bar at Sandy Hook and Mister Soames clambered over the side to jump down into his pilot's yawl, Jane made sure that his coat pocket was suitably filled with a bottle of her favorite port.

The first day at sea was dedicated to tightening the vessel. As the *Destiny* rolled over the swell and shifted tack, logs not firmly secured, cask lids insufficiently tightened, hammocks and sea bags improperly stowed, all caused a ruckus below as they were flung about. Sailors scrambled to tie down, tighten, batten and stow everything that had moved, leaving the schooner a tight vessel as she flew across the waves.

On deck, the watches fell easily into their customary rhythm, and Jane and her chief mate were able to take a noon sighting as the sun shone in a clear blue sky. Earlier in the morning, she had taken a land bearing and confirmed their position on her charts. It gave her a sense of satisfaction as she saw that the *Destiny* was making good time at an average speed of over eight knots. Perhaps she would beat the bigger ships to Cuba after all despite her being forced to cool her heels for an extra day in New York. Pushing to keep as straight a line as possible, adjusting the heading as the wind shifted, and refiguring her course, Jane kept herself busy throughout the first watches.

As the first day wore away, Mister Galsworthy had kept the crew busy establishing the watch routines. Cookie was hard at work turning out a simple but filling noonday meal in the galley at the fore of the deckhouse, while the ship's carpenter, Koopmans, perched on the starboard rail and worked at fixing several large blocks that had split in the storm the ship had weathered in April off Nantucket. The replacements had been installed during muster week, but the carpenter always liked to have extra rigging on hand.

By the end of the afternoon watch, the captain saw that all was in general good order on deck and she asked Dawkins to call the men aft. Once they were assembled, she climbed to the top of the stairs that led to the quarterdeck and looked out over her crew. Her two mates, Dawkins and Galsworthy, leaned against the starboard rail, the latter chewing a plug of tobacco as he stood with his arms crossed, while the two green boys, Robert Boniface and Billy Hitchens, were perched on the top of the afterhouse with their legs swinging as they elbowed each other. At fourteen and sixteen, they were old to be starting to sea, but Jane refused to have younger boys on her crew. Watching after them was too much like being their mother. These two lads, who were sons of Josias' business acquaintances, hoped to make nautical careers.

At the back of the bunch, Cookie and Koopmans kept busy with their hands while they listened. They had known the captain many years, and she could count on them to fulfill their duties taking care of the men and the vessel. Aside from Mister Galsworthy, they were the only two crewmembers who had been with Jane during her years in the coastal trade, and she was glad to have them aboard.

The rest of the crew were newcomers and Jane was eager to learn their strengths and weaknesses. Which ones could be sent aloft in a storm to cut loose a flapping sail? Which would do only what they were ordered to do, and which would seek out extra duties to pass the time? Above all, which of the men would earn the respect of the officers and their fellow men, and which would give sullen service and destroy the morale of the crew? If she and Mister Dawkins had read the recruits well, they had a hardy bunch who would make quick work of the business of sailing the schooner. If not, they would be fighting the problem till the end of the voyage.

"All right, men," she began, "we are finally off and you made a good job of it in the end. I should like to thank you all for signing on. We mean to make a lucky and profitable venture of this trip and see you all home with your skins whole and your pockets fat."

At this, a cheer went up from the men and Jane had to wave her hands to quiet them. She continued,

"We are bound for Cuba as our first port of call. We have a contract to pick up sugar, and will see to loading some for ourselves as well. That should give you something extra in your pay packet if we get a good price."

Another cheer interrupted her speech, and Jane waved again to settle them so she could finish.

"We have heard there may be fever in Havana, so we will make quick work of the cargo when we are there. I fear we may need to limit shore leave if the epidemic is raging, but I aim to make it up to you on the other side. Dawkins and Galsworthy here can be counted on to see you right with the work, and Cookie will keep your bellies well filled. Do your work, do it well and swiftly, and we will all arrive home by and by with gifts for our sweethearts and money to put in the bank."

A loud Huzzah. greeted this final remark, after which Jane thanked them once more and ordered her chief to dismiss the men to their duties. It was all Jane could do to keep a calm demeanor in front of the crew as she was feeling giddy with excitement inside. She was honored that her family placed their trust in her, and aimed to do well by them. But overriding her business sense at this moment was sheer joy at setting out to sea toward unknown horizons.

Wednesday, May 10 Lat. Obs. 38° 50'N Long. DR 74° 18'W Pleasant weather, moderate winds from SE, all sails set, people employed variously.

Steady winds carried the *Destiny* down the coast on their second day at sea. Galsworthy had the men busy swabbing the deck and polishing the brass when they weren't set to making small stuff or splicing rope. Unlike many captains, Jane did not expect the crew to work in silence and always enjoyed the sound of the old shanties the men sang as they went about their tasks. Fairchild showed himself the possessor of a fine tenor voice with a good ear for a tune, and the men were happy to let him lead the singing. More than once, Jane caught herself leaning a little too close to hear the words of a sad ballad, and rushed away in embarrassment when Fairchild would look up and directly into her gaze.

Jane knew the ways of men on the prowl. She had many years of practice holding off would-be suitors. While Galsworthy had helped hold the men aboard her family's fleet in line, her figure had drawn much attention in the ports she frequented over the years. It was important that her own rectitude of conduct never be called into question, and Jane had simply found it best to take a firm tone with any men who sought to gain favor, but she was finding that somewhat difficult to maintain in Fairchild's presence. Ever vigilant of the need to maintain the distance of command, Jane was nevertheless finding herself roaming the deck periodically throughout the day to see to the work that was being done.

Standing with Dawkins at the stern rail that afternoon after returning from her latest sojourn forward, Jane finally pulled herself up short. Her place was here by the helm, not interfering with the men under Galsworthy's command. She would have to rein in her impulses and make sure she kept to her station from now on.

V

Family and Friends

Thursday, May 11 Lat. Obs. 36° 42'N Long. DR 75° 02'W First part light winds from E. Tacked ship to S. Later stiff breezes from NNE. Heavy seas, rain in abundance, squally. Capt's birthday observed.

Jane was somber when she awoke at dawn. Today was her twenty-fourth birthday, and the ache of distant friends and relations felt particularly keen. As she sat down to the sparse breakfast in her cabin, she contemplated the price paid by the long distance seafarer. Leaving the bosom of her family for weeks at a time on her northern trading trips was as nothing compared to the many months that would pass before she sailed back up the Hudson River to the dock below her father's house in Newburgh. Getting out of her bunk and wrapping herself in her shawl, she sighed and hoped that the dear ones at home were missing her as sorely as she was missing them.

"Ma'am, are you presentable?" The query was accompanied by a gentle knock on the cabin door, followed by its swift opening at her assent. To her surprise, Dawkins bounded in with a broad grin, Galsworthy tight on his heels. The two of them seemed to be hiding something behind their backs to judge from the awkward positions they took up to her left and right.

"Whatever that is you've got in your grimy mitts, you'd better hand it over. And pray it's not another of those grotesqueries you've pulled out of the fishing nets, Mister Galsworthy. I would not be amused this morning." As a girl, Jane had often been the brunt of jokes among the crew involving various flora and fauna discovered stuck into the anchor chains and trolling lines. They learned quickly that she was squeamish about anything remotely resembling a snake and delighted in pulling pranks on her that largely featured eels in unusual locations, such as her berth.

With a flourish and a bow, Dawkins presented Jane with a stack of letters neatly tied with a large red ribbon. Galsworthy, not to be outdone, doffed his cap and sank to his knee as he held out a small cedarwood box in his weatherworn hand.

"Many happy returns of the day, Captain! And may you live a long and prosperous life. Huzzah! Huzzah! Huzzah!" The generous good nature of the lively greeting brought Jane to her feet. Throwing herself into the arms of the two mates, she allowed herself a few tears of happiness as she swiftly embraced them and then stepped back.

"And," added Galsworthy as he climbed back to his feet, "the men asked that we greet you on their behalf when we announced the occasion at the watch change this morning."

"You render me quite undone, sirs, and I am grateful for that." Jane's voice broke as she gathered the letters and gift in her hands. "And how have you come by these treasures, may I ask?"

"Your good uncle had them delivered while you were ashore, ma'am. I think you'll find correspondence there from your family and friends, all with directions to be delivered on your birthday. We have fulfilled the mission entrusted to us, and would like to suggest that you delay your appearance on the deck for a time in order to partake of the well wishes therein."

With that, Dawkins pushed Galsworthy back through the door and closed it gently behind him. Jane could hear them chuckling as they discussed the discomfited look on her face when she was sure it was another practical joke in the offing. Thank goodness there were no eels this morning.

Sitting back down in front of her breakfast, Jane cheerfully untied the bow and sorted quickly through the letters. Setting aside the thick letter from her sister Prudence, she opened a sweet note from her mother and father. Wishing her well on her adventure, and expressing confidence in her as a captain and sailor, Richard and Eliza Thorn had filled their letter with words of love and warmth that did much to brighten Jane's mood. She knew that her unconventional choices had been a worry to her mother, but her father's stalwart support and steady hand had brought her to a life she cherished aboard a vessel she adored. She thanked her stars for that every day.

Among the short missives from friends and relatives, Jane was pleased to see one bearing the name of E. Coffin. Friends since her childhood, she and Endeavor had shared a tender moment before she set off for New York and her new command. Her heart sped up a little as she broke the seal to read his words.

Dear Friend Jane,

Please forgive the greeting, if it is too formal for a communication between longstanding friends. As this is the first letter I have ever had occasion to write thee, there is no experience to guide me, other than good will and affection.

Perhaps it were better to begin with Dear Jane, Happy Birthday. There, thou hast succeeded in persuading me to acknowledge thy pagan practice of holiday celebration. Well I remember the indignant young lady demanding why she had no gift from me on the occasion of her ninth birthday. I fear the ensuing explanation of Friends' philosophy earned me no friend in that quarter. Fortune has provided years to correct that false beginning, for which I am earnestly grateful. Yet now, when I am honored to receive an invitation from Mother Thorn to observe the day, it will be without thee, to my great regret. I pray thee know that my earnest hope would be for our lives to draw closer even as thy path pulls thee away for a while.

May God favor thy voyage with fair winds, profitable and honorable commerce, and a swift return.

With fondest regards, I remain yours,
Endeavor Coffin

With a smile at Endeavor's plain style of speaking, Jane folded the letter and set it aside. She appreciated the peaceful nature and strong sense of moral right he displayed in the practice of his Quaker faith. Beguiling foreigners were an interesting distraction, but cherished friendships would stand the test of time.

Destiny's Gold

Picking up the last packet now, Jane settled down to read Pru's news from home and what was sure to be good sisterly advice.

My Dearest Little Sister,

I am feeling a little sentimental this morning, as I try to write a birthday letter for you. And perhaps I am wanting just a bit, to remind the High and Mighty Captain that she does have a life here at home with her family. It will be strange not to see you at the table, even as my son Silas cuts the cake alone for the first time. It never seemed a large thing, that you were always home on your birthday, what with your river trips being short, and the coastal voyages somehow always fitting around the date. It is strange, how dates, or even days, take on significance. That my first-born should have arrived on the very date of your 10th birthday, marked that date forever in red on my calendar. At least my seafaring husband is home for a while. I'm sure William will hold his son's attention in your absence.

It seems Mama has invited Endeavor Coffin to join us for the birthday dinner. I saw him yesterday as I returned from the apothecary with Mama's tonic, and had to tell him all I knew about your doings since you left for New York. He was most anxious to know the expected date of your departure for Havana, as he was writing a letter himself, and wanted to be certain to finish in time. I had to promise to include it with this one when it goes. Jinks, I hope you understand that young man, who is not really so young, clearly has hopes for you. You haven't told me if he has said anything, and you usually do tell me everything, so I suppose he's been admiring in silence. But do not mistake silence for lack of interest. You two have been such good friends for so long, you could be excused for failing to notice that he would like more.

Enough. Life will go on here on the Hudson, while you ply the high seas. Time enough when you return, to discuss your vision of the future.

There is little news here. The Ramsdell's ferry had to heave to and rescue a passenger's dog who had leapt overboard. Apparently the animal's mistress made such a furor that the captain was forced to order a boat lowered to chase the creature, who seemed determined to return to Beacon, regardless of its owner's desire to carry it to Newburgh. Father refuses to tell me the new nickname the ferry has acquired as a result, as I understand it is rather rude.

Silas would probably tell you the only important news is that Father has promised to give him command of the next sloop to Poughkeepsie. If all goes well, and I'm sure it will, there will be yet another Captain in the family. He has been on the river since before he could properly walk, and seems to think it his personal waterway.

Time for presents. You are invited to join us in eating cake – surely it would not be a proper birthday without cake! The package is from Mama. She would not tell me what it contains, only that it has languished too long in her box of treasures, and must now be put to proper use. Whatever she has selected I am certain it was to some purpose. I shall be consumed with curiosity until you return and tell me what and why and how!

My present to you is the promise of a new frock. Not one of those sturdy, sensible sea-going creations you insist we concoct together. This is to be a strictly shore-bound party frock, in a color to set off your lovely hair. The details will remain my secret until it can be unveiled for the proper occasion.

So dearest Jinks, Happy Birthday. Last Sunday Pastor Johnston closed the service with his usual solemn "May the Lord watch between me and thee, while we are absent one from the other." It has remained in my mind, as I contemplate the next months. Yes, Beloved Sister, may it be so.

Affectionately yours,
Pru

Wiping her eyes with the back of her sleeve, Jane straightened up in her chair. Pru's warm words were a tonic for a lonely heart. Curious now as to the contents of the box, she pried open the top to discover a loaf of rum-soaked plum cake that brought back memories of many a happy celebration as a child. Wrapped in oilcloth, she also discovered a lovely vial of French perfume. Pulling the stopper and holding it to her nose, Jane drew in the sweet smell of frangipani and jasmine. My goodness but she had never dared apply something so bold to her person before. She raised the stopper to her neck and dabbed a small drop behind each ear before replacing it and stowing the bottle in her sea chest. Feeling a tiny bit naughty, Jane drew herself up and prepared to face the rest of the day.

Much cheered from her hour with the birthday

correspondence, Jane dressed quickly and climbed the ladder to the quarterdeck. Seaman Griggs, a tough old salt they had picked up in Newport on their last trip south from Maine, stood at the helm. He had sought out the *Destiny* when she came ashore to land a cargo of dried fish from Penobscot, where the Mainers' talk had all been of their newfound status as one of the United States. Clad in his blue sailors' togs with a weather-beaten cap jammed down over his unkempt gray locks and an old pipe clenched firmly in the corner of his mouth, Griggs was the picture of the experienced sea hand.

To his right, Dawkins stood with his legs wide and his arms akimbo as he stared at the horizon with a frown. Looking past his shoulder, Jane could see the source of his worry. As the sun rose in the eastern sky, the clouds were colored a rosy hue that boded ill for mariners. The afternoon would start them on the swing that would take them around Cape Hatteras, and many a navigator had cut the bank here too closely only to founder on the shoals when a gale blew up. Jane had no intention of suffering a similar fate.

"The glass is falling this morning, ma'am. Like as not we shall see a blow before the day is over." Dawkins was less troubled than resigned as he issued this prediction. Leaving New York in early May meant they would be safely into the westerlies on the northern leg before the summer storms kicked up. But in the warmer waters of the Caribbean they were risking an early hurricane which could drive them far off course and endanger the vessel and her crew. Jane hoped her general good luck would hold and they would have smooth sailing down and back before heading east toward the north Atlantic.

On the foredeck, the men were unusually quiet as they went about their work. Seasoned mariners though most of them were, they had no experience of the young captain and her ability to navigate stormy weather and treacherous seas. Jane could see them watching her as they bent to their tasks, and kept her chin high and gaze steady. Turning to Dawkins, she commanded that the vessel be battened down and storm precautions taken. With most of the headsails taken in and the main reefed, the *Destiny* would lose speed, but she would run safely before a gale.

"Mister Dawkins, get the anchors loosed and ready to release. And make sure we have the extra haul line in the center of all of the booms."

Years of sailing through the narrows below Dunderberg Mountain on the Hudson had taught Jane to bridle her boat and ride it like a wild horse through the galloping current and swirling winds. A sailor hauling the booms from side to side as the variable winds shifted would help them ride out the storm. Should their luck not hold and they be blown toward shore, the crew would be ready to drop the anchors and slow their progress onto the shoals.

As the men scrambled to clear the deck, she watched Fairchild work to stow the heavy foresail and coil the sheets. Over the past two days, she had often caught him staring forward over the bow, lost in thought, when not entertaining the men with a song or story. She wondered what awaited him in Cuba, and had a thought that perhaps his presence aboard her vessel had greater import than a mere job for the mysterious Alan Fairchild of Ottawa.

Once the *Destiny* was ready for heavy weather, Galsworthy sent the port watch below to rest and eat. Keeping a crew in fighting trim was a job he took seriously, and he would not let his captain down by overtiring the men. Jane asked herself again if she had been too impatient to beat the fleet out of the harbor in pursuit of a commercial advantage. Perhaps she ought to have stayed another day or two and filled her final crew slot. Heading into a storm with so few men to handle the weighty spars and expanse of canvas carried by the schooner might be foolhardy. Nevertheless, she would have to make do with seven seamen, plus three officers and two non-watch standing crew, to see her through. At this point, she had no choice.

Two hours later, the starboard watch had taken the deck, and the weather still held off. The schooner was making excellent headway even under shortened sail, with the rushing seas under her hull and the thrum of the taught lines making for a thrilling ride. Jane took a noon sighting that put her within a hair's breadth of her dead reckoning latitude and showed continued good speed over ground. The wind had picked up slightly and lifted the schooner into a sustained rate of seven knots. Heeling slightly to starboard, the *Destiny* sliced through the water as she made her way south and east around the Outer Banks.

Jane paced the deck scanning the horizon. Watching and waiting had never been easy, and as the afternoon wore away and the light began to fade in the early evening, she scoured the low hills off the starboard bow searching for the Hatteras Light. The Gulf Stream swung close to the shore here, and the only way to make passage south was to thread the needle between the breakers off their windward beam and the northerly currents to the east. She knew that the Light was not to be trusted. It had been built so low, and the lamps were so weak, that it could often not be seen by passing vessels. She had Dawkins set a man as lookout for the tower even as they readied the lead to sound the bottom every five minutes.

As seven bells rang at the end of the first watch, the captain leaned over the starboard side amidships holding on to the pitching rail and squinting into the dark ahead. From behind, the freshening wind blew hair into her eyes as the anticipated squall finally prepared to make its appearance. Suddenly, the cool breeze turned warm as a quiet voice whispered into her ear.

"Happy birthday, sweet captain."

Stunned at the boldness, Jane froze for a moment before whirling around to see who had spoken. As she swung about, the first blast of the squall slammed into the starboard beam, throwing Jane to her knees when the *Destiny* shuddered under the onslaught from a new direction. By the time she had gotten her legs under her, the man had vanished.

"Call all hands, Mister Dawkins! Center the booms! Helm to starboard, hard over!" Jane bellowed her commands as the crew flew to their stations on the suddenly wet and slippery deck. The *Destiny's* nose swung to starboard as the crew released the main sheet and balanced the vessel with the wind coming over her starboard quarter. With reduced sail and little canvas forward of the foremast, the vessel was being driven from the center of her bulk, and hunkered securely into the waves as the gusty winds drove her forward. Throughout the next hour, the crew wrestled her booms back and forth across the deck as the wind sheared and gusted over 30 knots, always holding the wind well off her stern and wearing to keep the vessel away from the breakers they could hear crashing off the starboard beam.

Just as Jane was feeling confident they had the schooner well in hand for the choppy passage, a loud crack accompanied the parting of the extra line added to the main boom. Intended to help control the movement of the many hundred-pound spar as it swung in a giant arc, the line gave way as the deckhands hauled to center the boom over the keel. Manning the main sheet, seaman Parkes was pulled off his feet as the boom fought to swing out over the side and threatened to take the hapless sailor with it.

Before she could call out to the men, a dark shape sprinted through the driving rain across the deck and latched itself onto Parkes' legs. Bracing himself on the rail, Jane could see that Fairchild was fighting to hold the seaman on board while calling to Dawkins to take the sheet. Moments later, the two men collapsed to the deck as the rest of the crew brought the *Destiny* back under control and secured a new line to the boom. After shaking hands with the relieved Parkes, Fairchild worked his way back through the sheeting rain to stand by the helm.

"Nice work, Mister Fairchild," Jane shouted into his ear over the noise of the wind. Turning to look at her, the sailor allowed himself an insolent shrug and a nod, then grabbed the wheel as Dawkins ordered a change in helm. Jane felt her ire rise as his casual response made it seem he thought her appreciation his due. She opened her mouth to put him in his place when a shout came from the foredeck.

"Light ho!" Boniface on lookout had finally spied the lamp as it sputtered in the battering wind and rain. Marking the shoals eastward of the point, the light alerted the second mate that the time had come to sound the depths and keep the vessel well off the reef.

"Man the lead! Lead overboard!" Galsworthy roared over the storm and sent the sounding man to the rail.

"By the mark three! And a half two! By the deep two!" The bottom under her keel was drawing closer, and the *Destiny* had fewer than three feet below as she cleared the point at a distance of two miles.

Straining to see the white line of breakers through the water pouring off her brow, and holding her breath lest the boat come to a jarring halt on the shifting sands, Jane clenched the starboard rail with white knuckles.

"Steady as she goes, Mister Fairchild," Jane commanded. She knew that the *Destiny* could handle the blow, but didn't trust the unstable sea bottom. Just as she wondered if it was time to throw out the anchors and wait until morning, the lead sounding showed they had passed the shallowest stretch of the shoals.

"By the mark five," and the *Destiny* was once more headed out over deeper water.

"Full and bye, Mister Fairchild." Jane wanted as much speed as the sails would give her as they plowed their way south out of the gale.

The storm blew itself out as the first watch ended. Lamps were lit below and the crew hurried to hang their sodden clothing from ropes strung among the bunks. Cookie doled out precious hot coffee to the cold seamen while the larboard watch cleared the decks and prepared to set the jib. There was a lightness to the movements of the men as they came and went on the moonlit deck. Without a doubt, the captain had shown her mettle and had beaten her way through the challenging squall. Next time, they would stare down the weather confident that their master would stand strong before the storm.

Drained from her exertion and the need to show a strong face to the crew, Jane made her way aft to her berth as the second bell was struck. She was ravenous but did not want to disturb the galley where Cookie had at last put out the fire and found his berth. Rummaging in her sea chest, she located the tin of biscuits pressed into her hand by Uncle Josias' housekeeper as Jane departed for the wharf. The heavenly aroma of ginger and cloves assaulted her nose when she pulled open the top and plunged her hand into the contents.

Perched on her berth with the tin in her lap and a cup of watered wine in her hand, Jane pulled her hair loose and rolled her shoulders to ease the tension. Unlike the rest of her dark-haired family, Jane sported a mane of red hair that set off her green eyes. Her father always said there must have been a Viking somewhere in the family. With a broad brow and long nose, she was not conventionally pretty in the way of the society misses her mother expected her to emulate, but was undoubtedly beautiful in the way of strong, proud women. Leaning over to fetch her brush from under the mattress, Jane began her nightly ritual of taming her knots while contemplating the events of the day.

She was pleased with the way the vessel and crew had responded to the worsening weather and worrisome shoals. She also felt content at her own command of the situation and their safe passage through the dangerous waters. What brought her up short was the sudden memory of the whispered endearment.

With a flash of certainty, Jane felt sure it had come from that Canadian rogue. His audacity astonished her while creating a knotty problem. She could not deny that she felt a certain thrill when recalling the episode. She should certainly discipline him for taking liberties with the captain, but if no one else had seen the exchange, perhaps she could let it go. She wasn't certain of the right answer, but decided to put off thinking about it until morning.

Blowing out the lamp, Jane soon fell asleep to the gentle movement of her schooner as it sailed on its way toward the Caribbean and the sugar warehouses of Cuba.

VI

Reaching for Cuba

Thursday, May 18 Lat. Obs. 24° 02'N Long. DR 80° 02'W First part light wind from WNW. and thick foggy weather, Latter hours foggy. Saw two schooners heading to N by E, did not speak them, Spoke brig Jenny C. NB Hispaniola, y. fever in Havana.

After the excitement of the storm off Hatteras, the crew was relieved when the following week brought moderate airs steady out of the northwest. The morning fog was less dense for each day that passed, allowing for good land sightings at the start of each morning watch. The *Destiny* had settled into a slower pace, making no more than six knots much of the day, and at times coasting along at a rate barely above a crawl. After the heady speeds of the prior week, Jane was feeling a little anxious that her lead on the rest of the New York fleet was withering away. But by her reckoning, they were now less than a day out of Cuba.

In the captain's cabin, Jane was in earnest discussion with Galsworthy and Dawkins.

"We can't put in at Havana if that report is correct. The damned Danes will stick us in quarantine for weeks while the market cools and our competitors get their noses in the door. We just have to be headed north as soon as we can, and without bringing the fever with us." Jane paced the cabin and banged the navigation table with a closed fist on each pass.

Dawkins sat bent over the charts laid out on the table as he searched for a solution. Earlier in the day, they had hailed a brig bound northward from Hispaniola. The master let them know that a yellow fever outbreak had been reported on the island of Cuba and people were dying in Havana. The fever had struck in many places this year, including what was being reported as a growing epidemic in Savannah. The *Destiny* could not afford to risk her crew or cargo by exposing themselves to the pestilence, but they had to come away with a load of muscovado sugar or forfeit the contract and pay a hefty fine to the cargo owners.

"Matanzas." Dawkins stood up and pointed on the chart to an area about sixty miles to the east of Havana on the Cuban coast.

"This is where the sugar is actually produced, in the *ingenios* around Limonar. They bring it into the warehouses in Havana for trade, but I reckon we could waylay a load. Send a note to the consul to meet us, and we'll be in and out while the rest of the traders cool their heels in the Havana harbor."

"What if there is no sugar to be had there?" Galsworthy asked. "Ye'll have lost a day if we have to beat back west to come in to Havana, ma'am."

"I think the risk is worth the taking," Jane decided. "We'll hang on the anchor and I shall take the small boat in to make out the lay of things. Dawkins, you shall stay aboard and keep the men busy so they don't consider their chances of sneaking ashore. I will take one of the hands and be back quick as can be."

That evening, Jane leaned against the stern rail enjoying the warmer wind on her face and gazing up at the stars.

"Look there," she said to the chief mate leaning on the rail beside her. "That must be the Southern Cross. I've never seen it before. I fear I shall never want to come ashore again once this voyage is over. This world contains many things I'd wish to see before I die."

"Aye, captain, the world is indeed a wondrous place waiting to be discovered. Prosecute this voyage well and your uncle will be sure to entrust you with many a cargo to come. Perhaps even round the Cape and on to Calcutta. That would be something to see!"

Jane turned to him. "How have you managed it all these years? The coming and going and sailing away from loved ones at home?" Pru's letter had been in Jane's thoughts all week. Could she make a life ashore? Would someone like Endeavor find it agreeable to be tied to a wife who spent months at sea? Or perhaps he would wish to join her aboard, as did so many of the captains' wives and children. Not that she thought Endeavor would be happy on board. He did his best to avoid stepping foot on any sort of vessel lest he be tipped overboard and have to swim for shore. He had a deathly fear of deep water which no amount of coaxing or teasing by Jane had been able to ameliorate.

"Badly, I fear," was Mister Dawkins' wry response. "Mistress Dawkins, God rest her soul, never did find peace with my absences and was wont to harry me unmercifully to give up the sea and find employment on land. My promise to her that we should have our older years together in a fine cottage near the mountains went unfulfilled when she died ten years ago. It's a vow I wish I could have kept, ma'am."

As she lay in her berth that night, Jane tossed and turned, uneasy in spirit. Her life was on a path that she must either commit to, or turn away from at some point if she was to have the comfort of husband and children and a settled home. Time enough to make the decision once she was back in New York, but she was troubled by the choices that were rearing their heads and demanding that she follow one path or another. Falling asleep to the sound of the waves as they rushed past the hull, Jane promised herself a talk with Endeavor soon after she arrived home.

Friday, May 19 Lat. Obs. 23° 04'N Long. DR 81° 31'W First part pleasant wind N + W. of S, Matanzas sighted at noon.

The lookout sighted land the following day at the start of the afternoon watch. They had adjusted their heading overnight to make easting and approach the Matanzas harbor from the north. As they pointed the *Destiny's* nose south, they could see several ships at anchor in the bay and dozens of small boats pulled up on the shore. From the water, Jane could see the town as it spread out from the harbor and a central square. Beyond, the land rose abruptly to a hill with two rounded peaks, and then fell away to the surrounding plains.

"Prepare to drop anchor!" Galsworthy had the crew moving swiftly to douse sails and prepare for coming into port. As Jane swept the docks with her spyglass, she could see several men dashing for the boats and bending their backs to the oars. No sooner had her vessel come to rest than there were a dozen or more of them surrounding her vessel and shouting at them in a Spanish creole she couldn't hope to understand. Mister Dawkins, however, had spent a number of years in the Cuba trade bringing coffee to Boston, and he stepped forward now to negotiate with the wildly gesticulating crowd.

Several minutes later, the chief turned to Jane and announced that he had dispatched one of the lively fellows to fetch the consul, and another to alert the harbormaster that they were in need of his assistance. Before long, a flat-bottomed boat appeared in which reclined a solid gentleman under a large awning. The red and yellow flag at the stern declared him an emissary of the government, and indeed he proved to be the Health Officer. Handing over the ship's papers, Jane reported that all aboard were free of sickness and that the cargo to be landed consisted of dried timber from New England. Within short order, the vessel was pronounced safe and the officer was rowed back toward shore. No sooner had his boat cast off from the *Destiny* than another appeared with the immigration official aboard. Mister Dawkins showed the man into the captain's quarters where he inspected the crew's papers and ship's manifest. All being declared in order, the captain was free to land her timber and arrange for the acquisition of her onward cargo.

Shortly thereafter, a brightly painted island ketch slipped away from the dock and made its way to the *Destiny's* side. Seated in the bow was an elegant figure in a navy coat with brass buttons and a commodore's hat. Black serge trousers and a red sash completed an outfit marred in its grandeur only by the dusty bare feet peeking out below. This dandy turned out to be Señor Miguel Cabrera, the harbormaster, who was duly invited aboard and offered a glass of port in the captain's quarters.

To Jane's relief, Cabrera had an excellent command of

English and she soon communicated to the agreeable señor that she was interested in purchasing a goodly tonnage in cases of sugar. In addition, they had need of replenishing their fresh stores and salted provisions. Señor Cabrera nodded and allowed that he could, for the right inducement, certainly provide her with contacts able to supply the needed items and help locate a buyer for her ballast load of logs. Foreseeing the imminent disappearance of yet another bottle of her favorite port, Jane nevertheless smiled back at the man and indicated that she would follow him ashore in her own skiff to continue negotiations.

As she prepared to disembark, Jane motioned to Galsworthy to have the crew lower the skiff and asked Dawkins to select one of the men to row her ashore. Then, before she could rein in her tongue, she burst out, "And if Mister Fairchild is at leisure, he would do."

This earned her a dark look from Mister Dawkins, whose job it was to manage the crew, followed by an uncomfortable half hour as the grinning fool Fairchild swiftly and expertly piloted the skiff a mile through the harbor to land. At the dock, he offered to hand her up as the boat floated a good three feet below the pier. Deciding that an assist was preferable to a mad scramble that would expose her drawers to the eyes of the impertinent seaman, Jane took his proffered arm and reached for the edge of the pier. As she grasped the plank to pull herself onto the dock, though, she stepped on the edge of her skirt and tumbled backward into a pair of waiting arms.

Her mind screaming at her to pull away, Jane also found herself taking a moment to enjoy the embrace. Fairchild had caught her under the arms and was now pressing his palms to a most interesting part of her anatomy. Fighting herself loose, she rounded on the cocky man and slapped him soundly across the face. Then, without another word, she hoisted herself onto the pier and stomped her way to the harbormaster's office at the end of the dock.

VII
Timber and Sugar

Matanzas, Cuba
May, 1820

Jane's passage up the waterfront toward the central square of the city of Matanzas carried her through both mean squalor and extravagant opulence. She craned her neck to take in the imposing edifice of the new Customs House built in the style of old Spain, then gazed eagerly around the open plaza thronged with elegant ladies in volantes next to ox carts piled with cane. Ragged children ran barefoot down the packed dirt streets where dogs lay panting in the shade outside tropical houses painted in every imaginable color. She could see flowers everywhere, growing from pots in courtyards, hanging from roofs, and climbing gates and walls.

Jane felt herself relaxing as the scent of flowers wafted in the balmy air. Shrugging off the impertinence of that rogue Fairchild for the moment, she stepped into the cool corridor of the harbormaster's *casa* and prepared to do business.

"Señorita!" The harbormaster threw his arms out as he came forward from the shadows. Peering around behind her, he was clearly puzzled that there was no one else in attendance.

"Welcome to Matanzas! We are graced by your presence here! Perhaps you would care to take a tour of the city while your good mate attends to the business of trade? I hope he has not been detained long."

Jane let slip a sigh as she contemplated once more the need to educate a man on the ability of women to both command ships and broker business deals.

"Señor Cabrera, Mister Dawkins is attending to matters on board and will not be joining us. Now, 275 tons of the finest white oak in logwood is resting in my hold. Shall we adjourn to your parlor and consider who might be interested in such a

Destiny's Gold

cargo?"

Astonished at this speech, Cabrera stood with his arms frozen in mid-gesture and his mouth open in amazement. Before he could gather his wits and consider how to respond, Jane marched into his office and settled herself onto a divan placed under an open window. Arranging her hands on her lap, she sat with her back erect and an expectant look upon her face. She had no idea how this popinjay would respond to her overbearing manner, but Jane suspected his desire for her business would overcome his surprise at having to deal with her.

Indeed, within moments the harbormaster rushed in and bowed to her as he exclaimed, "My dear Capitan Thorn, I would of course be most honored to act on your behalf and assist you in locating a buyer for your timber. And shall we also discuss the matter of your sugar load?"

An hour later, Jane stepped back into the late afternoon sunlight satisfied that she had put things in motion for the sale of her cargo and the acquisition of her outbound load. She had refused to engage Cabrera as her agent, but had hinted that he would receive a generous acknowledgement of his assistance should she be successful in both disposing of the timber at a good price and purchasing enough sugar to make the trip worthwhile.

A few minutes' walk brought Jane back to the dock where she expected to see that dog Fairchild waiting with the boat. The tide had come in and raised the gunwales a foot closer to the edge of the pier, so at least her descent into the skiff would be less fraught than her exit from it, but peering down the dock, she could see no sign of the man. Instead, a dapper older gentleman in a white tropical suit accompanied by a younger man in a dusty black one appeared to be awaiting her return. Lifting his hat, the former figure bowed slightly in Jane's direction and introduced himself as she approached.

"Captain Thorn, I believe? I am Thomas Rodney, United States consul, and very pleased to make your acquaintance. May I present my clerk, Mister Betancourt."

"A pleasure to hear a familiar accent, Mister Rodney. I

would offer you refreshment aboard the *Destiny*, but I seem to be missing my oarsman. Perhaps we might repair to an establishment I passed on the way down for a cup of what I hear is most excellent coffee here in Cuba." Jane proffered her hand to the consul, who hesitated a moment as he seemed uncertain whether to shake it, or kiss it in the manner of the Spaniards among whom he lived. In the end, he settled for a firm grip and a discomfited smile.

The small party located a table in the shade of the courtyard at the bustling cafe. Around them, Cubans of all colors and castes engaged in lively intercourse with friends and associates. Notable to Jane was the lack of women in attendance, but she shrugged off the stares and concentrated on listening to the consul.

"Your presence here comes as a surprise, Captain," Rodney began. "We would have expected a trader like yourself to have landed a cargo in Havana and loaded from the warehouses there. May I ask what brings you to Matanzas?"

"Yellow fever. We simply decided not to risk the unhealthy air of Havana and thought to try our luck with the port here. I understand that the local plantations are in the habit of sending their product to Havana for sale to the merchant ships, and thought one or two might be persuaded to cut the freight cost and sell to me here instead."

Rodney smiled as he took in the implied message; without the need to pay for carrying the sugar to the capital, a producer would be expected to offer his product at a lower price to the schooner master in front of him.

"And are you traveling in ballast, or do you have a load to sell in addition?" he asked.

"White oak. Cut last year from the finest stands in New England and dried straight and true. Finer timber cannot be had, and would hold up a roof against any tropical storm. There is enough for twenty houses aboard, and any carpenter would be glad to have it. I've conversed with Mister Cabrera on the matter and he seems to think he might find me a buyer locally."

At the mention of the harbormaster's name, Rodney

exchanged glances with his clerk and pursed his lips as he replied.

"I fear you may have been given some poor advice, Captain, if you have entrusted your affairs to Señor Cabrera. While I work diligently to maintain cordial relations with the local officials, I can't with all honesty recommend that others rely on them in any manner. Rumors abound of his being in partnership with those captains who continue to smuggle in contraband slaves despite the agreement ending that sorry trade. He is also known to collaborate with those who would prefer that their exports not draw the attention of the crown's excise man."

Jane smiled at the consul, and tilted her head in amusement. "Mister Rodney, I can assure you that Mister Cabrera's expectations and motives are well understood by me, not to mention his illicit practices. I have been running duty goods up and down the New England coast for years and am well acquainted with men of the harbormaster's disposition."

Throwing himself back in his chair, the consul guffawed as Betancourt allowed himself an open grin. "Captain, I warrant old Cabrera is about to learn the true meaning of Yankee grit."

"Oh no, Mister Rodney. He is now dealing with a New Yorker, and that is much worse."

By the time she had completed her transactions with the consul, the dinner hour was approaching and Fairchild had yet to return. Taking her leave of Rodney and his clerk, Jane made her way back to the skiff and contemplated rowing herself back to the *Destiny* on her own, the impertinent seaman be damned. He could swim if he hadn't decided to jump ship and stay in Cuba. She rather hoped he had, not that she couldn't use his service on the next leg. But he had signed articles only to Havana and was within his rights to seek another berth. If he didn't show up to retrieve his papers by the time they left, she would just leave them with the consul. In the meantime, she would consider what measures she might need to take to keep him in his place.

No sooner had she resolved to leave him ashore than Fairchild came dashing down the dock. With his sailor's jacket slung over his shoulder and his tunic open at the neck, he was far too attractive. She faced him square on with her hands on her hips and a piercing glare. He had the good sense to look embarrassed and removed his hat to beg her pardon.

"It truly was not my intent to offer you insult earlier, ma'am. If in making myself useful to you I happened to overstep a boundary, I am most sorry for that." Delivered in a contrite tone with his head ducked so she couldn't see his eyes, Fairchild was almost believable. At least believable enough that she was willing to get back in the boat with him and head out into the bay where the *Destiny* awaited the return of her captain.

As she clambered up the boarding ladder to the deck, Jane could swear she felt a warm hand placed on the skirts covering her backside. Whipping around to face the insufferable bastard, she nearly lost her grip. Fairchild stood below her holding the skiff to the *Destiny's* side with one hand while using the other to scratch the back of his neck. He was staring off toward the town with only a slight smirk to give him away.

That tore it. She would have him handed his papers as soon as they were aboard and have Dawkins pay him off. Both furious and disturbed by how much she responded to his touch, Jane stalked to her cabin and confronted the chief mate.

"Mister Dawkins, please see to it that Mister Fairchild is compensated for the voyage and put ashore with all dispatch. He is to be gone by the time I have finished consulting with Mister Galsworthy on the unloading of the cargo. Send a note to the consul that Fairchild is now under his jurisdiction and is at liberty to ship aboard another vessel."

"Aye, aye, ma'am." A confused Dawkins rose from the saloon table where he had been reviewing the list of the ship's stores and made for the companionway. He threw Jane a questioning glance as he passed out of the cabin, but knew better than to question her command.

The captain took a moment to compose herself and straighten her skirts. That infuriating man was not only insubordinate and dangerously out of line, but she suspected he was also engaged in something that could put her vessel in danger of crossing the Spanish authorities. She noticed that his apology had not included any explanation of his whereabouts that afternoon, and as he had returned without packages she knew he had not visited the shops. Mister Rodney had made it clear to her during their visit that everyone in Cuba was suspected of treachery by the Spanish crown. The consequences for the *Destiny* should any of her crew be accused of comporting with enemies of the government would be drastic, including the possible impoundment of her vessel. All in all, she was better rid of him even if she was now down two crew berths again.

That evening, as she sat at mess with her officers, Jane decided to bring the whole matter out in the open as a means to assure them of the restoration of her balanced mind and attention to the needs of the voyage. They could not have helped but notice her distraction over the past days and it was high time that she return to the business at hand.

"I believe an apology is in order, gentlemen. It cannot have escaped you that personal matters have from time to time occupied my thoughts of late. I wish to assure you that I am no longer in danger of being drawn into a situation that is unbecoming."

The silence that followed spoke volumes both about the concern her mates had been harboring with regard to her inappropriate attention to the attractive sailor, and to the uncomfortably personal nature of her remarks.

Clearing his throat, Galsworthy lifted his glass and gestured toward the captain. "To the master, may she have fair winds and a following sea."

Dawkins likewise hailed the captain and threw back the dregs of the wine in the bottom of his tumbler. Setting the glass back down, he stretched his legs out in the narrow space between the table and the unlit warming stove.

"Looks like we have a busy day afore us tomorrow if we are to make sail again by the end of the week," Dawkins observed. "Shall I pay a visit to Cabrera in the morning?"

"Yes, let us see what he has been able to arrange. But let us also seek our own contacts. Mister Rodney suggested a visit to one of the local landowners, a Monsieur Jean Baptiste Sarrazin, who may wish to both buy our load and sell us the muscovado we are in quest of. I will send a note to him in the morning."

The moon that evening lit the harbor and the widening in the bay that would take them back out to sea. Looking down over the side, Jane stared in wonder at the silvery glow around the anchor chain. She had heard of the phosphorescent algae that populated the waters in warmer climes and was enchanted to see the twinkling lights as they swirled in the gentle current. A warm breeze lifted the hair off the back of her neck and Jane was sure that she would never tire of new sights, new ports, and new places that made her heart yearn for adventure.

VIII

Monsieur Sarrazin

Jane was up early on their second day in port having slept badly, tossing and turning in her berth in the close confines of the cabin. She had opened the skylights and windows, but the air was hot, still and oppressive. Tonight, she would arrange for a hammock to be strung on deck where she could feel the sultry evening breeze across the bay and watch the stars.

In the meantime, she had affairs to arrange. Donning a simple white dress, she covered it with a navy muslin coat sporting brass buttons. A billowy cravat, tall boots, and a beaver bicorne hat completed the outfit and marked her as the master of the *Destiny*. Cookie had left her breakfast on the saloon table, and she picked it up on her way to the deck. She would eat it sitting on the quarterdeck where she could enjoy the feel of the breeze and the song of the tropical birds that thronged the masts above her.

As Jane stepped out from the companionway, she caught sight of Riggins on anchor watch.

"How goes it this morning, Mister Riggins? Are we secure to the bottom here?"

"Aye, ma'am. The flukes are holding at ten fathoms. We have ample room below us to come further into shore if needs be."

"Thank you, Riggins, I am counting on it." Unlike the brigs, which fully loaded would often draw over fourteen feet below the waterline, the *Destiny* could slip into any quay that had a scant ten feet of depth. If she could make it into the Matanzas wharf, they could unload and load without using lighters and reduce their time in port by a day or more. Without having to ferry the goods down the harbor to their vessel, they would also save the cost of the boats and their crews. If all went according to plan, they would have the *Destiny* at the dock in the morning and be ready to head back out to sea within twenty-four hours, fully loaded with sugar.

Peering across the bay, Jane could see a contingent of fruit and vegetable merchants headed their way in the flat-bottomed boats that seemed so popular here. Within minutes, several were alongside the *Destiny's* bow where Cookie and Dawkins were waiting to trade with them for supplies. She went forward and handed a note to the chief mate, asking him to see to it that it was delivered to Mister Sarrazin as quickly as possible. Nodding, he took the folded paper and passed it to one of the fruit sellers with a small coin and some quick instructions.

As she waited for Mister Dawkins to complete his transactions, she settled on the stern rail with her mug of coffee, now gone cold, and the biscuits and jam she had for breakfast each morning. Cookie had added a plate of mango to tempt her, and Jane spent a pleasant half hour watching the harbor come to life.

As the crew would not take shore leave, Mister Galsworthy had set the men to small chores to keep them occupied, including keeping the deck awash to prevent the seams from drying out in the hot sun and leaking. Mid-morning, he ordered the small boat made ready and assigned Boniface to row Jane and Mister Dawkins to shore.

Standing on the pier as they approached the town was a young boy in livery who appeared to be awaiting their arrival. His dark features suggested that he was likely one of the many enslaved Africans on the island, and Jane found herself both curious and repulsed. She had heard that half of the population of Cuba were slaves, brought there on the slave ships, or born into that sorry state. She had never traveled in the south of her own country, and had no prior contact with these unfortunate people, even though she knew there were many slaves living in New York. Confronting one now brought an acute sense of discomfort and helplessness.

Jane and Dawkins clambered onto the pier as Boniface made fast the skiff.

"Thank you, Boniface. We shall be at least two hours about our business if you would care to tour the town in our absence,"

Jane said.

"Aye, aye ma'am, and thank 'ee!" The young Boniface, who had signed aboard for his first long voyage, was eager to be off and exploring the fascinating streets of Matanzas. "But take care to stay on the main streets and look out for trouble. Return to the boat immediately should anything untoward happen and we will meet you there."

With a salute, Boniface clapped his straw hat on his head and set off to discover what delights were to be had in the town as the young liveried boy approached and held his hand out to Jane.

"Mademoiselle, c'est pour vous, s'il vous plaît."

Taking the proffered note with a thank you, Jane opened it to find a message from Monsieur Sarrazin, the sugar planter. He inquired if she would do him the honor of accompanying his messenger to his home off the main plaza, where he would meet her to discuss matters of mutual interest. She handed the missive to Dawkins and told him she would rejoin him at the harbormaster's office within the hour.

Smiling at Sarrazin's messenger, she waved to indicate that he should lead the way to his master's house. A short walk soon brought them to the front door of a small townhouse where the brightly colored shutters framed windows and doors thrown open to the morning sun. Following her guide through the front entry, Jane was struck by the mannered beauty of the house. The entire establishment spoke of French gentility and refinement, no less in the furnishings than in the way the staff, most of whom appeared to be Africans, tended to their work. She was hailed from an open door on the left, where a diminutive man in knee breeches and dark coat stood with his hand outstretched. His curly dark hair, styled in the latest Paris fashion, framed a long face with a prominent nose and square jaw.

"Mademoiselle la capitaine, you are most welcome to my home! I am Monsieur Sarrazin and I was pleased to receive your message this morning. Monsieur Rodney does me great honor in referring me to your notice for the handling of your affairs. Please, please, *entrez s'il vous plaît."*

Removing her hat, Jane ducked through the open door in front of the man, who closed it behind him after motioning to one of the servants to bring refreshments. Waving her into one of two gorgeously upholstered chairs in front of a set of open doors leading to the garden, Monsieur Sarrazin sat opposite her and threw his arms wide.

"And how may I be of assistance, *Capitaine* Thorn?"

There ensued an enlightening three quarters of an hour wherein Jane and the effusive Frenchman discussed the current state of affairs with regard to the sugar business in Cuba. Like many of his countrymen who had fled Haiti in the wake of the revolution over ten years prior, Sarrazin had set himself up as a coffee planter in Cuba. While business was booming and the world was purchasing all of the beans he and his fellow planters could produce, Sarrazin was looking to the future. Rumor in the markets was that the American coffee buyers had found a new source of product in the mountains of South America. If the Brazilian farmers could produce their superior harvest less expensively, the Cuban coffee planters would soon need to find another source of income, and Sarrazin believed that sugar could play a role.

Sarrazin explained that five years earlier, Cuban landowners had been accorded the freedom to clear-cut their lands, making way for the plantation of thousands of hectares of sugarcane in the newly deforested fields. As Jane listened to the eager planter describe how he had raised two successful crops this year and constructed the first buildings for his sugar works, she became certain that all of the labor he needed for this mammoth undertaking was being supplied by slaves. In recent years, Jane's father and uncle had been increasingly vocal in their abolitionist ideas, which accorded well with her own view of the subject. She was loathe to profit on the backs of these unfortunate souls, and yet profit she must if she were to complete the mission entrusted to her. It bore thinking about, she reflected as she listened.

Sipping from a cup of excellent strong coffee delivered in the company of a tray of small cakes, Jane decided the time had come to find out if Sarrazin could provide the sugar she needed in sufficient quantities and at a price she could accept.

"I am most pleased to hear of your success in the production of muscovado, monsieur. May I inquire if you will be bringing a quantity to market at the present time?" she asked.

"Most assuredly, ma *capitaine*," he replied. "Although I fear I may not be able to supply it easily in the quantities you seek."

Jane let this reply linger for a moment as she tilted her head to look up at him with a small smile. Clearly, the man was angling for a premium price to turn loose of his stock. "Well, monsieur, that would be unfortunate, as I have a bank draft in my possession to be used for the purchase of the full load from a single producer. The terms of the contract are quite clear."

Of course, the contract contained no such language, but Jane thought the early threat of needing to turn elsewhere for her cargo might bring the negotiation to a head more quickly.

"Well, *bien sûr*, we will do our best to fill your contract, *capitaine*," Sarrazin exclaimed with a worried look.

In the end, Jane agreed to purchase the Sarrazin plantation's entire output, which was currently sitting in a warehouse in Matanzas awaiting shipment to Havana. She was most satisfied with the price she had negotiated once she also made pointed reference to the savings the planter would realize by no longer needing to pay for storage and shipping of the inventory. The quantity would be enough to complete her contract with Bernard & Banks, but would leave nothing over for her own family's speculation, however. She would have to locate another several hundredweight before they returned to the dock today.

"Very good, monsieur, we are in agreement," Jane said as she leaned forward and held out her hand. "Once I have disposed of the lumber in my hold, we will look to load as soon as tomorrow if you can manage it."

"Oui, *bien sûr*, we will be ready. But what lumber are you carrying?"

As luck would have it, Sarrazin was in need of her timber as he was engaged in an expansive building project to increase the output of his sugar works. He was, in fact, so eager for the wood that she managed to sell it to him for more than double her expected price. She was well pleased with the visit and felt no small amount of satisfaction that she had made her outbound load pay so handsomely. Her uncle would be pleased to see the letter of remittance from the agent in Havana when it arrived in New York. Sarrazin agreed to meet the *Destiny* at the wharf in the morning with carts and men ready to offload the logwood and assist with the loading of the sugar boxes. In the meantime, she would send word to the consul and her agent to draw up agreements and arrange for the export taxes to be remitted and invoices settled.

As she took her leave, Monsieur Sarrazin extended an invitation to return with him that evening to his *ingenio* located in the valley south of Matanzas toward Limonar.

"It is but an hour's drive and my wife would be so pleased to make your acquaintance. I am returning there myself after several days spent here in town, and would be accompanying you on the road. In the morning, we can join your vessel and oversee the cargo transfer, if that would be agreeable to mademoiselle?" Sarrazin seemed eager to show her the progress he had made in his new enterprise, and Jane had to admit to herself that she would find it educational, if somewhat unsettling, to see the workings of a slave plantation first hand. Accordingly, she accepted his gracious invitation and arranged to be collected at the dock in the early evening.

The walk back to the waterfront was marred only by the sight of Fairchild lounging about at one of the cafes on the plaza. Catching her eye, he looked far from chagrined or put out by his abrupt dismissal. Indeed, he grinned broadly at her when he noticed her gaze, and tipped his hat with a slight bow. Infuriated, Jane considered marching up to him and putting him firmly in his place, but then decided it was beneath her to engage with him since he was no longer a member of her crew. And if she were honest, she wasn't sure she trusted herself to maintain the censorious tone the occasion called for. She was acutely aware that when it came to Mister Fairchild, her mind seemed to compel her to behave in ways that were utterly foreign to her balanced nature. Better to leave it alone and ignore the man.

Well back at the harbormaster's house, the captain was surprised to see Dawkins standing on the street in front of the building with a deep scowl on his face.

"Negotiations not going well, Dawkins?" Fresh from her success with the agreeable Sarrazin, Jane was feeling a tad more chirpy than her chief's dark look would call for.

"The man is either a scoundrel or an ignoramus, and I fear he may be both." Dawkins pronounced this estimation of Cabrera in a low growl Jane recognized. He was wont to employ it with any seaman who failed to live up to the exacting standards Chief Dawkins expected from his men. "He thinks me a fool who doesn't know the value of a pound, or of the worthless sugar he just tried to palm off on me."

Dawkins had been promised a highly favorable deal on a particularly fine load of sugar that Señor Cabrera knew about. It had been sitting in the warehouse for a month waiting for just the right conditions to ship it to the capital for sale, but the harbormaster was sure he could get the owner to consider a reasonable offer from the mate of the *Destiny*. Leading Dawkins along the quay to a ramshackle building at the far end, he threw open the doors to reveal several thousand cartons of sugar stacked to the ceiling of the cavernous space. Dawkins slid a knife into the closest box to test the quality of the product and was pleased to taste the dark, rich sweetness of fine muscovado. Then he stepped between the towering rows to the back of the shipment and repeated the test. This time, the knife brought out a sandy, grainy clump of poorly refined, molasses-heavy inferior sugar.

Cabrera feigned surprise when shown the results of this second test, and made a great show of demanding that a third and then a fourth test be done from different boxes. When all save the initial case turned out to be poor quality dross, he finally allowed that perhaps he had been misled as to the contents of the cases. Without a word, Dawkins turned on his heel and strode back to the veranda in front of the harbormaster's office to await his captain.

Upon hearing the chief's report, Jane walked inside to face Cabrera, who was ensconced behind his desk with his feet balanced on an empty barrel. The room was filled with tobacco smoke and she paused to open a window before bearding the once-again astonished little man.

"Señor Cabrera, I am not a fool and do not like to be taken for one. I am in the market for eighteen hundred pounds of first grade muscovado or refined sugar. Anyone who wishes to sell such product to me may bring it to the dock first thing in the morning. All cases presented for sale must be opened and will be subject to inspection." She then named a price ten percent less than what she had just paid Sarrazin, and well below the going price in Havana. Reaching across the desk to pluck up one of Cabrera's fresh cigars, she held it out for him to light. Inserting it between her lips, she asked, "Do I make myself clear, Señor Cabrera?"

When he nodded assent, Jane reached out to shake his hand. "Thank you, and I look forward to showing my appreciation in a suitable manner when my hold is filled and we are cleared for an early departure with the tide on Friday. I will be most grateful for any assistance you can render us in that regard."

With that, she walked back out into the sunshine where Dawkins fell in at her side.

"Negotiations going well, Captain?" he asked on seeing her smile.

"Yes, Mister Dawkins," Jane observed as she drew in a mouthful of strong tobacco before tossing the cigar at her feet, "I think we can say that the business will be concluded in a satisfactory manner."

IX

Ingenio Prospérité

The clock tower on the square chimed five as Jane stood on the dock with Galsworthy in attendance. She had returned to the *Destiny* with Dawkins earlier in the day to pack a satchel with her overnight things and let Mister Galsworthy know that the crew would need to bring the schooner to the wharf face at first light. To her surprise, the second mate had insisted on accompanying her on the visit to Sarrazin's ingenio despite her protests to the contrary.

"Surely there is no danger to me in a simple overnight visit to a genteel family?" Jane had argued.

"Begging your pardon, ma'am, but the roads are perhaps not safe, and the presence of another man might be a good idea. Besides, I've always wanted to see one o' them plantations, and this might be my only chance."

Jane knew herself bested by her old friend. A smart captain listens to her mates and, while the final decision was always hers, she would be a fool to ignore the advice of her officers. In the end, she decided she was rather glad of the company. Much as she trusted in the good will of the Frenchman, it was safer to have her own friend along, and she had sent a note ashore to Monsieur Sarrazin that there would be two guests that evening.

Before long, a volante pulled by two shiny black ponies pulled up, and Monsieur Sarrazin leaped from the step to hail them.

"*Bonsoir, mes amis.* I am very pleased to make your acquaintance, Monsieur Galsworthy, and it is good to see you again *ma capitaine*! I feel we have become friends already, and it is with pleasure that I look forward to your visit to my family home at Prospérité. Please, join me in the carriage."

Motioning for them to board the unfamiliar equipage found only in the islands, Sarrazin climbed in behind them and called for his driver to set off. This personage, mounted on the off horse, was as grandly outfitted as a general and rode with the staid decorum of a funeral coachman. Jane was enchanted by these unfamiliar sights and felt that she had truly left home for the first time in her life.

The route up the Yumurí Valley to *ingenio* Prospérité followed the banks of a lazy blue-green river dotted with sandbars and small islands. Birds flew from tree to tree along its banks emitting calls unfamiliar to the northern visitors. Before long, Jane could see low white buildings with tile roofs amongst what appeared to be expansive stands of cane. A great number of people were busy wielding long knives as they trimmed the foliage from the sides of the stalks.

"Are those the sugar fields, Monsieur Sarrazin?" Jane inquired.

"*Oui*, the cane will be ready for harvest next month and we are preparing the stalks to be processed. Once we start cutting them, we must move swiftly to bring them to the grinders and the boiling house so that the syrup is as sweet as it can be. We work day and night for many weeks then, and it seems we do nothing but ladle syrup and haul cane." Sarrazin exclaimed proudly.

"And may I ask, are those your slaves at work there?" She did not wish to offend her host, but Jane wanted to understand how the plantation functioned and how the work was accomplished.

"Some of my best people! They are well taken care of by me and strive to make the harvest as abundant as possible by caring diligently for the crop. We farm this land together, me as master and they as labor, and *enfin* we all profit by it!" His enthusiasm and conviction could not be mistaken.

"But," Jane insisted, "they are slaves are they not? And subject to your will and unable to leave should they so desire?"

"Where should they go if they were at liberty to do so?" Sarrazin seemed genuinely puzzled by the query, and Jane let the matter drop.

They passed through the gate of a walled yard and drew up before a low house fronted by an arched colonnade that opened into a shaded veranda. Crossing into the interior of the house, Jane was struck by the formal grandeur of the marbled floors, lofty ceilings that peaked below the roof, colorful wall paintings, and massive furniture. The general effect was of a cool, shadowy interior through which rays of light played from the open windows and doors. No expense had been spared to bring the finest France had to offer to this outpost in the Caribbean as evidenced by the display of brocaded hangings and cut crystal that greeted them on arriving in the main saloon.

Perched on a silk settee was the lady of the house, who rose to shake their hands and introduce the young lady to her right. This was Madame Sarrazin and her daughter Amelie, a girl of not more than sixteen or so. Madame was a small, elegant woman dressed in the finest of silk gowns with her hair simply piled atop a fine-boned face graced by a charming smile. Amelie was a younger version of her stylish *maman*, and displayed a similar warmth of manner as she stood to receive their guests.

"*Bienvenues*. It is a delight to have you in our home, and we are so happy to see fresh faces." Madame Sarrazin cried out. "*Mon mari* is so busy with his affairs in town we are often left to amuse ourselves on our own out here. *Bon*, we have a special meal ready for you. Eugenie will show you where to freshen yourselves before we eat."

After shaking the dust off her clothes and combing through her hair in the bedroom to which she had been shown, Jane made her way to the dining room. A small table had been set to one side of the large chamber, around which the five of them now gathered. The sumptuous meal of meats and vegetables prepared in the island way, served with rice and fruit, was new to Jane's palate. She found herself taking seconds and then thirds of the dishes on offer, and thought that she would have to ask *madame* for some recipes to bring back with her to the family's cook in New York.

Dinner conversation was lively and covered a variety of topics, from the politics of the French families in Cuba to the innovations being introduced in the production and refining of sugar. Steam engines, which looked to become a viable source of power for everything from factories to shipping vessels, were beginning to revolutionize agriculture as well. Jane shared her own thoughts on the coming change in maritime cargo.

"It's the future, that's what it is. Much as I love my schooner and delight in sailing her, steam power allows one to move a cargo from place to place in as near a direct line as can be achieved. The North River Steamboat Company has been transporting passengers up the Hudson for ten years now, and has shown it can be done profitably. And I was most impressed at the feat the Woods brothers accomplished two summers ago when they brought their little steam powered tugboat from Glasgow."

"What will you do, my dear, if the merchants no longer hire your schooner?" Madame Sarrazin asked as she beckoned to the servants to clear away the table for the final course.

"Well, it will be many years, I reckon, before we see a wholesale loss of the Atlantic trade to steam, but if we do, I shall just have to learn to shovel coal." Jane smiled as she lifted her glass in a toast. "To progress!"

It was a merry company that repaired to the saloon after dinner for port and cigars. To Jane's astonishment, it appeared that even the ladies were expected to smoke. Notwithstanding her performance for the harbormaster earlier in the day, Jane had never held with smoking and did not wish to partake now. The port on offer, however, was rich and sweet, and she was glad to sample a glass or two.

As the evening wore on, the talk turned to the growing and harvesting of sugar cane as it was being developed on Cuba.

"May I ask," Jane inquired of her host, "if it is necessary to rely on the work of slaves to make the *ingenio* a going proposition? Would it be possible to produce the sugar using labor you pay a wage to instead?"

"Ah, dear *capitaine*, not at a price you traders would be willing to pay. Should I replace my slaves with hired workers, my product might have to double or even triple in price. You see, the provision of the wage is not *enfin* the sole of the matter. Since I already pay to house and feed my workers, a wage would merely replace those costs. No, *mademoiselle*, it is my ability to control my workforce that makes them so valuable and productive. They come to work when I need them, they work long hours because I make them, and they do exactly the work I tell them to do because it is their duty. In turn, I take care of them the way a father takes care of his children. "

"And can you not pay for such hard-working labor? Surely a high enough wage would bring you people willing to work long hours and do as you command them," Jane replied.

"*Mais non*, I have not found that to be the case, *capitaine*. A man who is free to make his choices about if he will or will not work will often choose not to do so. There you have it. I cannot rely on the willingness of people to come work for the wages I wish to pay, and to do the work I require of them," Sarrazin said as he shrugged his shoulders.

Jane was returning to her bedroom later that evening when Galsworthy tapped her on the shoulder and indicated that he would like a word outside.

"Sorry to bring a sour note to the evening, ma'am, but I thought you should be made aware. When you went upstairs before dinner, I saw that Sarrazin fella' step into his office. I can't say for one hundred percent certain, but it looked to me that he was meetin' with a couple of gents who were awaitin' on him there. I'd wager next month's pay that one of them was Fairchild, ma'am, or else someone who looked mighty like him."

"Here?" Jane was astonished at how the reprobate seaman kept popping up wherever she went. Obviously, he had business here in Cuba, as she had suspected, and it behooved her to get to the bottom of it. Although she had severed his connection with the *Destiny*, she had still brought him here aboard her vessel and the consul had made it clear that the Spaniards might decide to hold her responsible should he be found culpable of any offense while ashore.

"Leave it with me, Mister Galsworthy. I shall ask Sarrazin what the man is doing here," Jane assured him.

"No, ma'am, I'm not sure that is a good idea. These French stick together like thieves and he is most likely here by invitation.

I doubt ye'd get a straight answer from that planter fella' on the matter."

"French? Why no, Mister Galsworthy, Fairchild hails from Ottawa. Surely the English Canadians have no truck with the Quebecois, and he is most decidedly English."

"No, ma'am, I doubt that too. Alan he may style himself, but I suspect he is really *Alain*. One of the crew was boastin' how he had left a string of broken hearts behind on his last trip through Montreal, and that Fairchild looked like he took the slur on the fair denizens of that town quite personally. He allowed as how French lasses were so comely that a man could be excused fergettin' himself, but French men would not take such an insult lying down. I thought he might be fixin' to deck the other man, I did."

"Well, that is scanty evidence for your notion, but I'll not mention it to our host. However, I would certainly like to speak with the man if he is skulking about the place. I'll take a turn around the garden and see what is what. Good night, Galsworthy." With that, Jane set off down the path that led to the cultivated remains of what was once the coffee plantation at Prospérité in search of the mysterious Mister Fairchild.

She had gone no more than a few steps around a curve at the bottom of the garden when she was abruptly waylaid and had a hand clapped over her mouth. Struggling to free herself, Jane felt herself being pulled into a stand of trees and pushed up against the trunk of a large willow. Hidden from the gaze of anyone at the house, it was the perfect spot for an assignation, which is apparently what Alan Fairchild, for it was he, had in mind. Removing his hand from her mouth, he replaced it with his lips, and Jane found herself responding to his embrace. Pulling his head down to hers, she swiftly twisted him around so that his back was up against the tree and leaned into his arms.

"*Ma cherie,*" he murmured against her neck as he kissed his way across the skin exposed above the edge of her blouse. "*Que tu es si belle et si adorable. Je te désire… mon dieu!*"

This last remark had been occasioned by the knife wielded in Jane's hand that was resting against his cheek just under his left eye. She was holding him firmly by the collar and pressing his back into the tree behind him while threatening to let the blade slip at any moment and remove a strip of skin.

"So, Galsworthy was right. Apparently you are not what you represent yourself to be, *monsieur* Fairchild, if that is really your name." Jane applied a little more pressure on the blade to see how he would react.

His eyes widening in shock as he felt a trickle of blood start down his cheek, the moonlight revealed the erstwhile seaman to be dressed in a fine suit of broadcloth and a shirt of white silk that felt smooth under Jane's hand. This was no deckhand merely seeking a berth and three square meals.

Fairchild recovered quickly, but did not dare move as long as her knife was poised next to his eye. Speaking quietly, he owned that he perhaps had not been entirely forthcoming with her.

"*Oui, ma capitaine.* My name is Alain Bonenfant. If I promise to tell you what you wish to know, will you remove your weapon from my person?" Fairchild had already released her and his hands now hung at his sides. Stepping back a pace, Jane let go of him but kept her blade pointed in his direction.

"Yes, I would consider that a very good idea if I were in your position. You've apparently abused my trust in you as a crewmember to further some plan of your own here in Cuba. Tell me why I should not shout out for the night watchman and have you turned over to the authorities as an imposter."

"Because we would see to it that he was spirited out of the country before they could arrest him," someone behind her said. Without taking her eyes off Fairchild, Jane turned her head to address the familiar voice.

"Ah, Mister Betancourt. I might have guessed. Does Consul Rodney know of your involvement with this brigand?"

"The affairs of the US Consul bear no relation to this matter, Captain. We merely seek to put right that which has gone so terribly wrong. And to serve the honor of France." As he finished speaking, Jane heard him step close behind her. Before she could bring her knife around to hold him off, Betancourt threw her down, knocking the blade from her hand, and was soon using her sash to lash her hands together. At her feet, Fairchild was likewise engaged in wrapping her ankles. A handkerchief between her teeth completed their efforts to disable her and prevent her from crying out.

"*Alors, ma cherie*, I am sorry for this insult. But we must be well away this evening and cannot risk you setting the hounds on us. Perhaps we will meet again someday and finish what we have started. *Adieu, ma capitaine.*" Fairchild's voice in her ear was the last she heard of the two men as they slipped away into the night.

X

Secrets and Lies

"Stupid. Stupid, stupid, stupid." Jane was more angry than anything else. Galsworthy had told her that Fairchild was accompanied by a second man; how could she have overlooked that? The answer, she had to admit to herself, was that she had allowed herself to be momentarily swept up by a pair of strong arms and warm lips. Stupid.

It took Jane a number of minutes to lever herself onto her knees and locate the knife her father had given her when she first climbed on a boat as crew.

"You never know when you may need to cut a line, or a man, in a hurry," he had said. "Keep it on your belt at all times."

Glad now that she had heeded his advice, Jane set about freeing herself from the hastily tied bonds. Too bad Fairchild had turned out to be a real seaman; the knot around her ankles was well tied and did not yield easily to either her prying fingers or the sharp blade. She had just succeeded in tearing the gag from her mouth when Galsworthy appeared, panting from exertion.

"My stars, ma'am! What have ye gotten yerself into?" he exclaimed as the moonlight revealed his captain seated on the ground covered in dirt and surrounded by ragged bits of white cloth.

"That, Mister Galsworthy, is exactly what I intend to find out." Brushing herself down, Jane leapt to her feet and marched quickly toward the house with her mate hard on her heels. On the way, he explained that he had waited a half hour for Jane to return, and then set out to find her when she had not appeared. In return, she related her misadventure and the sorry outcome of her attempt to reckon with the false seaman. Galsworthy couldn't help but smile at the thought of Fairchild with Jane's knife against his face; too bad she felt restrained by her good nature not to take a larger chunk out of the man's hide.

"What do ye intend on doing, if I may ask, ma'am?" Galsworthy queried as the house came into view at the top of the rise.

It was a very good question. Whatever Fairchild, or should she call him *Bonenfant*, was up to, it involved their host. Her main concern was for the welfare of her vessel and its crew, and she could not afford to entangle either herself or them in some political intrigue on the island. Slowing her steps, she finally came to a halt when they were still some distance from the veranda.

"I don't aim to bring trouble on us, Mister Galsworthy, but it seems that trouble has found us. While I would like to forget this sorry episode, I am afraid that it may be only part of a larger problem that will dog us until we leave this place. It will be at least another day before we can cast off for the Baltic. During that time, we will be doing business with this Frenchman Sarrazin who, I have to believe, is consorting with men who are harboring secrets and a dangerous agenda."

Galsworthy nodded and then waited patiently as Jane considered her next move.

"Come, let us retire for the night and see what may be learned from our host over breakfast. Perhaps we may discover what intrigue is being played out here without showing our own hand. In the meantime, I will bar the window and lock the door of my sleeping chamber. I suggest you do the same."

Their plans for worming some sort of truth out of Monsieur Sarrazin in the morning were thwarted when they discovered that he had left early on his horse for the dock. Madame Sarrazin was most apologetic as she explained that her husband wanted to order the opening of the warehouse and arrange for storage of the oak logs before the *Destiny* arrived to offload her cargo and take on her new load. She insisted that they sit down to breakfast before departing, as there was still time before the schooner would arrive and work would begin in earnest.

As captain, it was not Jane's role to oversee the unloading and loading of the cargo. That job fell to the capable Mister Dawkins, who would be sure to have prepared all of the papers necessary for the accurate accounting of the loads. However, the crew would be missing the steady guidance and strong arm of Mister Galsworthy, and they made haste to finish as quickly as good manners would allow.

Out in front of the house, they waited with Madame as the volante was made ready and brought round.

"Thank you again, Madame, for your kind hospitality," Jane said. "We have enjoyed ourselves immensely and will tell all our friends of the warm island welcome we have encountered here. We were gratified to see that the customs of France have been kept alive here in Cuba although it lies so far away."

"*Mais non*, mademoiselle, it is not Cuba that nurtures the heart of our country here. We are from Haiti, and it was with great sadness that we had to leave that beautiful place when we were threatened with our lives. My poor Amelie's father was butchered by his own slaves, and we were spared only because we were visiting relatives in town that night. Monsieur Sarrazin, God bless him, took us in when we had nothing, and made me his cherished wife. He feels deeply the wrong that was done us, and we pray every day that we may have restored to us that which was taken."

Jane knew of the slave revolt that had taken place in the islands some years previously. The mass slaughter of white plantation owners and their loyal servants had shocked the world. She was aware that many of the dispossessed that had managed to escape had ended up here on Cuba, where they sought to rebuild their lives.

Grasping Madame Sarrazin by the hand, Jane let her see how touched she was by the tale, and that she was grieved by Madame's loss. Whatever the justness of their cause, the acts of barbarity and inhumanity perpetrated by the revolutionaries were beyond the pale.

"I wish to express my sincere condolences, *madame*. You are far stronger than I can imagine myself to be in similar circumstances."

"No, my sweet girl, I expect that strength lies at the very core of your soul. It is what draws people to you and makes them want to follow where you lead. Be careful what path you choose, for many are willingly led by those who know their own minds." With those parting words and a fond embrace, Madame Sarrazin turned back into the house as the carriage set off on its swift passage through the valley back into town.

Jane and Galsworthy arrived at the dock to a scene of great activity. Mister Dawkins had brought the schooner in on the early flood tide as the sea breezes picked up with the rising sun, and she was now snugged to the near end of the wharf where men scurried up and down the gangplank. Although it appeared that chaos reigned, there was an orderly movement as some men shouldered heavy oak beams and bore them ashore while others moved cases of sugar to the weighing station for inspection before they were placed in the hold. Galsworthy jumped down from the carriage before it came to rest, and set off at a near run toward the dock, bawling at the men as he advanced. Among the busy throng were the excise man and his assistant, as well as the ubiquitous Señor Cabrera.

"Ah, *senorita capitan*. It is a pleasure to see you this morning." Waving his arms to indicate a line of carts drawn up on the wharf, Cabrera beamed at Jane. "You can see that your offer has been accepted, and there is plenty of sugar for your consideration."

"Indeed, Señor Cabrera, it would seem that you have succeeded in spreading the word. I commend you, and look forward to revisiting our business with you before our departure tomorrow."

Leaving the beaming man to attend to his duties in the port, Jane walked down the pier past where the *Destiny* had tied up shortly after dawn. Gazing past her bowsprit, Jane could see a ship setting out to sea. By shading her eyes with her hand and squinting, she was just able to make out the flag waving from the ship's top spar: a swallowtail blue field with a yellow cross. Jane couldn't recall having seen her in the anchorage the past few days, and wondered when she had arrived. She would have to remember to ask Cabrera.

The walk back up to the wharf was slow going as Jane

dodged piles of sugar cartons and bales of provisions. Cookie was preparing the vessel for the weeks of sea time ahead of them on their way to St. Petersburg. While they could put in at Orkney for supplies, Jane was hoping to make it all the way to the Kattegat before they needed to reprovision. If the Danish health official was at all suspicious they might be carrying yellow fever, there was a good chance they would be told to head back to the quarantine bay on Känsö island in Gothenburg harbor; but if they escaped into the Baltic with a clean bill of health, they could put in at one of the ports in southern Sweden for basic supplies.

Rounding the head of the gangway, Jane caught sight of their host from the prior evening. As she raised her hand to hail him, she noticed that he was in heated conversation with someone. Huddled together at the end of the warehouse, they were looking around and appeared to be arguing. A minute later, the second man shook Sarrazin's hand and turned toward Jane to step into a waiting volante. She spun on her heel to hide her face as she recognized the consul's clerk. What was he doing here, and what had Sarrazin to do with him and his plans? Certain that they were plotting something that would affect the *Destiny*, Jane continued on her way to intercept the planter and find out what she could.

Monsieur Sarrazin was still flustered from his encounter with Betancourt when she approached, and was hard pressed to assume a pleasant smile with which to greet her.

"*Bonjour, mademoiselle la capitaine.* I am most sorry to have missed you at the house this morning. I trust you were well taken care of in my absence?"

"But of course, monsieur, and we are grateful for your kind invitation. The evening was most delightful, though I fear we may have kept you from your other guests. I thought I saw Mister Betancourt at the house last evening in the company of my former crew member, Mister Fairchild."

"Guests? *Mais non, mademoiselle.* You were our only guests last evening, and I am afraid that I am not acquainted with the gentlemen you named. Now, shall we inspect the cargo and verify that it meets with your approval?"

Stunned by the bald-faced lie, Jane followed Sarrazin back to the warehouse.

XI

All Aboard

As she followed Sarrazin through the gaping warehouse doors, Jane had to duck to avoid being knocked down by the sugar boxes being moved about with cranes suspended from the ceiling. Traveling on huge iron rails that spanned the space, the clanking chains of the cranes' windlasses created such a noise that men had to shout to be heard. It would take most of the day to stow the cargo in the *Destiny's* hold, and then another several hours to batten the hatches and prepare the schooner to set sail.

"Ahoy, Captain!" Dawkins' voice was raised above the din as he shouted to Jane. "Over here!"

Excusing herself to Monsieur Sarrazin, Jane strode through the piles of boxes to join the chief in front of an opened case.

"Here, Captain, have a taste." Dawkins held out a knife on which he balanced a small pile of deep brown muscovado sugar. Taking a pinch in her fingers, Jane placed the granules on her tongue. The flavor was exquisite. She was sure it would fetch a high price in the markets of St. Petersburg.

Smiling, Jane asked, "Is it all this good?"

"Aye, Captain, that it is. We should make a fine profit on this load trading on our own behalf. Perhaps Banks and his partner did us a favor by shorting us on the shipment. We should seek to carry as much of our own sugar as we can on this voyage, and use every square foot below decks for it."

Jane knew what Dawkins was getting at. Stowed far forward in the lockers was that goodly shipment of brocade from Lowell. Jane had lost several days in New York waiting for the load, and she would be glad to see the back of it. Although well wrapped and carefully packed, fabrics were subject to mildew and rot on the long transatlantic passage, and if she could fulfill the terms of the contract by selling it now, she would be much relieved.

"We have a bottom price contract, and as long as we can

exceed that here in Cuba, perhaps we can offload the goods right now and use the stowage for our own sugar," Dawkins suggested.

"Perhaps we can indeed, Mister Dawkins. I see the consul has just arrived. Let's see what we can do."

Mister Rodney was quite sure that they could put the word out to several of the local planters and merchants who would be interested in purchasing quantities of the beautiful fabrics. He thought Jane might get an even better price in Havana, but she was willing to settle for the local market as long as they could meet her minimum price. With the help of a local seller's agent, the *Destiny* held a wharfside auction late that afternoon and sold every bit of fabric from the hold. Jane was thrilled as she signed the agent's bills of sale and did a rapid sum in her head. The load had fetched a premium price, and Banks' firm would see an immediate return on the cargo they had entrusted with her family. She hoped they would do as well with the sugar.

Jane left Dawkins to oversee the rest of the loading and sought out the consul once more in his office on the plaza. He looked up from a desk piled with papers as she entered, and rose to offer her his hand with a smile.

"You have made a fine profit of your visit to Matanzas, Captain. May you make many more!"

"No small thanks to you, Consul Rodney, and I am grateful for that assistance. We were able to settle our affairs without extending our credit with the bank here, and that will make my uncle well pleased. I do wonder if I might trouble you on another matter. You see, the *Destiny* is in need of two more crew. Are there any likely seamen adrift here, aside from the one I have dismissed, who might like a billet on a schooner?"

Rodney hesitated a moment before answering. "There might be, Captain, but you'll need to consider the cases carefully. I can recommend Daniel Macy, a fine able seaman out of Nantucket who lost his place last month when the *Martha* went down in the bay. He's cooled his heels here hoping for a trading ship instead of heading home with the rest of the crew. He might do, but I don't know how he will feel about serving under a woman, ma'am. My apologies for being so plainspoken."

"Well, those Quakers make hardy sailors as long as they keep their opinions to themselves. Let us see if he passes muster. Send him along to see Mister Dawkins if he's willing. And the other?"

"The other is a harder choice. Perhaps you have heard that slaves in Cuba have the right to go before a judge and request that a price for their person be determined. Anyone, including the slave himself, who pays that sum has the ownership of the man to do with as he pleases."

"A curious system, but pray tell what that has to do with my crew?" Jane asked.

"A fellow named Jean Vaugine has put in for his price and let it be known that he was in search of a ship owner who would buy his title. It seems he is anxious to be quit of Cuba and make his way in the world. I think he hopes eventually to buy his own freedom if he can but find a captain to take him on with a seaman's wages."

"Can you arrange for him to be at the dock this evening so that we may take the measure of him? I will need to consult with my officers to hear their opinion of the matter before I can make a decision." Jane was intrigued, but wary of taking on someone who came with the potential for problems down the road. She could not in good conscience have a slave aboard her vessel, but perhaps there was another solution at hand if the man proved sound and agreeable.

"One matter remains then, Consul Rodney. The man I am leaving ashore, Mister Fairchild, here are his papers." Jane reached out with the small packet and dropped them on the consul's desk. "I would like to warn you that he may be the cause of some trouble for you, I am sorry to say. He and your Mister Betancourt."

The consul raised his eyebrows in astonishment. "My assistant?"

"Indeed. I encountered them at the Sarrazin *ingenio* last evening and was set upon by them in order to delay my alerting the guard of their presence. It would seem they are involved in some scheme together. You may wish to look into it."

"Set upon?" Consul Rodney rose in alarm.

"Aye, but I have come to no harm and have no desire to press charges as it would delay our departure. I leave it in your hands, Mister Rodney."

Having concluded her business with the consul, Jane thanked him and handed over a packet of letters she asked him to see posted on the next vessel headed for an American port. In addition to letters from herself and the crew to friends at home, Jane had sent along detailed reports of the journey and cargo to her uncle.

That evening after the lamps had been lit in the *Destiny's* cabins and the crew quarters at the bow, two men arrived and hailed the watch. They were shown separately to the captain's quarters, where Jane and her officers were reviewing the day's work.

Macy proved to be a hale young man of twenty or so who had worked the Nantucket fleet since he was a lad. Dressed in seaman's togs with his dark hair covered in a flat cap, he walked with the rolling gait of the seasoned mariner. Tired of the stench and greasy smoke of the whaling ships that went on voyages lasting two years or more, Macy was hoping to make his way on the vessels that plied the Atlantic in the merchant trade. He professed not to care whether the captain wore trousers or skirts or nothing at all, so long as the ship was well run and his wages paid. His plain speaking and simple manner brought to mind her dear friend Endeavour, and inclined Jane in his favor. Both Dawkins and Galsworthy could find no fault with the man, so he was offered a berth to New York by way of St. Petersburg and sent forward with his sea bag to join the men in the forecastle.

Vaugine was another matter entirely. A man of thirty or so years, he appeared strong and healthy, and was well spoken – in French. He commanded enough English to explain that he had worked as an overseer on the coffee plantation, but was eager to try becoming a sailor. His demeanor, while marked by the deference expected in someone whose every moment was at the disposal of a master, was nonetheless proud and upright. Without the bonds of slavery to hold him down, it was clear that Vaugine would make a name for himself in the world.

Jane was torn. The month's advance he would be given as a green boy aboard the *Destiny* would be ample to serve as a down payment on his manumission. She could easily collect the remainder of the freedom price from his further wages so that he would be free to seek his own way once they returned to New York. But she needed seasoned crew, and was loath to bring aboard another hand who would need training and supervision from Galsworthy.

In the end, she decided to leave the choice to her mates. If they thought it worth the extra work, she would advance the sum to the court and take him aboard. It took only a few minutes for them to agree that if they could be the path to liberty for but one man, it was a worthwhile project. Vaugine was sent home with instructions to gather his things and appear with the magistrate in the morning so that his papers could be settled and the money paid.

Once the men had left, Jane climbed to the deck to breathe in the tropical evening air for the last time before the *Destiny* got under way in the morning. She was troubled by the unsettled state of affairs with Fairchild and the deceitful Sarrazin. The encounter with Fairchild and Betancourt the night before had shaken Jane more than she had been willing to admit to herself at the time. The pair were in collusion with Sarrazin in whatever business they were conducting, and had used her schooner to bring Fairchild to Cuba. That much was clear. She wondered if the frigate she had seen beating out to sea had carried him aboard. Well, good riddance to him and may she never see his face again. The scoundrel.

Shaking her head, Jane gave up thinking about it for the moment. She couldn't see how any of it could harm the vessel under her command, but she would not truly relax until they were out on the ocean and well away from the island.

Back in her cabin, with the gentle slapping sounds of the wind in the rigging floating down through the open companionway above her, Jane lit her lamp and settled down at the desk to write one last letter. She had already written to Prudence and her uncle and sent a quick note to her dear parents to assure them of her health and wellbeing. Now, there was the letter to Endeavor to consider. Poking her nose with the end of the quill as she pondered, Jane finally dipped it into the ink and began to write.

Dear E.

Thank you for your birthday letter. It did brighten the day for me. I heard from my dearest sister that you planned to take my place at table. I trust William did not terrify you with tales of hairsbreadth escapes from perils at sea. You must believe he exaggerates for the amusement of my father and nephews. My voyages, at least thus far, are so tame as not to bear retelling for fear of putting my audience to sleep.

That said, things have not proceeded entirely as anticipated, yet I believe the results will be satisfactory. I do now find myself in a most fascinating and peculiar part of the world, among people who have ideas and ways of life more foreign than I had imagined. The island of Cuba is beautiful, almost beyond description. Flowers are everywhere, of exotic varieties I have never before seen. The warm weather, at least in the morning and evenings, brings people out of doors so the streets are busy, but in a more cheery and lively atmosphere than one would find in New York. Then the city is suddenly deserted as the noontime sun becomes oppressive, and all retire for the afternoon sleep, or siesta as it is called here.

There is not time now to relate more, as tomorrow if all goes as planned, we leave Cuba for more northern climes. Also tomorrow, I expect to take an action in accordance with a cause dear to both of us. No details now, but I hope to please you with the tale on my return.

Even as I embark for yet more distant ports, the thought of home and friends anchors my heart. I sometimes find myself thinking "I must tell Endeavor about this!" The coming months will surely afford many such moments, and I look forward to long conversations when I return. Until then, I am

Your wandering friend,
Jane

Jane sealed the letter and set it aside to hand to the consul in the morning. She blew out her lantern and again mounted the ladder to the quarterdeck. Nodding to young Hitchens, who was keeping watch on the quarterdeck, she worked her way forward to where her hammock still hung from the mizzenmast. She unhooked one end and hung it from a cleat on the main mast, then climbed in to watch the stars and finally, dreamlessly, fall asleep.

XII

Making Northing

The crew was called on deck early on their last day in Cuba. Jane planned to catch the outgoing tide in the early afternoon and there were still last minute provisions to stow and affairs to conclude. She had sent a note last night to Consul Rodney to arrange for a solicitor to accompany the magistrate and Vaugine, and she was now in her cabin awaiting their arrival.

Before the start of every voyage, long or short, Jane made it a point to spend time reviewing her charts one last time. Word had come in with the ships at Matanzas that the Gulf Stream was indeed shifting eastward and swinging north sooner than was usual. She considered following a route that would take them past Bermuda, but with the chance of running into the eastern edge of the stream, she decided to play it safe and ride the Antilles current to Florida and then follow the coast. They would make easting south of Hatteras and cut straight across the Gulf Stream, picking up the westerlies out the other side. If her luck held, they would be well north before the hurricanes began to build in the Caribbean. It would mean sailing on a beam reach for two or three days, but the *Destiny* did well at that point of sail. It was just when they got closer to the wind that she began to fall off and refuse to come to weather.

Satisfied that she had chosen a passage that was both prudent and likely to shorten their voyage to the North Sea, Jane stowed the charts and tidied her cabin in preparation for departure. Neat by nature, she nevertheless tended to allow things to lie about loose while they were in port. Unless she wanted to be on her knees hunting for things over the coming weeks, it was best that she stow everything away in her trunks and behind doors.

Built to accommodate a couple, the captain's cabin was relatively generous by ship standards. A wide berth lay atop a set of latched drawers, with a large closet taking up the space between it and the bulkhead. Deadlights brightened the room on sunny days and lanterns mounted to the beams provided a cheery atmosphere at night. Amply supplied with a desk, armchair, and bookcases, the glowing teak-lined chamber was warm and elegant, and Jane appreciated the care that had been taken to make the captain's quarters comfortable, even if they were a little lonely at times.

She had just finished her housekeeping when Griggs appeared at the cabin door. He had been sent by Galsworthy to alert the captain that Vaugine had arrived with the magistrate and a solicitor in tow.

"Please ask them to join me here, Griggs, and let Mister Dawkins know that I request his presence as well."

"Aye, aye, ma'am." Griggs saluted and disappeared, then returned a minute later with her new recruit, the magistrate, and a man who introduced himself to Jane as Señor Carlos Fuego.

"I have here the documents you wrote to me about, Captain Thorn. Perhaps you would like to look them over before we proceed?" Fuego asked as he extended a sheaf of papers to Jane.

She did so as she waited for Dawkins to join them. Out of the corner of her eye, she glanced at Vaugine from time to time. She was impressed by what she saw; even in this fraught moment, he radiated a sense of assurance and calm. Outfitted in something approaching the typical sailor's garb of canvas trousers and a short navy jacket with a sea bag leaning against his leg, he appeared ready to take up his duties the moment the documents were signed.

"They appear to be in order, Señor Fuego, thank you."

As soon as Dawkins joined the group, she turned to Jean Vaugine and fixed him with a stern gaze. "You understand that with this document I am paying your valuation, and thereby purchasing the rights to your person?"

"*Oui, Capitaine*, I understand."

"Very good. Then let me explain these other three documents. The first is your manumission papers. I will sign these now and provide you with a copy that testifies to your status as a free man as of this moment. Make sure you keep them about your person once you land in New York. There are slave traders still at work there although the practice is banned in our part of the country. As for the second, you will serve aboard my vessel as any other man, and be paid your wages like the rest of the crew. These sea articles set forth the terms and duration of the voyage. This final document is a promissory note stating that you will repay Thorn Shipping for the purchase of your freedom. We are retaining your first wages as a down payment against the debt you owe, and you will pay a portion of your further wages after that toward it. Do well on this voyage, and there will be a place for you on our ships in the future, Mister Vaugine. Is all of that agreeable to you?"

There was a tear in the corner of his eye as Vaugine stepped forward and quietly held out his hand to the captain. She shook it, and felt an answering tear start down her own cheek.

"You are most welcome aboard, seaman Vaugine, and I am certain we will all be well satisfied with our business this morning. Now, Señor Fuego, Mister Dawkins has arrived to serve as our witness. Perhaps you could bring this matter to a swift conclusion so that we may be about our work preparing to depart."

Spreading out the papers on the desk, the solicitor pointed to the places where Jane, as representative of Thorn Shipping and Cargo, should affix her signature. Then it was Vaugine's turn. Jane was pleased to see that he signed his full name; someone who could read and write would find it easier to make his way as a free man.

Picking up a bottle of her favorite port, Jane poured small glasses all around. "Let us toast to Mister Vaugine and his future."

"*Oui, ma capitaine.* And to the lady who makes it possible." With a slight bow followed by a firm salute, Vaugine followed Galsworthy out of the cabin to begin his new life as a deckhand aboard the *Destiny.*

As soon as the paperwork was in order and the money handed over from the vessel's cash box to the magistrate, Jane took her leave and set off ashore alone to accomplish one final task.

The scent of flowers carried on the warm breeze from the southeast as Jane made her way one last time across the central square of Matanzas. The busy streets were filled with people, causing her to duck aside more than once to avoid being knocked into the gutter. Wiping sweat from her forehead, Jane turned into a cool alley that led behind the courthouse. The consul had mentioned that a number of tattoo parlors were to be found here, and named one that he heard had a reputation for being clean. She was determined to follow the tradition of the sea and commemorate her first visit to this foreign port with a flower tattoo. A simple outline of a mariposa, it would serve to remind her of this first foray into the wider world aboard a vessel under her command.

Baring her forearm in the inking den, she showed the man with the needle a drawing she had done last night. A scant inch across, it would not mar the look of her arm while still marking her as a member of the sailing fraternity, even if she was a woman. She smiled to herself as she thought of the fainting fit her dear mama was likely to have when she saw it. Jane didn't try to upset her mother, but sometimes things just worked out that way.

Afterward, her arm still stinging from the needle, the captain walked slowly back to the dock, enjoying her last moments on the island. She had delighted in the warm, pleasant climate and the hospitality of the people, but she was deeply troubled by the entrenched practice of slavery. The growing sugar exports could only be sustained through the use of slave labor as far as she could see. The government in Spain would surely consider the garnering of wealth more important than the freedom of man. It was a knotty question the Thorns would have to confront if they wished to continue to carry the products of the Caribbean economies to the world, she thought.

Jane made one last visit before embarking for departure. She found Señor Cabrera stretched out on the divan in his office partaking of the daily siesta. Handing him a bottle of her favorite port, Jane thanked him for his assistance with the acquisition of their cargo, and with helping them clear their paperwork with the authorities that morning. She left a packet on his desk that would handsomely reward him for his efforts, and shook his hand. The little man still made her wrinkle her nose, but he had held to his promise and their success in Cuba was due in no small part to the harbormaster.

"By the by," Jane said in a casual voice as she passed back out the door, "I saw an East Indiaman standing out to sea this morning. Was she recently arrived? I don't recall her in the harbor these past days."

"*Si, Capitan* Thorn, she came in on the late evening tide yesterday and turned again this morning before anyone could make their way out to her. Very peculiar, but since she did not land a party ashore, she was free to go."

"Did you not go out to her last night then?"

"No, *Capitan*, the wind in the harbor had risen and it was so late, I thought to wait for the calm in the morning." Señor Cabrera shrugged as if the whole thing was of no importance and took his leave.

Curious, Jane thought. A ghost ship that appears and disappears and no one is the wiser as to her intentions or destination. However, Jane was sure that she would recognize her if she ever saw her again, and perhaps she might discover the answer to the mystery then.

Dawkins and Galsworthy had the men moving rapidly about the deck during the captain's absence, readying the lines to be cast off, raising the foresail to pull them off the dock when the tide turned, and stowing away the last items delivered for the galley.

Shortly after the afternoon watch came on deck, Galsworthy called out that the tide was running. Dawkins gave the command to cast off the bow lines, and the *Destiny* slowly swung about to turn her nose to the north. As the breeze filled the foresail, the stern lines were cast loose and the schooner headed out of the bay, heeled well over to larboard as she surged toward the open sea.

Destiny's Gold

Tuesday, May 23, 1820   With light wind from east and proceeded with all possible despatch to the Gulf of Mexico, Thursday comm.c. with mod. Winds from SE + Pleasant and ends the same. Left dock Matanzas at noon from which I take my departure. Lat. (chart) 23° 04'N Long. (chart) 81° 31'W.

Once out on the open water, Jane called to Dawkins to assemble the crew midships.

"Ahoy, men," she called from her customary spot at the top of the quarterdeck ladder. "We have made a profitable venture of things thus far. With luck, we will beat the hurricanes to the north and have smooth sailing this month. If not, I know I can count on you men to handle the vessel. We welcome Mister Vaugine and Mister Macy to the crew and ask that you all help them find their feet. Mister Vaugine will be on larboard watch, which makes you, Billy Hitchens, the acting ordinary on the starboard watch." She pointed to the young man as he lounged on the hatch covers. "All right men, look lively, we are St. Petersburg bound!"

Within the hour, Cuba had fallen away astern and Jane gave the order to bring the heading around to west by northwest. They would pass south of the Bahamas by evening and turn north as they drew closer to the Florida coast. By hugging the shore, they would stay well inside the rapidly flowing body of water that tracked its way at a speed of five knots up the eastern seaboard. Since winds out of the north could blow up at any time and churn the sea in the Gulf Stream into a roiling cauldron, experienced mariners knew that the potential for a few extra knots of speed over ground was often not worth the storms and high seas the Gulf Stream was ready to throw at any foolhardy captain green enough to try taking what seemed like the easy path.

Hourly soundings and speed log readings kept the larboard watch busy as the evening wore on. Just as dusk began to settle, Boniface on lookout spied the breakers off the southernmost outcroppings of the islands to their north. Skirting well away from the shoals where the sea floor rose to low hills that barely broke the surface, the *Destiny* picked a careful path through the beautiful but treacherous waters of the Antilles.

Friday, May 26   Lat. DR 28° 35'N Long. DR 79° 27'W Comm.c. with light winds from SW, light rain but getting better; some crew sick; have left the Bahamas.

Dawn broke on Friday with a clear sky and steady winds out of the southwest. During the night, Jane had the helmsman turn the bow to the north, but she was ready to seek a closer inshore path now that the sun had come up.

Galsworthy had reported at the forenoon watch change that Vaugine and Boniface had taken to their bunks. Vaugine had seemed healthy when he had come aboard, but was struck with a bout of seasickness as soon as they had left the harbor. Two days of purging had seemed to put him to rights, but now he was lying in his bunk sweating and complaining of a sore head. Boniface lay on the facing bunk listless after having been up heaving over the side for much of the night.

"Is it yellow fever, Dawkins? You've seen it before," Jane asked with a frown as she conferred with her chief mate in the saloon that afternoon. She knew they had run this risk by putting in to Cuba, and feared their luck had run out.

"We will know soon enough, ma'am. Doctor Devèze in Philadelphia proved that the fever does not transfer from person to person, so I doubt the lad has taken it on from Vaugine. And there was no fever at the *ingenio* where he was living, so Vaugine may simply be a case of ennui from the purging. We will move them to the forward bunks away from the other crew and watch for signs of yellow in the eyes."

"See to it that Cookie keeps them provided with gruel and plenty of fresh water. And let's get them on deck into the sunshine as soon as they are able," she ordered.

The afternoon saw light rain building and passing over them as the *Destiny* sailed under single reefed canvas. Jane loved this part of sailing; the cresting of the waves as the schooner surged forward, finding its line in the sparkling ocean and carrying them all toward their next adventure. She knew she was being romantic, but it was her love of the sea, and the boats that plied their trade on it, that had brought her out here. She felt she had been set free by her family to make her way in the world, and she relished every minute of it. The next leg of the voyage would take them to waters new to her, and to places she had only read about. While the unknown called to her, she was also at heart a hardheaded businesswoman. If she could make a good profit for their client and themselves on this voyage, she would be well satisfied, and knew the sentiment would be shared back in New York.

Saturday, May 27 Lat. DR 30° 07'N Lat. Obs. 30° 07'N Long. DR 78° 12'W Comm + ends wind from South east, wind variable to East. Ends same. Crew much improved.

Jane went on deck with the morning watch and sought out Mister Galsworthy on the foredeck, where he was supervising the resetting of the jib, for a crew report.

"How are things below; any change in the men?"

Galsworthy pointed forward to where Jane could see the lookout astride the bowsprit with his legs dangling over the side.

"That's Boniface, ma'am. Crawled out a' his berth this morning and insisted on standing watch. He is much improved and looks to be on the mend. We'll keep an eye on the boy, make sure he is steady on his legs afore he goes back to full duty."

"Very good. And Mister Vaugine?"

"Much the same, ma'am. No signs of yellow in the eyes yet nor any purging of blood. He may just need more time to get his sea legs, this being only his second time aboard. He tells me he was most distressed on the passage from Haiti to Cuba; it is a wonder he made up his mind to follow the sea, ma'am!"

"Let's get him up on deck then. Make him up a stable seat where he can see forward and let us see if we can make a sailor of him yet," Jane ordered. "And what of Mister Macy; how goes it for our whalerman?"

"That Macy fellow is a born seaman, handy with a line and always at the front when it's time to douse a sail. He'd make a fine mate, that one would, and you should seek to keep him on once we return, ma'am. Glad he came aboard," was Galsworthy's enthusiastic assessment of the young man.

The next day, Jane ordered a sharp swing to starboard to make a quick transit of the Gulf Stream. They made good time and crossed its eastern edge a day and a half later. Soon, they had picked up the first puff of a westerly breeze, and the *Destiny* was off and running to the northeast, bound for the cold waters of the north Atlantic and the rugged string of islands at the top of Scotland.

XIII

Deep Blue

Friday, June 9   No sighting. Lat. DR 42° 30'N   Long. DR 55° 31'W
Throughout the day strong gales from NE + N + N by E under close reef of sail.
Dolphins sighted.

The second week in June brought the first gales of the northern passage. The last two days had been foggy and cool, but with no heavy winds or rain. The air pressure had dropped overnight and Jane ordered the vessel prepared for a storm. To the west, Nova Scotia lay off their port quarter, sending cold gusts from the northern reaches of Canada across the broad expanse of open water. Despite it being early summer, the crew was bundled in wool coats with knitted hats pulled down over their ears as they worked the deck. Jane commanded Cookie to have hot drinks available to the men all day, and at noon took her own glass of hot, strong tea back to her cabin after she and Dawkins had attempted to take a sighting at noon. The low clouds turned the sun into a soft orange glow without defined edges and they had abandoned the attempt.

Once below, the captain stowed her sextant in its mahogany case and stripped off the layers of clothing that had kept her warm and dry. She then spooned some of the muscovado sugar saved for her own use in a small silver box into her tea. The rich flavor was a treat she looked forward to sharing with the family at home. Jane tucked herself into her berth and set to working out their position based on the headings and speed log. An hour later, she was pleased to see that they were still working their way at a goodly clip toward their next waypoint at sixty degrees north latitude and three degrees west. With steady winds, they should make the turn south as they passed through the Northern Isles of Scotland in about four weeks.

A knock at the cabin door heralded the arrival of Dawkins,

who dripped his way in and dropped into the chair by the navigation table.

"It's started to rain, ma'am. Good thing we reefed earlier; looks like a real blow headed our way."

"And Vaugine? How goes it for our greenest hand?" Jane wondered. "Is he ready for the next test the sea is going to throw at him?"

Over the past two weeks, Vaugine had learned to ride the rhythm of the sea and keep his stomach settled. To Jane's relief, they seemed to have escaped Cuba without being afflicted by the fever, and she considered herself lucky indeed. The yearly trouble with the many plagues in the tropics, and the unfortunate use of enslaved peoples to produce exports, had given Jane much to think about as she contemplated future trading voyages.

Dawkins couldn't keep from smiling now as he remembered the look of terror on the inexperienced seaman's face as he stared out at the approaching storm.

"Aye, he'll get the hang of it, ma'am, just give him time. He's willing, I'll say that. And the men like him well enough. Once he gets a few more sea miles under his belt and lives through a storm or two, he'll be all right."

Jane knew how he must be feeling. The sight of nothing but deep blue water in every direction with dark clouds and rain showers barreling down on you could be daunting to any man. Over the years she had learned to trust her vessel and her own skills to bring them safely through weather like this. As any mariner knew, you tried your best to avoid trouble, but had to be ready to handle it if it came. They would seek to keep their compass heading through the gale, but it was more important to angle the bow across the waves while making enough headway to allow the helm to steer. Reducing canvas would slow the vessel down and keep her from heeling over too far while the storm blew itself out.

Soon enough, Jane could feel the schooner start to move up and down as the waves built astern. She climbed back into her oilskins and joined Dawkins at the helm from whence she could see Vaugine standing amidships with the rest of the watch while clinging tightly to a halyard. Together, they rode out the storm as the seas poured over the leeward rail and the rigging whined above.

By late afternoon, the storm had blown itself out and the vessel had been put to rights. The bilges showed little increase in the water level, and Jane was glad to hear that the hull seams were holding under the tremendous forces of the raging seas. The first dogwatch came on deck in time to see the sun burst through the clouds. A cheer went up as a pod of dolphins suddenly breached the surface of the ocean just off the starboard bow. The hands lined the rail and cheered them on until the dolphins disappeared as suddenly as they had come.

Wednesday, June 28 Lat. Obs. 55° 23'N Lat. DR 55° 25'N Long. DR 22° 30'W This day a continuation of yesterday's weather. Light airs and at times calm. Squally from NE to West round to N Picked up a cache of codfish oil exceedingly covered with barnacles from which we filled two barrels.

As June came to a close, the *Destiny* ploughed her way through the north Atlantic, often fighting squalls and gales or sitting in calm, sunny waters waiting for the wind to find them. Dawkins assured Jane that the shifty conditions were typical of these waters, but they were making good time. All in all, he thought they were several days if not a week ahead of any brig captains who had left Cuba when the *Destiny* had departed from Matanzas.

The men entertained themselves during the calms by fishing, although none were successful in landing anything that could be called dinner, and Vaugine was teaching the men Haitian tavern songs accompanied by Griggs on the pipes. Vaugine had adapted well to the crew and Jane was pleased to see that the men had taken the former slave under their protection. They were improving his English and teaching him the ways of the sea. He was a quick study and could soon tie all of the important knots more rapidly than most of the crew. The boys, Boniface and Hitchens, benefited from the lessons in seamanship too, and Jane could see their confidence growing daily. She had instructed Galsworthy to keep the pair busy with studies and work so they did not have too much idle time on their hands.

Once or twice a week, they spotted ships and brigs headed west, but did not exchanges messages with any as they were too distant. The captain was quietly pleased to see that the *Destiny* overtook and left astern the other vessels headed north along their path.

They had been at sea over a month when seaman Parkes on lookout spied a dark shape floating in the water. It bobbed on the waves about a hundred yards off the larboard beam, neither approaching nor receding over the two hours they watched. Jane ordered out the skiff, and Boniface and Hitchens put themselves forward, eager to fetch the object and bring it back with them if possible.

"All right, boys, take a line with you and see if you can lasso it like a bronco!" Jane commanded.

Except for Riggins at the wheel, the rest of the crew lined the rail to watch the entertainment as the boys rowed out to the mysterious object.

"Ahoy!" Hitchens shouted, "It's a cask, ma'am. We'll have a noose on it in a trice."

In short order, the cask was secured and dragged behind the small boat as the boys pulled vigorously for the *Destiny*. Riggins and Galsworthy helped the pair over the side and then hoisted in the small barrel.

"It's oil, ma'am," Galsworthy said. "Look, it's stamped here. Cod liver oil."

"Must have fallen off a ship, probably from Norway," Dawkins observed. "We'll have plenty for the lamps and Cookie can throw some in the grub to keep the crew fit, ma'am. That was a lucky find."

XIV

Inbound to Elsinore

Monday, July 10   No sighting. Lat. DR 57° 52'N   Long. DR 10° 53'W   A number of ships to P and S. Sighted the Jeremiah out of NY. Did not speak as too distant.

By the time they had crossed the North Sea, the boys could no longer be called green. All of the men had come together into a practiced crew. Jane was confident in their abilities and she was pleased that Galsworthy and Dawkins shared her opinion.

The *Destiny's* passage across the sea had been notable for the great increase in the number of vessels she passed both north and south bound. There were so many that Dawkins ceased to keep a tally in the daily log and merely noted that there were "a number of ships." Then, as noon was approaching on the tenth of July, and they were rounding the promontory of Skagen on Denmark's northernmost peninsula, Jane spied the *Jeremiah*.

Captain William Duncan had taken his brig south out of New York while Jane was still cooling her heels at her uncle's house awaiting her final cargo. She knew that he would be bound for Havana and then on to St. Petersburg with a load of sugar, the way he had for the last four years. Each time, the papers had reported on the *Jeremiah's* success in the Russian trade, and the profits he had brought to its owners. It had been Jane's notion to beat Duncan at his own game and use her schooner to bring sugar to the Baltic market ahead of the large cargo the *Jeremiah* would carry. She was sure she could outpace him on the windward legs of the passage, and hold her own across the northern reach where they would be pushed downwind by the westerlies.

The delay in New York had been frustrating for Jane, but without a letter of guarantee for the load out of Cuba, the journey would have been too risky for Thorn Shipping. She had been hoping for weeks that they could make up the time with their quick turnaround in Matanzas and the run up the coast. Seeing the brig just ahead of them now, inbound to Elsinore under full sail, brought a grin to the captain's face.

"Dawkins! Do you see her?" Jane called as she pointed north off the larboard bow. "She's making good time, but we are faster, I'll reckon. A shilling says we beat her to Elsinore!"

"Ah, ma'am, I would be betting against myself to take that wager. But I reckon you are right. Let us hope that Captain Duncan finds himself the guest of the quarantine authorities longer than we are held up."

Jane returned her spyglass to her eye and watched as the *Jeremiah's* crew clambered aloft to set more sail. She was taking advantage of every scrap of downhill wind to make port the following day, and Jane was determined to be ahead of her.

"Mister Dawkins, if there is another half a knot to be found anywhere under the *Destiny's* keel, I pray that you locate it and put it to good use. I'll stand a round of grog for the crew at the first tavern we find if I see the *Jeremiah* astern as we come into Elsinore."

This challenge brought a rousing cheer from the men when it was relayed by Mister Galsworthy. Soon, sails were being carefully trimmed and the helm brought as close to the wind as possible without threatening to throw the boom across the deck. The chip log was sent over the rail to check their progress every few minutes and gradually the *Destiny* settled to leeward and picked up speed.

By the time the sun had set an hour into the first watch, mist had begun to build over the Kattegat. The *Destiny* had been tracking down the Swedish coast at a distance of ten miles, and would have to turn south at Varberg to keep from running into Laholmsbukten in the coming hours. To avoid missing their waypoint, Jane ordered the schooner hove to, and soon the *Destiny* was drifting cautiously at less than half a knot with a man stationed at the bow with a lantern to watch for obstacles. The slow current flowing out of the Baltic, however, could carry them backward onto the rocky islands that dotted the coast, and a second lookout with a lantern was put at the stern.

Hitchens was sent to the mast to ring the *Destiny*'s bell every fifteen seconds, pausing at intervals to listen for the Nidingen bell off the shore south of Gothenburg. If they could hear it, they were in danger of running aground and would need to throw out an anchor. In the eerie quiet of the deck, only the hushed sounds of the waves lapping at the topsides, and the whispers of the men, could be heard as the leadsman called out the depth.

At the start of the middle watch, the depth was holding steady at fourteen fathoms, and Galsworthy sent the larboard watch below. By the time they returned for the morning watch, the sun would have been up for half an hour and they would be ready to set out for Elsinore as soon as the fog had burned off.

"Brings to mind the mists off Stony Point," Jane murmured to the second mate as he stood by her side at the mizzenmast. "I've said for years we need a fog bell there, or even a light if someone could be convinced to put up the money. You remember when we ran my sloop aground there two years ago? I don't wish to repeat the experience this night."

"A good reminder that caution is the sailor's friend!" Galsworthy's rejoinder was interrupted by Macy crying out urgently at the helm.

"Ahoy, Captain! I hear a ship to starboard. There, hear her spars a'creakin'? And that be her riggin' flappin'. There, her bell."

"Ring the bell hard, Hitchens!" Galsworthy roared to the boy where he stood at the mast. "Ring like your life depended on it!"

"Throw out an anchor," Jane directed. "We'll stall until we know where she is."

Grabbing the speaking trumpet, the captain ran to the starboard rail and began to call out.

"Ahoy! Ship to starboard! This is the schooner *Destiny*. Ahoy! We are southbound at half a knot, coming to anchor now. Ahoy! You are off our starboard beam." Jane shouted out repeatedly, pausing every few seconds to listen for a reply.

Several minutes later, she finally heard an answering hail.

"Ahoy *Destiny*! We are the brig *Jeremiah* southbound at a knot. We hear you off our port quarter. Ahoy! Can you see our lamps?" The deep voice carried across the water toward them and helped Jane locate the ship in the mist.

"Aye! This is Captain Thorn speaking. We have your lights now. You are a hundred yards off our starboard bow. Hold your course."

"Aye Captain! This is Captain Duncan. We will set anchor shortly when we are well away. Whither bound, *Destiny*?"

Should she tell him? No need to lend any more urgency to Duncan's plans for arriving in St. Petersburg, which he was sure to feel if she revealed their destination or cargo.

"Bound for Elsinore on the morrow. Godspeed!" With that, Jane stepped away from the rail and headed for her cabin. On the way, she stopped to speak with Galsworthy, who had overseen the dropping and setting of the stern anchor.

"Are we fast, Mister Galsworthy?" she asked as she leaned over the bow and followed the lay of the anchor chain with her eyes.

"Aye, Captain, that we are. With luck, the current will hold us pointing south until morning. We just need a good breeze, and we'll leave that devil astern while they are still a'sortin' out the gaskets."

Although the close call had been unnerving, Jane was glad to know that the *Jeremiah* was within overtaking distance once they could see their way in a few hours.

"I'll be below, Mister Galsworthy. Roust me out if anything changes. Otherwise, I will see you at first light." Jane dropped down the companionway into her cabin. She peered through the open saloon door to find Mister Dawkins with his head on the table fast asleep. Leaving him to get what rest he could, she lay down fully dressed on her bunk and was soon sound asleep herself, matching her chief mate snore for snore.

Tuesday, July 11   No sighting. Lat. (chart) 56° 05'N Long. (chart) 12° 37'W
Entered customs port at Elsinore. Many ships at anchor. Jeremiah inbound late
afternoon. Health officer aboard, quarantine order Känsö.

The weak northern sun peeked through the shrouds of fog a few hours later. Thankfully, the short nights and long days at these latitudes made the job of sailing the unknown waters less nerve-wracking for the unfamiliar navigator. Much as she had stared at her charts and calculated and recalculated the passage, Jane was never confident that she had got it right the first few times she ventured into a new harbor or stretch of sea. When the mist finally cleared, she was relieved to see that they were still many miles from land and safely away from the rocky shoals. What gave her even more satisfaction was to see the *Jeremiah* motionless half a mile away, with all of her sails furled and an anchor chain running from her bow. It would take them at least two hours to weigh anchor and get themselves under way, and Jane planned to be long gone before their first sail filled with wind.

As the sun continued to rise and warm the surface of the water, the fog cleared and the wind picked up. The afternoon watch took the deck as they sighted the forested point at Kullaberg with the Kullen light perched high on the rocky cliff. They would arrive in Elsinore that afternoon if the wind held, and it was time to prepare their papers for the Danish authorities.

"Mister Dawkins, pray join me below," Jane said to the chief. Once in her cabin, they pulled out all of the crew's papers, the cargo manifest, their port clearance from Matanzas and their lading order for St. Petersburg. From her desk, Jane drew forth a folded letter that bore the seal of the US Consulate in Matanzas.

"I don't know if they will pay attention to that, but Consul Rodney gave us a clean bill of health that we did not have yellow fever aboard when we left. And that the city had not had any new cases in over two weeks. Perhaps they will at least look more kindly on us."

Dawkins looked over the paper before handing it back with a shrug. "I have my doubts, but it is worth the try in any case, ma'am. They may at least shorten the time they hold us. Just pray that they send us to the new quarantine station in Sweden, not up to Norway. We'll lose more than a week in transit if we have to go to Kristianstad."

Pulling the quarantine flag from the locker, Jane followed Dawkins back on deck. They now had a clear view of the harbor and the sight was breathtaking. From where she stood, grasping the rail as the schooner rolled across the building waves of the busy channel, Jane counted over a hundred ships at anchor, many flying the quarantine flag and waiting for the health officer. With a sigh, she turned to peer out over the stern and smiled when she saw no sign of the *Jeremiah*. She would owe the crew a drink when they landed in St. Petersburg, and she was glad to do it.

Soon the *Destiny* was dropping her anchor in the harbor in the lee of a huge frigate flying the Union Jack. As Jane looked around, she realized that over half of the vessels she could see were likewise flagged. Well, the British had a good run of it during the blockades of the war, but now that it was over and American ships were free to ply the oceans without harassment, she and her fellow captains were determined to rake back the profit to be made in shipping goods both ways across the Atlantic.

The duty officer at Elsinore kept a sharp eye out for ships entering the channel from the east and the west so it wasn't long before the lookout called, "Cutter, ho!" and pointed to a small vessel headed their way from the shore.

Jane was impressed with the swiftness and attention to detail of the health officer, for it was he, once he had been hoisted aboard the *Destiny*. Without more than a simple "Good day, my name is Pinstrup. Where is the captain?" the official, dressed in an impeccable uniform much decked out in gold braid, asked to be shown to the officers' mess. Ducking his head to enter, the tall Dane silently held out his hand and sat down to peruse the papers he was given. If they wanted to put in to St. Petersburg, they had to have a clean bill of health from the man sitting in front of them.

"May I see your sick list?" he asked after finishing his scan of the docket.

"We have none, Mister Pinstrup. All on board are healthy and have shown no signs of fever. I have here a notice from our consul in Matanzas attesting to the crew's condition when we left the West Indies." Jane handed over her letter, which was promptly tossed back onto the table.

"We are not interested in the assessment of your consul, Captain Thorn. I would like to see each man of the crew personally. I ask you to arrange to have them presented to me on deck. Now, I see here that you are carrying sugar. Have you no other cargo in the hold?" Pinstrup looked suspiciously at Dawkins, who answered in the negative.

"We do not, sir. Nor are we carrying dunnage. The sugar is packaged in cases and we have used wooden chucks to secure the load. There is no cotton aboard." Dawkins knew that the presence of cotton in the hold would get them sent to quarantine immediately. Other captains had tried arguing with the Danish gatekeepers about the list of exclusion items that would force them into quarantine, and every one had either lost the argument or ended up in court.

"Very well, I will look in the hold and then see you topsides. Pray have the crew ready."

The inspection of the hold and the men was swift, and Pinstrup was soon handing Jane his quarantine order.

"You are remanded to Känsö for five days. The cargo may stay aboard, and the crew is cleared for shore leave on the island. You may return here for duty clearance no earlier than the eighteenth of July. Pray see to it that you have a Bill of Health from the officer on Känsö before you leave. Good day to you, ma'am."

Before Jane could reach out her hand to thank him, the officer had turned to the ladder and climbed down to his boat. Within a minute, he had sailed from sight and they were left to ponder their fate.

"Well," said Galsworthy, "wonder how his wife likes that when he comes home. Bet he looks under the bed for dust afore climbin' into it at night."

"Aye," agreed Dawkins, "he probably lines his children up and counts them too before giving them marching orders for the day."

Jane knew they were just trying to lighten her mood, but she was actually feeling rather relieved. The trip to Känsö island outside Gothenburg would only take them a day or so each way. Unless the health officer was equally lenient with the *Jeremiah*, which probably carried a more diverse cargo, they still had a good chance of making the Russian port well ahead of Captain Duncan. They could sell when the market was still high and might be back to sea while the brig was sitting in quarantine. Although Jane was not superstitious by nature, she made sure to cross her fingers and knock on the wooden beam over her head as she wished for a long internment for her rival.

Given the late hour of the day, Jane decided to hang on the anchor for the hours of darkness and take advantage of the early morning breeze to make their way back north. She urged Galsworthy to have the men well rested since they would be departing at the end of the middle watch when the sun first rose. Below, Cookie was breaking into the last of the barrels of stores and had sent word to the captain that provisioning would be advisable before heading for the Baltic the following week. Jane was feeling the pressure of time, but knew she would have to make port sooner or later. She pulled out her charts and began working on a plan.

An hour later, she was hailed from above.

"Ahoy Captain! Skiff inbound from the *Jeremiah*!" Dawkins shouted down the companionway. "Looks like the captain's on his way over, ma'am."

The brig had arrived while Jane was poring over the coastline of western Sweden and was now resting a scant hundred yards away at the edge of the anchorage. Jane swiftly gathered her papers together and stowed them out of sight. No reason to leave any clues as to their destination for Captain Duncan to see. She would have to find a way to satisfy his curiosity without revealing her mission.

Standing up, she brushed at her clothes to remove the worst of the wrinkles, and smoothed back her hair. Jane donned her blue coat, buttoning it up tight to the neck, and shoved her hat on her head. Drawing herself erect, she took a deep breath and prepared herself for a game of wits with the master of the *Jeremiah*.

No sooner had she pulled herself together than Captain Duncan was being shown into the saloon by Dawkins. At over six feet tall, the bear of a man dwarfed the space. With his hail-fellow-well-met demeanor and loud voice, he made Jane both want to laugh and flinch away.

"Welcome aboard, Captain Duncan," she greeted him with a smile.

"Ahoy, Captain Thorn! I hope you'll forgive the intrusion, but once I worked it out last night who you were, I had to take the first opportunity to pay my respects. Your uncle and I are old acquaintances, and he's spoken of you often. It is a real pleasure to finally shake your hand!" Which action he promptly carried out by grasping Jane's right hand and giving it a solid pump followed by a slap on the back that almost knocked her off her feet.

Grinning at her, Duncan pulled off his hat and waited for her to indicate that they should sit at the saloon's small mess table. Setting her own hat down, Jane motioned to Dawkins to bring the glasses of port.

"The honor is all mine, captain. Uncle Josias has shared with me his own regard for you, and it is always a treat to raise a glass with a friend of the family." So saying, Jane motioned with her tumbler toward Duncan and took a sip while she contemplated her guest.

She wasn't fooled for one minute. This visit, undertaken so soon after the brig's arrival, was not a mere friendly passing of the time. Duncan was surprised to see her here with the *Destiny*, and was intensely curious about her business. Above the jovial smile lurked a pair of piercing eyes that were avidly watching her face for clues.

For the next half hour, they exchanged bland pleasantries about friends and family back in New York and Boston. While fascinated by her career as a schooner master, Duncan was clearly torn between learning more about her command and ferreting out the details of her current voyage. It would be impolite to ask outright if the master did not volunteer the information, but her visitor left her plenty of openings to share it if she so desired.

She did not. In response to a question about her passage to Elsinore, Jane avoided giving any clues about when she had left New York or where her vessel had been in the intervening `weeks. Let him think she came straight from America.

"Yes," she answered, "we had good weather all the way across with the exception of a squall or two. Nothing that would challenge the *Destiny*, mind you. And your own trip, how was the passage over?"

She continued to parry and thrust with him for another few minutes before he gave up and stared at her. Finally, lifting his hat from the table and rising to make his way back to his brig, he blurted out,

"I'm sure you know your own business best Captain, but I have a feeling we will be seeing each other again before too long. Good day to you, and my regards to your uncle."

With a nod to Dawkins, Duncan clumped his way up the ladder and was soon being rowed back to his own command.

"Whew. My goodness but that was a sweaty job! Do you think he is suspicious that we may be trying to steal a march on him and take his business from under his nose?" she asked Dawkins.

"He is mightily puzzled, that much is sure. He didn't see the *Destiny* in Havana, so he won't have a thought that we might be carrying sugar. But your lack of candor about our presence here is sure to have him suspecting that we have something to hide. He'll go to sleep tonight wondering what that is."

"Well, better that he suspect something than know

something for sure."

XV

Quarantine

Wednesday, July 12   No sighting. Lat. (chart) 56° 05'N Long. (chart) 12° 37'W Bound for quarantine Känsö.

At dawn, Jane gave the order to weigh anchor and put about to head north. The dense pack of vessels surrounding the *Destiny* blocked any breeze that might have helped her gain a heading, so Galsworthy had the crew put out the skiff to pull her around in the gentle northbound current. Soon, they were moving slowly out of the anchorage and were able to hoist sail for Sweden within the hour.

Eager to begin her five-day quarantine, Jane had Dawkins keep the *Destiny* under as much sail as she could bear in the moderate winds. They sighted the station tower at Känsö by the middle of the afternoon watch and turned north by northeast to approach the harbor. A short time later, they were startled when a cannon shot was fired as they passed the entrance to the channel in anticipation of coming about to enter it downwind.

"Are they shooting at us?" Jane exclaimed.

"I think it was a warning, ma'am. In case we intended on passing them by." Dawkins seemed unperturbed by the noise. "Look, there comes the pilot."

Jane gave the order to heave to and then waited at the rail for the small rowing boat to pull alongside. Aboard were two men at the oars and a rather nattily dressed person who appeared to be some sort of official.

"*God dag, kapten!* May I have your orders please?" Declining to come aboard to fetch them, the official sent a man up the ladder just far enough to take the papers from Dawkins' hand and then sat down in his boat to review them. He took out a logbook and made several notations, then finally addressed the captain.

"*Kapten* Thorn, you are to follow me in to the mooring field. There you will tie up and remain aboard your vessel. Since we will not be offloading any cargo or treating any of your crew, you will not approach the dock. While you are in quarantine, you may not visit any other vessel or crew, nor may they come aboard your own vessel. The crew may land and make use of the field to the south for recreation between the hours of ten and twelve in the morning. In five days, we will conduct a further inspection of your vessel and issue you with a bill of health." All of this was delivered in a stern voice that brooked no argument.

"Very good, sir, we will follow you to the mooring and remain aboard our vessel." Jane confirmed.

"Are you in need of any supplies during your visit here, *Kapten*?"

"Fresh water perhaps, if it could be had?"

"Very well, we will bring you several barrels tomorrow to be returned prior to your departure."

The pilot boat turned and made its way to a mooring field at some distance from a row of large buildings that lined the shore. Each house seemed to rest on its own man-made island with short bridges linking them one to another. In the center of the front wall, an opening had been left in the stone foundation through which the bay water flowed in two of the buildings. Over the next few days, they would watch in fascination as crews were taken one by one in boats to this opening, stripped of their clothing, shaved of all hair, and rowed inside. Other buildings appeared to be warehouses for the cargoes being offloaded. A sulphurous smoke emitting from their chimneys indicated the station staff were fumigating the goods inside.

The following five days were enervating for Jane and the crew. They were restless to be on their way to the Baltic, and the rainy coast of Sweden was not conducive to lengthy sojourns on the deck. Regardless of the weather, the captain insisted that everyone take a turn ashore each day to stretch their legs and feel terra firma under their feet. Galsworthy had them busy aboard clearing out the crew quarters and scrubbing every surface until it gleamed. There were ample fish in the bay, so

Cookie and Koopmans had taken to dropping a line overboard and filling buckets of water on the deck with live catch. When he also found wild sorrel, carrots, and onions in the field where they were allowed to roam, Cookie whipped up tempting dishes each night that went far toward improving the morale of the crew.

Jane made good use of the long, wet days to catch up on her correspondence. The letter from her dear sister had brought to the fore conflicting feelings she had hoped would be washed away in the salt air of the north Atlantic. But the excitement of foreign travel tempted her away from home, and she thought it would for many years to come. She was at a loss how to reconcile that yearning with the longing for hearth and home that tore at her heart some nights as she lay in her solitary berth.

Tuesday, July 18 No sighting. Lat. (chart) 57° 38'N Long. (chart) 11° 46'W Dep. Känsö with clean bill. Making Varberg for provisions.

On the morning of the eighteenth, Jane was eager to be on their way. She waited impatiently as the morning wore on and was frustrated when it took the quarantine officer until nearly midday to arrive. This time, he climbed aboard with one of his men who was ordered to load the now-empty water barrels into their boat. As had the health official in Elsinore, he asked that the crew be brought on deck for review, followed by a tour of the cargo hold. Having seen no sign of sickness in the men, he handed Jane a clean Bill of Health and wished them a speedy and safe voyage.

Jane was leaning over the rail watching him descend to his boat when he stopped suddenly.

"*Kapten*, I nearly forgot! The station commandant received a message for you to be delivered today. My apologies that it slipped my mind." The official shoved his hand into his pocket and withdrew a sealed letter addressed to "The Captain of the Schooner *Destiny*" which he handed up the ladder to Jane.

"Thank you," said a surprised Jane as she stuck it in her pocket to be read after they were well on their way back south.

At a sharp command from Dawkins, the crew sprang into action and the *Destiny* was under way before the quarantine skiff had returned to the dock. The afternoon breeze had picked up and they beat quickly southwest then south to round the island and head for the open water. Along the way, Jane kept a sharp lookout for the *Jeremiah*. To her consternation, she had not seen the brig arrive at Känsö and worried that Duncan had talked the Danish authorities into letting him pass. If so, Jane would be a week behind him to St. Petersburg and would arrive to a glutted market. She would either have to seek another port for her cargo or sell at a lower price. She didn't relish either option, and hoped that the *Jeremiah* was sitting in quarantine somewhere.

The starboard watch was at early mess when Jane retired to her cabin to review her charts and the ship's log. She had been too busy to look over Dawkins' daily record beyond verifying the recorded positions and weather state, and she wanted to add any pertinent notes. She was famished, and glad to see that Cookie had sent along her meal. Pulling off the lid, she breathed in deeply as the smell of poached cod fillets served with roasted root vegetables and a sorrel sauce rose in the air. She wasn't sure exactly how he did it, but there was no doubt that her cook was a magician of the first order.

Galsworthy joined her shortly and the two spent a lively hour finishing the last of a bottle of Jane's port and discussing the coming Baltic leg. Once her second mate had retired with the watch, she set about going through the log, making corrections and additions. In the middle of a recalculation, Jane suddenly remembered the letter in her pocket. She pulled it out and squinted at the seal on the back. It appeared to be some sort of coat of arms with a large eagle in the center. Jane eased the wax open and unfolded what proved to be an invitation to dinner, in Varberg, tomorrow night.

Frowning, Jane grabbed the coastal chart off the pile of papers on her desk. She had intended to put in at Halmstad the following afternoon for supplies. If she chose to accept this invitation, she saw they would need to change course immediately and make for Varberg this evening. They could anchor in the bay and run in to the dock in the morning. A day spent ashore in town would do the crew good and allow for a full reprovision of the schooner.

Lifting her head, Jane shouted up the stairs. "Mister Dawkins! Are you about?"

A moment later, Dawkins' head appeared in the opening. "Aye, Captain! Is aught amiss?"

"Here, have a look at this," Jane said as she passed the letter up to him.

The chief studied the letter in the light shining up from her cabin, turned it over to inspect the seal, and then read it through one more time. Lifting his head with a frown, he asked, "Where did you get this, ma'am?"

"The quarantine officer delivered it with our Bill of Health. What do you think?"

The invitation, signed by someone calling himself Armand, Marquis d'Otrante, requested her presence at a dinner in her honor to be given the following evening at what sounded like a country house near Varberg. The note indicated that the marquis and his party were anxious to meet the famous *Capitaine* Thorn and hoped the visit might be to her profit. They would arrange for a carriage to meet her and would be delighted if she would consider stopping the night.

"Do you intend to go, ma'am?" Dawkins asked, equally surprised, as he handed the letter back down the ladder.

"Aye, I think I just might. We're in need of friends here in the north, and perhaps this marquis and his guests would be a good connection for the Thorns. Let us turn for Varberg and plan to provision there tomorrow. Please give the orders and see to it that I am awakened by the morning watch at six bells."

"Aye, aye, Captain. Pleasant dreams," and Dawkins' head disappeared back into the night.

Jane's head was full of questions as she prepared to crawl into her berth for a few hours' rest. Who was the Marquis? How did he know of her? What business could be of profit to her family? And most importantly, did she have a suitable dress to wear?

Jane blew out her lantern and settled down to sleep as she felt the *Destiny* turn to port toward the city of Varberg and the mysterious marquis.

XVI

Dinner Plans

Varberg, Sweden
July, 1820

Sailing to Varberg the next morning was accomplished in short order and the *Destiny* was tied up at the commercial dock in time for the crew to have breakfast ashore. Port clearances were handled swiftly, and the harbormaster gave Dawkins a list of shops at which to procure the supplies they needed. Not forgetting her promise to the men, Jane handed Galsworthy a sum sufficient to purchase a glass of rum for each member of the crew and cautioned him not to let anyone become too drunk to stand. Departure was at mid-morning the next day and she needed her crew in top form.

Before she set off on her own errands, the captain cornered Dawkins on the deck.

"I've decided that you are coming with me, so make sure your boots are polished and your hat brushed. I'll send a note to our host to let them know we will be two this evening and hope they do not find it presumptuous of me. But I want you at my side to hear what this marquis and his friends have to say. Let us take Vaugine as well. He can make himself handy among the household and overhear anything that may be useful to us later on."

Dawkins grinned at her and tipped his hat.

"You have the mind of a fox, ma'am, and it will be my pleasure to accompany you this evening. I'll square it with Galsworthy and be ready for the carriage. I'll send Vaugine to your cabin now so you can have a word with him."

When Vaugine joined her, Galsworthy, who looked both curious and alarmed, accompanied him.

"Ah, Mister Galsworthy, we are perhaps being put in the way of some new business at this dinner, and I should like

Vaugine to be our eyes and ears in the forecastle, if you will. Can you spare him to me overnight?"

His face clearing, Galsworthy gave a laugh. "Ah captain, not much escapes you does it? Aye, we'll get by without him this evening if he's willin'. What say you, Vaugine? Up for a little spying?"

"*Bien sûr, ma Capitaine*," Vaugine replied with a bow.

"Most satisfactory, Vaugine, and we will of course add to your wages for the extra service this night." Jane felt a modest remuneration was due the man in all fairness for acting as their mole below stairs.

"*Non, ma Capitaine*, this would be an insult. I am at your service and hope to repay you in some small way. I shall be ready this evening." With another bow, and then an erect salute, Vaugine returned to his duties leaving Jane and Galsworthy staring at each other.

"I say," Galsworthy said after clearing his throat, "maybe ye ought to just send that feller instead. He's got the manners of a lord, that's for sure!"

Having set things in motion, Jane headed off to find a ladies' dress shop. She had packed one of the gowns Pru had made, but thought it would not be grand enough for a dinner with a marquis. Jane's taste ran to simple fabrics of one color that would fit under her greatcoat. Today, she thought to find a lively sprigged muslin like those she had seen on all the fashionable young girls in New York. She had never owned such a dress, with all its embroidery and lace, and had made up her mind to acquire one for this occasion.

The weather had finally cleared and the streets were filled with people speaking a language that sounded like singing to Jane's ear. She quickly located the postmaster and delivered to him the packet of letters written by herself and her crew during their enforced idleness. She then set off down the streets that ringed the central square and soon came to a district filled with shoemakers, haberdashers, tailors, milliners, and a ladies' dress shop. Jane pushed open the door of *La Mode du Jour* and was immediately engulfed in a wave of feminine voices chattering and laughing as they fingered the gowns on display.

"*Bonjour, mademoiselle. Kan jag stå till tjänst med något idag? En fin klänning, kanske?*" The query came from an elegant older woman dressed in black who smiled at Jane from behind a counter.

"Yes, hello. Do you perhaps speak English? I am afraid I am a visitor here." Jane smiled back and hoped that she would be able to communicate well enough to accomplish her task.

"But of course, *mademoiselle*, and we are always happy to see a visitor! How may I be of service?"

Jane explained her need and the circumstances of the dinner she would be attending. The woman's eyes widened when she heard the name of the house where the event was to be held.

"*Mademoiselle*, only the finest will do for such an occasion! Did you have something in mind already, perhaps?"

Jane proceeded to describe the summery modern dress she had envisioned and watched the French modiste's frown grow deeper with every word.

"*Non. Non, non, non.* This is a dress for a silly girl that you describe. A woman who does not know who she is and so dresses like everyone else. Such a dress would look like you had borrowed it and you would feel *maladroit* all evening. Come, we can do better for you."

Madame took her by the hand and led her past a dozen or more mannequins wearing exactly the sort of dress Jane had in mind. At the back of the shop, the modiste stopped in front of a gown that made Jane gasp. The long skirt and empire bodice were done in an emerald satin that fell like a shimmering column from small puffed sleeves. A layer of gold filigree adorned the upper part of the dress and formed a second, shorter layer over the skirt. In its simplicity and brilliance of color, it stood out magnificently from the feathered frippery around it.

"Oh my. It is simply beautiful. Would you be able to have one for me this evening?" Jane asked, not taking her eyes off the ravishing gown.

"This one was made for a customer who changed her mind and I think it would fit *mademoiselle*. Shall we see?"

Once she had been fitted into the dress, the woman Jane saw in the mirror was more elegant and refined than she had ever considered herself. Madame had pinned her hair in a simple chignon and added a gold shawl. With her kid slippers, Jane knew this gown would hold its own among the ladies this evening.

"Thank you, *Madame*, you have saved me and I am forever in your debt!" Jane gave the woman a swift embrace and then picked out a simple headpiece to finish off the ensemble. The bill was far more than Jane had ever paid for anything to wear in New York, but she knew this dress would stand her in good stead for a number of years. Or so she told herself as she imagined explaining the purchase to her father.

That evening, Jane stood on the cobbled street near the entrance to the docks with Dawkins and Vaugine by her side. Both men had seemed taken aback at the change in the appearance of their captain, and she smiled to herself as she anticipated having a similar effect on her hosts. In addition to the kid slippers, she had added a thin gold chain with a locket from her sister and a pair of white elbow length gloves. Topping it off with a dab of her mother's perfume, Jane felt ready to present herself to the marquis.

Mister Dawkins had climbed into the blue serge coat with brass buttons and red sash that marked the officers of the Thorn shipping line. White knee breeches and black boots completed the outfit and were topped by a black mate's chapeau. Vaugine had managed to locate a respectable jacket among the crew and had polished his shoes. Altogether, they were a well-turned out party ready to make a good impression on potential business partners.

Within short order, a carriage drawn by two prancing chestnut horses arrived to carry them out to the countryside home of the d'Otrante family. This proved to be a large hall in yellow stone with an imposing colonnaded entrance at the top of a flight of wide stairs. Urns overflowing with purple vines marched up each side of the staircase and brought the visitor to a large front door flanked by burning torches. In the open doorway stood a tall blond man who must be the marquis, to judge from his open arms and welcoming smile.

As Jane's party climbed from the carriage, he came down the steps crying out, "Welcome, welcome! I am Armand. Welcome to my home. It is an honor to have you here. This must be Captain Thorn, though I would not have thought you such a hardy sailor, *mademoiselle*. You are as lovely as one of the flowers in my garden, or perhaps a rare orchid that blooms along the seashore, *hein?*"

Equally effusive was his welcome to Dawkins, and he soon ushered them into the hall while indicating to his coachman to have someone fetch their bags upstairs and show Vaugine to the kitchens.

Through an open door, Jane could see a goodly group gathered in the drawing room engaged in lively conversation. They turned as one toward her when the marquis clapped his hands and announced the arrival of his American guests. He then escorted Jane around the room, introducing her to the French and Swedish dignitaries he had gathered for the evening. There were over two dozen people in attendance, and Jane hoped that Dawkins was memorizing some of the many names that were flying at her. As they circled back to where they had begun, the marquis motioned to someone standing in the open doorway.

"*Et enfin*, let me present my dear friend *le comte* who has been looking forward to your visit this evening. *Capitaine*, may I present Count Bonenfant, cousin to the Swedish king."

Jane slowly raised her eyes up the expanse of brilliant blue brocade and Chantilly lace in front of her until she reached the well-known visage she had hoped never to see again.

"Good evening, Mister Fairchild," she said.

XVII

Monsieur le Comte

Jane's outward calm belied the turmoil within. She had thought him handsome before, but this tall, elegant figure in a gorgeously embellished coat matched by a pair of tightly fitted breeches and the whitest hose, simply took her breath away. Count Bonenfant held her gaze as he took her hand and bent over it.

"*Ma capitaine*, it pleases me to hear that name on your lips again." The look he gave her as he softly kissed the back of her hand spoke volumes. Jane found herself quivering at the touch and pulled her hand away quickly. Straightening her back, she gave him a cool stare.

"Perhaps, Mister Fairchild, you would like to grace us all with an explanation. When I saw you last, I had not only thrown you off my vessel for the second time, but also found it necessary to mend your manners at the point of my knife."

Around her, the guests broke out into peals of laughter at the discomfited nobleman. He had clearly not expected her to be so boldly confrontational in this formal setting. European manners be damned, Jane wanted to know what the blazes was afoot and she was determined to have her answer.

Behind her, Jane could feel the stalwart Dawkins standing with his legs squarely planted as if still at sea. His solid presence helped settle her feelings and she dropped her chin ever so slightly.

"Ah, *mademoiselle capitaine*, that is a long tale which I will be happy to tell if you would accompany me to the table," he held out his elbow for Jane to take. She couldn't very well ignore the gesture without looking a petulant child, so Jane found herself pacing the long hall at the side of the tall nobleman.

"You could start with telling me where you actually call home, you bastard. And what you are doing here." Jane blushed as she heard the epithet slip out. But by god, he deserved it.

The Count smiled down at her. "As you may have deduced,

my family is French. When my cousin was elected king of this country ten years ago, many members of my family and our friends, such as the d'Otrantes, joined him here. I have been visiting my cousin Oscar in Stockholm to bring him word of his mother from Paris."

Jane was temporarily distracted from her interrogation by the bustle of being seated at the table and acknowledging the gentleman to her left. Once the host had welcomed them with a glass of strong liquor, which she learned was to be drunk in the Swedish manner in a single gulp, her name was called out as the guest of honor and another round was poured so they could raise their glasses again. At this pace, Jane thought, they would all be snoring under the table before the final course was served.

She took the opportunity to observe the assembled throng as the various glasses were filled and chargers removed in preparation for serving the first course. Dinners with business clients at her uncle's house in New York had taught Jane how to behave at the table, and she was glad for her upbringing now as she watched her host in conversation with his guests. The marquis struck her as supremely self-absorbed, assuming that all those around him would bow in deference to his position and find him endlessly fascinating. Fortunately, his great good humor and genuine desire for others to have a good time somewhat offset his arrogance, Jane thought.

The other guests were an even mixture of gentlemen and ladies, most of whom appeared to be well past their middle years. Their gorgeous gowns and fashionable coats brought to mind the flocks of gaily-colored birds Jane had seen in Cuba, and truth be told, they were nearly as noisy.

A line of footmen entered carrying trays of dishes. With her first course on the table in front of her, Jane was determined to continue her inquisition of the perfidious Frenchman at her side.

"And what in tarnation were you doing on my vessel?" She demanded as she picked up her fork. "Looking back, it seems you went to awful lengths to get yourself aboard. And," she realized now, "to get yourself thrown off!"

"*Ah, oui*, I must excuse my terrible behavior, *ma capitaine*. I had taken a berth with Captain Jamison south out of Montreal. When I expressed my desire to hire on for a berth in New York, he was kind enough to recommend me to his friend Captain Thorn. I did not expect the master to be such a captivating woman, and I confess I was taken by surprise and could not contain my admiration for you. Perhaps I was too ardent, and for that I do most sincerely beg your forgiveness." This pretty little speech was accompanied by the contrite mien Jane had seen on earlier occasions.

She was debating whether to call his bluff and accuse him outright of lying when the marquis called down from the head of the table.

"*Monsieur le Comte!* Do regale us with the tale of how you come to be known by our friend the captain as Mister Fairchild." He raised his glass yet again for another toast. "To the count and his many adventures. *Alors*, Alain, *commencez-vous!*"

With a glance in her direction, Bonenfant began a long tale in French that, judging by his theatrical display, appeared to include at least one pitched sword battle and several attacks by pirates. He ended with "*Et voila!* I arrived in New York aboard the *Betsy Lee*. Captain Jamison provided me with a letter of recommendation to his friend Captain Thorn, who he knew was heading to Cuba. I am afraid I was somewhat lacking in my conduct and the good captain had me put back on the dock with my tail between my legs." Here, he glanced over at Jane with his familiar smirk. "I had the great good fortune to encounter Mister Dawkins here a few days later as he was in search of a replacement for an injured man, and after expressing my contrition for my earlier behavior, I was hired on again as Mister Fairchild."

His tale of derring-do earned Bonenfant a round of vigorous applause from the somewhat inebriated company, which he accepted with a seated bow and a smile. For her part, Jane figured they had heard a pack of lies. She was weary of the man's company and turned to the partner on her left.

This was a solidly built merchant by the name of Hans Törngren whose family owned a pottery in the town of

Falkenberg some sixty miles to the south. He was eager to show Jane samples of his factory's wares should she have occasion to visit the area again. He was sure they would appeal to the American market with their simple botanical motifs and sturdy glazes. Jane was intrigued, and wondered if there were any examples in the house for her to see. As luck would have it, the man never travelled far without at least one bowl in his satchel, and he promised Jane to produce it after dinner.

She continued her discourse with the jovial potter until her attention was drawn back to the head of the table where her host was once again having the glasses filled in her honor.

"*Mesdames et messieurs!* To the intrepid Captain Thorn, may she have fair winds at her back and success in all her endeavors. *Skål!*"

Jane decided to merely sip this round as the caraway scented alcohol was going straight to her tongue and loosening it in ways she thought she might regret later on. In combination with the wine that had been served with each course, she was finding that the repeated toasts had taken her past the place where she was pleasantly warm to one where she was decidedly hot and dizzy. As the meal came to an end and Bonenfant pulled back her chair, Jane stumbled slightly and was once more caught in the arms of the fetching count. This time, she did not resist his support and allowed him to hold her close at his side as they made their way back to the drawing room.

Placing her gently into a blue and white silk-covered chair near the window, the count leaned over and whispered into her ear, "*Que tu es si belle, ma capitaine.* The dress is ravishing and I have been bewitched by your scent all evening. Perhaps you might permit me to make its closer acquaintance later tonight."

Far too slow to react to this outrage with the slap it deserved, Jane was still searching for a reply when he melted back into the crowded room and left her with her mouth gaping like a fish.

"You seem at a loss for words, ma'am." Dawkins had finally made his way to her side and was now proffering her a cup of black coffee.

"My lord, Dawkins, but that man has a way of knocking me off balance. Please stay with me now and make sure I don't put my foot in it any more tonight."

"Aye, aye, ma'am. It will be my pleasure. And what have we learned to our advantage this evening?"

They chatted for a while about the possibility of buying pottery for the return trip home, especially after they had gotten a look at the charming fired bowl Törngren had brought from his room to display. They agreed to sit down with him early in the morning to discuss business and make arrangements for placing an order on their own behalf to be picked up on their return trip from St. Petersburg.

For his part, Dawkins had been seated next to an iron mine owner from the north. This worthy gentleman had held forth for some time on the relative merits of raw pig iron from Russia and the more refined bar product sold in Sweden.

"He says we can make a better profit carrying their iron to New York since it is heavier and will take up less room in the hold for the value we are to purchase. We would have excess tonnage capacity we could fill with the pottery and other lighter goods. And the iron would be worth more at the other end, ma'am. Many vessels were involved in that trade before the war and did well in it, I remember. Perhaps it is time to try again."

"That bears thinking about, Dawkins. Let us talk more with this man in the morning and perhaps come to some agreement that would be beneficial. It does begin to sound as if we might make a better load by buying just enough iron in St. Petersburg to make ballast and then filling our hold in Sweden."

With that, Jane resolved to put business out of her mind for the rest of the evening and enjoy the company of her host and his guests. She joined in a good-natured game of whist with the ever-attentive Dawkins stationed at her shoulder waving away any servant who approached with a tray of liqueurs. The ladies proved to be well-disposed toward her and were eager to ask her questions about her time aboard. A number of them claimed to be envious of her freedom and her authority to command herself and others. Jane assured them that while the burden of command was not light, she did relish her life on the water in the company of seagoing men. She couldn't help but glance at Bonenfant as she said this, and she was sure he caught the meaning in her look as he locked eyes with her.

At the other end of the room, a group of gentlemen were laughingly engaged in solving the mystery of the puzzle jug Herr Törngren had brought with him. Scarce ten inches tall, the jug sported half a dozen or so spouts. The upper rim was perforated with multiple round holes making it impossible to simply lift the jug and pour out the contents into a cup. The potter stood to one side grinning as he watched the men try one spout and then another only to end up with ale poured onto the table. As Jane joined him to watch the fun, he pushed his hands in his pockets and rocked back on his heels.

"*Ja, fröken*, I think we will try this in the factory! Perhaps I will have some for you to take to New York, *va*?" Törngren seemed well pleased at the success of his experiment and Jane was sure she could find a buyer for the charming gag among her customers.

"And how, pray tell, does one in fact pour out the contents?" Jane asked.

"One must put the mouth on the correct spout and cover the small hole inside the handle. Then simply draw the ale up through the handle by sucking hard. Clever, isn't it?"

Clever indeed. Jane had seen other puzzle jugs, but this one was notable for both its charm of form and the unexpected nature of the trick.

"Very nice, Herr Törngren, and I look forward to seeing how they sell in New York."

Jane realized she had once again been thinking first of trade in the exchange with the potter, and reminded herself that she could be too much of a businesswoman sometimes when she was meant to be enjoying herself at a party. Vowing to spend the remainder of the evening avoiding all topics that might lead to talk of shipments and cargoes, she settled herself on a lovely blue divan that complemented the airy colors of the room. She had been admiring the patterned wall coverings and filigreed furniture that was so foreign to her American sensibility. As she turned to engage the lady seated next to her in conversation, Jane decided to talk with her uncle about decorating one of the rooms in his house in this uplifting modern style.

The clock had struck midnight before the party began to disperse. Jane was glad to be shown to her room by one of the maids and stripped off her finery as soon as the door was closed. Pulling her night-rail over her head, she threw a shawl over her shoulders and took up the candle that had been left on the bedside table. She opened the door to scan the hallway and then made for the room she had seen Dawkins disappear into a few minutes earlier. Jane intended to ask him if he had spoken to Vaugine, but there was no reply to her gentle knock. The chief must have collapsed on the bed fully dressed and fallen sound asleep. He was accustomed to standing the early watch and was probably dead tired after being awake for so long. Jane gave up and turned back to her room.

Was she surprised to see Bonenfant leaning against the wall when she arrived back at her door? If she were being honest with herself, she would admit that she was hoping he would find his way there. Jane opened the door, then grabbed a fistful of the front of his shirt and pushed him inside.

XVIII
Business at Breakfast

Jane woke to a brilliant sun streaming in through the open curtains. The tall clock in the corner, which had startled Jane when she entered the room last evening, thinking it a person, showed it to be just past four thirty in the morning. She got out of bed and put her ear to the case to verify that it was working; surely it could not be so early and so bright outside. Hearing the ticking of the mechanism, she concluded that the time was correct and that she had slept a scant two hours.

Much as she thought she needed more sleep, Jane was too restless to return to bed. Her mind was turning over the events of the evening, and of the most enlightening interlude with the handsome count once the candles had been blown out. No prudish miss, she was well acquainted with the goings on between men and women and had a generally good idea of what to expect. The true nature of the interaction, however, had been well beyond her imaginings and left her quite sure that a staunch Yankee like Endeavor might need some schooling in the way of things to measure up. It bore thinking about.

In the meantime, she had no intention of repeating the episode and would seek out an opportunity to put the count firmly back in his place before leaving this morning.

Quickly, Jane completed her morning ablutions and packed her things into her satchel, then pulled on her usual captain's garb. This morning was going to be devoted to business and she wanted to look the part. Leaving her bag on the bed, she descended to the lower floor and let herself out through the French doors in the drawing room. The garden was still cool at this time of day and the flowers were at their abundant midsummer best.

As she leaned to smell the early roses and admire the tall daisies growing in a bed along a stone wall, she heard voices further down the garden path. Soon, the marquis appeared on the arm of the stylish young man who had been seated to his left at dinner. *Sven something* was all Jane could recall of his name. Clearly besotted with each other, the two were laughing and waving two wine bottles about as they weaved their way up the stone walk.

They stopped in front of her and the marquis greeted her with a wide smile.

"Bonjour, ma capitaine! What do you think of my garden?"

"It is truly lovely, my lord, even at this early hour," Jane replied, charmed by the young lovers who had obviously not slept since the festivities of the evening before.

"Bon, we are all friends here! Do call me Armand, if we may call you Jane, *mademoiselle?"* As he was speaking, he threw his free arm around her shoulders and pulled her in for a hearty embrace.

Good-naturedly, Jane extracted herself from Armand's grasp and nodded to Sven.

"But of course. It would be my pleasure to be on a first name basis with two such charming gentlemen." Jane shook her head with laughter as she said this, and then looked Armand square in the eye.

"Now that we are well acquainted, I do wish you could satisfy my curiosity on one point, my dear Armand. How ever did it come about that I received your gracious dinner invitation? I would not have thought that the presence of one small schooner in your quarantine bay would have brought the attention of someone as illustrious as yourself."

"Ah, oui. For that you must thank my friend *le comte.* He arrived here a week ago rather suddenly and informed me that he would be grateful if I would arrange something for the day after your anticipated departure from Känsö. I am always happy to accommodate my friend and must admit I was rather curious to meet you myself. He spoke quite warmly of your skills as a captain and trader. I confess I did not expect you to also be so beautiful."

This last remark was delivered with a deep bow that nearly toppled the marquis over onto Jane. Sven hauled him back upright with a giggle and the two of them were soon on their way toward the house and what Jane hoped was a few hours of sleep.

Pondering this new information, Jane headed inside to see if she could locate either of her crew. She was not surprised to find Dawkins already up and partaking of coffee the staff had set out in the dining room. Pouring herself a cup, she sat down at the table with him and pulled the sheaf of papers he was perusing toward herself.

"Good morning, Mister Dawkins. I see you have already worked out the freight margins for the bar iron. It would appear that we have room in the hold for the other goods we discussed, more than what I had thought."

"Aye, ma'am, that we do." Dawkins pointed to a column of numbers he had scratched at the edge of what appeared to be the prior day's newspaper. "That bar stuff is fetching a high price in the market just now. The Swedish restrictions on production are keeping the value up and the Russian bar product is of inferior quality, if that fellow I talked to last night is right. We'd do well with a load, I reckon. The British have been raising the tariffs so high the Swedes can't sell much there anymore, and they are starting to ship to the American market again. If we are successful, we could send larger vessels next year. Shall we give it a try, ma'am?"

"Have you included a calculation for the purchase of ballast pig iron from St. Petersburg? I refuse to carry stones that don't earn their passage."

"Aye, I have indeed, ma'am. We'll let that make up part of the contracted load and hold back some of the bar for our own trading. It should make this a very lucrative voyage."

"All right, then, let us see how we do. What shall we use for the rest of the load?"

The next hour consumed the pair as they pushed prices and tonnage around on paper, finally arriving at a valuation for a load of crockery they thought would be of sufficient margin to make the cargo pay. No sooner had they agreed on the price they would offer than the factory owner himself joined them for breakfast. Over herring and rye bread, they came to an agreement that seemed satisfactory to all parties. The load would be delivered to Gothenburg by September first, where they would stow it in the lockers for the trip across the Atlantic.

Once they had arranged for the Törngren shipment, they debated the remaining available tonnage. It was not enough for a significant payload, but Jane wanted to make the most of the *Destiny's* hold on this voyage. In the end, they decided to wait until they arrived in Gothenburg to see what else might be available for export.

The morning was wearing on and Jane was eager to head back to the wharf to rejoin her vessel. She had not seen her host again since their impromptu meeting in the garden and was afraid she would have to depart without taking leave of him. Bonenfant had also been noticeable for his absence, but Jane suspected he was recouping his lost slumbers of the night before. She smiled to herself as she called to mind what he had been doing instead of sleeping.

"Dawkins, would you and Vaugine have our things put into the carriage? I will join you shortly. I would just like to pen a note to our generous host."

Jane rummaged in her holdall for a pencil while sending the footman to search out a piece of paper. He returned in short order with the paper and a note addressed to her.

Mademoiselle,

Urgent matters have taken me to Stockholm early this morning so I shall not be in a position to bid you adieu personally. Mon amie, it pains me to write it, but I must beg that you not attempt to further our liaison to your benefit. It has been a pleasure to have made your acquaintance. However, the gulf between our positions would preclude any interest I might otherwise have in deepening our friendship and must therefore renounce with sadness the possibility of any such amitié intime. In sadness, I remain

Yours truly,
Alain, Comte de Bonenfant

Stunned, Jane read through the missive twice more before she could comprehend what the son of a bitch was actually hinting at. Unless she was gravely mistaken, that bastard thought she had sought him out to catch him as a matrimonial prize! Jane was certainly grateful that he harbored no expectations of her. But by god it was lucky the coward didn't have the backbone to say farewell in person. She had fully intended for this to be the last time *le comte* would put his hands on her, with or without her permission. Were he in front of her now, however, she might find it difficult to refrain from putting *her* hands on *him*.

Leaving her note for Armand with the obliging footman, Jane ran down the steps and hopped up beside Vaugine and Dawkins. The driver called to the horses and they were soon off down the dusty drive on their way to the waterfront. They made good use of the half hour to look about themselves, noting the few houses in the environs of the town and the dense forests that crowded the hillsides. Varberg seemed more of an outpost of civilization than a thriving community, but the activity along the docks led her to believe that things might be changing.

The carriage had reached the docks before Jane had managed to master her temper completely. Alternately huffing to herself from embarrassment and scowling with anger, she had struggled to keep her emotions to herself. While she did not regret her encounter with the man last night, she most certainly would have boxed his ears this morning.

Back onboard, Jane called Galsworthy to join them in the saloon. She had sent Vaugine on his way to lend a hand with departure preparations and said they would talk to him when he came off watch later that day.

"So Mister Galsworthy, how goes it with the stores? Is Cookie satisfied that we are well provisioned until we reach St. Petersburg?" Jane asked through the open door from where she was kneeling on the floor of her cabin stowing her things back in her trunk while Dawkins sat at the table scribbling on his notes from breakfast.

"Aye, ma'am, that we are. The butcher was a thief as thought we didn't know the value of a side of mutton, so it may be more salt pork on this leg than the crew would like, but we have plenty of rations to stand us. Mayhap we take on fresh water again if we decide to put in somewhere," Galsworthy pronounced as he stood by the table twisting his hat in his hands.

"All right, Galsworthy, spit it out, man. What is troubling you?" Jane had noticed his unease.

'I didn't like the look a' those fellers ya' sent to inspect the cargo this morning, ma'am. Seemed to me that they were no Swedish officials. Unless Swedish officials speak French when they think no one is looking, ma'am." Her second mate stared at her belligerently as if she had personally wounded his pride in some way.

"What in blazes are you talking about, man? I sent no one to inspect the cargo!" Jane jumped up in her astonishment.

"Why, they had a signed paper from you ma'am, saying we were to give 'em free access to the hold so they could look over the consignment. Make sure it didn't break any quarantine laws or some such. I told 'em we had clearances already, but they insisted they had to come aboard. The paper looked all right, so I figured I had no choice. We did station someone at the hatch to make sure they didn't try to make off with anything. Ma'am."

At this point, Galsworthy realized that he had been duped and was beginning to look angry, while Dawkins had dropped his pencil and risen to his feet.

Without further word, the three of them raced as one to the hold and began to search it.

"Open the hatch!" Dawkins shouted to the men on deck and soon sunlight flooded the space, illuminating the tightly packed boxes of sugar that filled the hold. Ten minutes of poking around the cargo brought them up empty-handed.

"What the devil do you suppose they were doing?" Jane was greatly perturbed that someone had been amongst her shipment. As far as she was concerned, the *Destiny's* hold was a sacred charge that she tightly controlled. She knew to an inch what was stored there and to whom it belonged. The crew was forbidden from entering the cargo area and one of the officers supervised every bit of goods as it came aboard or left her vessel.

Jane stood by the aft bulkhead scanning the space over and over. Nothing seemed out of place, and every box was where it had been put when loaded. Frustrated, she slammed her hand on the door panel as she stormed back to her cabin.

"It's that blasted Frenchman. I know it. Damn his eyes, what game is he playing?" Jane knew her mates were not responsible for her temper, but she had no one else to berate at the moment.

"Let us make haste to cast off, Dawkins, before we are subject to any further indignities, and bring Vaugine to my cabin once we are well out to sea. I want to hear what he may know of what is going on." She had no great hopes that her spy would have heard or seen anything helpful, but it was worth the try. For now, she would put the puzzling "inspection" out of her head and help get the *Destiny* off the dock and under way.

XIX
On to Russia

Thursday, July 20   No sighting. Lat. (chart) 57° 07'N Long. (chart) 12° 14'W
Unknown parties conducted insp. for unknown reasons. Making for Mölle.

Tonight's destination was the small fishing village of Mölle south of the Kullen Lighthouse. Jane planned to reach the anchorage by sundown and approach the toll station at Elsinore at first light the next day. The narrow Kattegat channel, bounded by rocky shores and hidden boulders, and trafficked by hundreds of ships each day, was no place to bring the *Destiny* in the dark. She would wait out the few hours of the nordic night in a protected cove.

Once under way, Jane and Dawkins went below after sending for seaman Vaugine. Jane had been mulling over all she had experienced since first setting eyes on the troublesome Bonenfant, and wanted to talk over her thoughts with Dawkins and the Haitian crewman.

"Ah, Mister Vaugine, join us if you please!" The sailor had knocked on the doorframe and stood waiting to be invited in. "And pray shut the door behind you," Jane said.

Waving him to a seat, Jane poured Vaugine a glass of the port she was sharing with Dawkins, and then sat back to contemplate the man. Dressed in his nautical garb of light blue tunic and navy pants, he made an interesting figure. Well above average height, his broad shoulders lent him an air of strength and sturdiness. His hands had finally hardened after the early weeks of bleeding palms and peeling skin, and he walked now with the true sailor's rolling gait.

"So, Vaugine, what have you to tell us?" Jane began. She watched as Vaugine leaned forward to set his empty tumbler on the table and shifted in the seat to face her.

"*Alors*, I believe the captain is right to be concerned. The valet of the comte and the marquis' driver spoke in French and talked much of the travels of the *comte* since he returned from Cuba. He arrived here at the house of the marquis but a week past and was heard to ask the marquis to find a way to bring you and your vessel to Varberg, *Capitaine.*"

"Do you suppose he saw us in Känsö, Dawkins? And took advantage of a friend to waylay us here?"

"You are most assuredly correct, ma'am. But it does beg the question of why." Dawkins said.

"He must have wanted to see me," Jane mused. Looking up, she blushed as she realized both men were staring at her. Neither seemed surprised at her notion, and she suspected her assignation of the night before was not a secret.

"More likely, ma'am, he wished to see the *Destiny,*" was Vaugine's dry comment.

But of course, Vaugine was correct. The realization came to Jane and Dawkins at the same moment; the visit from the imposter inspectors was the reason for the whole subterfuge. By getting Jane off the *Destiny*, the *comte's* emissaries could gain access to the cargo.

"Back to the hold, Dawkins," Jane ordered as she ran from the saloon.

"Thank you, Vaugine, you have been most helpful. You may return to your duties," Dawkins said as the sailor rose to his feet. With a salute, Vaugine climbed back to the deck and Dawkins set off in hot pursuit of his captain.

He found her standing by the door to the cargo bay, which had been flung back against the bulkhead in her haste.

"What have they done, Dawkins? And why?" Jane was at a loss to understand what was going on around her and around her vessel. She had thought that they had left trouble behind in Cuba, but it would appear that it had followed them here.

"Nothing is disturbed, and nothing is missing. What were they looking for?"

"Perhaps, ma'am, they were simply looking to see that the cargo was still intact and aboard," Dawkins suggested.

Jane considered that for a moment.

"You may be right, Dawkins, but what would that tell

them?"

"It would tell them that you were still on your way to St. Petersburg, ma'am."

The *Destiny* was settled at anchor well before sundown and the crew had gathered on the foredeck to sing and tell stories before heading for their hammocks. She had Dawkins reduce the watch to anchor duty so the men could get a few hours of sleep before rising for the early departure for Elsinore. For herself, she felt too worried to sleep, and tried lying on the roof of the deckhouse to stare up at the stars.

The voyage had been a tremendous success thus far; Jane had already remitted a tidy sum back to New York from her business in Matanzas, and her crew had brought the *Destiny* safely across the Atlantic. She had two new hands who looked to be a good investment in the long run, and who would be a blessing to the firm if they decided to stay with her crew. But as she lay on her back looking out into the night, she contemplated the trouble that now seemed to be brewing on the far side of the Baltic. If Dawkins was right, someone was waiting for them to arrive in St. Petersburg with the cargo from Cuba. There could be no explanation for it but that Bonenfant had put something aboard and it was hidden in the cargo. But he had played his hand too boldly, and Jane was now alert to his ruse. She couldn't very well order the hold emptied and the cargo searched without delaying them more days than they could afford. She didn't see that she had much choice but to continue on her way. They would, however, inspect every box as it left the *Destiny* in St. Petersburg, and she would find whatever it was that Bonenfant had sent with them to Russia.

Friday, July 21   No sighting.   Lat. (chart) 56° 05'N Long. (chart) 12° 37'W Have cleared duty at Elsinore, entered Baltic this afternoon. Winds SSE.

Dawn saw the *Destiny's* crew preparing to weigh anchor once again. They made the channel by the end of the morning watch and dropped anchor among the hundreds of vessels at Elsinore awaiting the duty collectors. Jane scanned the field for any sign of the *Jeremiah*, but was unable to find her among the many ships blocking her view.

In due course, the excise man appeared and demanded their health clearance before he would come aboard. Satisfied that they were in compliance with the Health Inspector's orders, he followed Dawkins to the captain's mess to review the *Destiny's* cargo manifest and collect the toll. Jane knew this was an established part of trading in the Baltic, but that did not assuage her feelings of being waylaid by a highwayman in a narrow canyon. If they wanted to trade in Russia or other points to the east, they would have to pay, but she did not have to like it.

They were on their way again by noon, heading south through the Öresund past Copenhagen on the Danish side and Malmö in Sweden. As they skirted Saltholm to starboard and then the Falsterbo peninsula to port, Jane looked ahead to the open waters of the Baltic. They would anchor tonight on the far side of the peninsula during the few hours of darkness, and then set off for the eight hundred mile passage up the coast of Sweden and into the Gulf of Finland.

Sometimes, Jane had to pinch herself to believe that this all was real. She was as far from home as she had ever been, with the wind in her hair and a new adventure in every port. While she was concerned about what might be waiting at the other end, the captain was determined to enjoy the trip north. Throwing her arms wide, she nearly knocked Griggs off his feet. Grinning at her, the helmsman observed,

"Sure is a mighty fine sight, ma'am. It never grows old, seeing the world."

XX

Bumblebees

Sunday, July 23 Lat. Obs. 56° 17'N Long. DR 17° 18'E Gusty winds SSE Jib boom crack discovered purs. to accident NY harbor. Will need repair prior to return Atl. Passage.

The crew made good use of fine weather as they sailed north up the Baltic to the Gulf of Finland. Moderate breezes gave way to the occasional gust that forced them to reduce the *Destiny's* sails, but they made good speed as they worked their way up the coast of Öland.

Jane was taken by the limestone cliffs and low-lying beaches of the islands they passed and wished she had leisure to explore. Colorful buildings perched on the rocks like charming dollhouses, and small villages gathered around stone churches with fantastically shaped steeples. She vowed she would make time on her return voyage to go ashore, to climb the hills, and explore the intriguing streets.

Two days out from Elsinore, Galsworthy approached her with ship's carpenter Koopmans in tow. Jane was standing on the deckhouse looking out over the water and from the corner of her eye could see them making their way toward her. To judge from the scowl on Koopmans' face, the news was not good. With a sigh, she clambered down onto the deck and faced the tidings head on.

"Report, Mister Galsworthy," she said in a mild tone.

"Aye, ma'am. Koopmans here has discovered we did not escape the smash with that sloop in New York undamaged as we thought. All these stiff winds have put a lot 'a pressure on the spars and it looks like she's got a crack in the jib boom that's a' startin' t' open up."

"Show me, Mister Koopmans," Jane commanded, and headed for the bow.

Koopmans crawled out nearly to the end of the eighteen foot spar and pointed at a crack that appeared to run for six inches aft of where the jib stay was attached. Wrapped around the jib boom in his worn seaman's togs as he showed her the fault, he looked like a bundle of rags topped by a gray shock of wool that had been thrown onto the spar by the wind. It was all Jane could do to keep from laughing at the ludicrous sight. She vowed that he would be given a new suit of clothes at the first opportunity, although she suspected he would refuse to wear them. Old seamen were superstitious that way.

"Ye can see that she's a' pullin' herself apart here, ma'am," the carpenter called.

"What do you recommend, Koopmans?" she asked once he returned to the deck. Dawkins had joined them and was peering over the bow to see the problem.

"I'll be able to repair her for the voyage home once we are at a dock with a good ironmonger, but out here I'll just have to shore it up with a wooden brace. I can't guarantee she'll hold unless we move the jib stay back aft of the damage, ma'am. It'll give us a bit 'a weather helm, but I could rig a temporary chain plate and move the stay back a bit. I'll strap that fore bit too so she's more solid."

"Have you got what you need aboard?" asked Dawkins, who had not sailed with the carpenter before this voyage and did not know of the man's adoration for the boats on which he sailed.

"Aye, sir, that I do. I'll take care a' the old girl and we'll fix her up the first chance we get."

They turned to watch as Koopmans made his way to the companionway and went below to his workbench.

Looking over at Dawkins, Jane remarked, "He's rebuilt every bit of my vessels over the last few years, I reckon. If anyone can keep her together, it will be he. Galsworthy, please keep me informed of the repairs. Dawkins, let the helm know we will be dousing the jib."

As she returned to the quarterdeck, Jane wondered whether they could make a claim against the sloop's owner at this late date. She would have to consult with her uncle, who would not be any more pleased about paying for this repair than she was.

Three days out from Elsinore, the captain decided she had to solve the mystery of the cargo. She did not want to bring smuggled goods into the Russian port and run the risk of having her sugar and vessel impounded. She needed to know what she had aboard that was valuable enough to send a man to Cuba to get it.

"Mister Galsworthy, can you spare me Mister Vaugine for a bit today? I'm going to search the hold and would like his assistance."

She could see that Galsworthy had the hands working on polishing the woodwork and thought he would not miss one man.

"Aye captain, and I'll join you for a bit too. Those inspectors got my goat and I been itchin' t' figger out what they was up to, ma'am. Vaugine! 'Hoy man!" the mate called out.

Jane had the men lift and secure the hatch covers to provide light below and then led them into the hold.

"All right, gentlemen, let us think of a plan before we begin. What might they have seen if they were looking for something in particular?" Jane asked as she stood scratching the back of her head and gazing around at the tightly packed space. Cases of sugar were stacked in neat rows along the centerline of the hold, each pile strapped together and then strapped to the one behind it. Wooden slats were inserted wherever there was the smallest gap between the boxes to hold everything secure without movement. Additional cases had been wedged into the cargo lockers that lined the hull, and the doors secured with latches tied in place. There remained but a narrow walkway inboard of the lockers the width of Jane's shoulders.

"Let us begin with the lockers ma'am, see if any of 'em has been opened," suggested Galsworthy.

"Very good. Vaugine, you take the larboard lockers and I'll look over the starboard side. Mister Galsworthy, could you fetch a couple of lanterns so we can get a closer look at the boxes here in the middle."

When none of the latches appeared to have been tampered with, they turned to the cases in the center of the hold.

"Do you suppose they were just counting the cases, ma'am? Making sure we still had 'em all aboard?" suggested Galsworthy.

"No, I think they were looking for something specific. It sounds like they were here a goodly while, which is more than they would have needed to ascertain that we had not offloaded anywhere before arriving at Elsinore."

Jane paused to think as the others continued scanning the load for anything out of place.

"Ma,am," said Vaugine, "perhaps what they were looking for is *in* one of the boxes. And they just wanted to make sure the box is still here."

"Excellent, Vaugine, I think you must be right. Unless there is contraband in all of these boxes, and heaven help us if there is, they must have a way of telling which case contains their goods. I would bet my next glass of grog they've marked the box somehow. All right, we know what we're looking for, let us get at it."

Galsworthy found the first one.

"Ahoy, ma'am, what's this?" He was bending over and pointing to a small gold mark at the bottom left corner of a case in the first stack. Jane held the lantern close to peer at the mark, which did not appear on the otherwise identical boxes above and below it.

"It looks like some sort of insect. What do you think, Ezra? I don't remember seeing anything like this in the warehouse where we loaded. I don't think it can be a plantation mark since it is so small."

"It is a *bourdon, Capitaine,*" came Vaugine's voice over her shoulder.

Jane and Galsworthy straightened to look at him.

"Go on," the captain said. "What's a *bourdon?*"

"It's a, a, ah what is it called? It makes a bzzzz noise?" Vaugine's English, which had been improving rapidly over the prior two months, did not always stretch to more uncommon words.

Jane looked back at the mark and pronounced, "A bumblebee."

"*Ah oui,* a bumblebee. *C'est Napoleon.* The emperor, it is his symbol," he declared.

"Oh good lord, have we stumbled into some sort of French politics, Mister Galsworthy?" Jane yelled and threw her hands up. "All right, let us see if there are any more."

A careful search of the remaining visible cargo revealed nine more cases marked with the golden bee. They had to assume there were more cases with the symbol buried in the center ranks of boxes and in the lockers. It was time to find out what was in them.

"Galsworthy, let us have Koopmans down here with his tools without alarming the rest of the crew. And please put a word in Dawkins' ear about what we've found."

Koopmans arrived within short order carrying his hammer and crowbar.

"Mister Galsworthy says we are going to open some a' the cargo ma'am?" he asked.

"That's right. We'll need to extract this box from the pile," Jane said as she kicked the first case Galsworthy had found. "There's nothing for it but to pull apart the bindings and restack the boxes on top. Vaugine, lend a hand here."

Between the two of them, they managed to lift away two boxes after Koopmans cut the ropes binding the pile and removed the wedges. Galsworthy returned and took Jane's place to help move the next two and leave the suspect case on top. With his crowbar, Koopmans pried up the lid to reveal a smooth layer of brown sugar covered by a piece of oiled paper to protect it from the wooden crate.

"We shall have to empty the sugar. Vaugine, please fetch

the bucket in my cabin."

It ended up taking four more buckets scrounged from a puzzled Cookie in the galley before the case was empty. And all that was in the buckets was sugar.

It wasn't until Vaugine attempted to pick up the empty case and move it to the floor that they discovered the secret.

"*Mon dieu*, but that is still heavy." Vaugine exclaimed.

Koopmans elbowed him aside and crouched down to look carefully inside the box. He took out his hammer and tapped around the edges of the interior until he heard a hollow sound. Picking up the crowbar, he inserted it into a crack at the seam and yanked back to pop out the plank. The four of them stared at what had been hiding in the false bottom.

"It is gold, is it not?" Jane said in a disgusted voice. "They are smuggling gold, of all the blasted things. I feel like a pirate, dammit. All right, let us have it open and see how much there is."

Koopmans pulled up the rest of the planks and they counted out two hundred coins marked *Napoleon Empereur* on the front and *40 francs* on the back. Doing a quick calculation in her head, Jane estimated that the ten boxes they had found contained 80,000 francs if they were all loaded equally. It was a small fortune, of which this might only be a part.

"Galsworthy, please take the coins to my cabin then see to it that the hatch is replaced. Vaugine, Koopmans, please repack the sugar in the case and put the cargo back together. Not a word about this to the rest of the crew, if you please."

Jane picked up the lanterns and followed Galsworthy aft where she hung them from hooks in the decking overhead. Entering her cabin, she scooped the coins Galsworthy had dumped on the table into a leather bag and stowed them in her trunk. She then went on deck to confer with Mister Dawkins.

"Dawkins, we've got a bit of a sticky situation," she confessed to her chief once she had walked him away from the helmsman's ears.

"We shall have to deal with the people whose gold it is, but I am thinking about the crew right now. Vaugine and Koopmans will keep it under their shirts, but the crew knows something is up. What shall we tell them? They have a stake in our success and will want to know if there is a problem with the shipment. And they'll spread rumors if we don't give them something they can chew on."

From the stony look on his face, Jane could tell that her first mate was still struggling to comprehend the enormity of the betrayal by Bonenfant, and the jeopardy into which they were sailing. After a protracted silence, he shook himself and bent to speak quietly into her ear.

"Ma'am, we shall just tell the crew we discovered we've been shorted on the sugar. It's the truth, anyway, so we won't be hard pressed to keep up a front. We shall let them know we will expect full compensation from Sarrazin after the matter is put in the hands of our agent in St. Petersburg. If word of the gold gets out, we shall think of something then."

It was the best they could do at the moment, and Jane knew it.

"Make it so, Mister Dawkins, and I will consider what is to be done with our unexpected cargo."

XXI

Treasure Chest

Wednesday, July 26   Lat. Obs.   59° 37'N   Long. DR 23° 38'E   Moderate winds
SSW   Preparing cargo for delivery St. P.

"Mister Koopmans," Jane asked the carpenter, "what's the longest excess line we have aboard? Something we could spare until we replace it in Gothenburg?"

"Well, ma'am, we might be able to do without the extra anchor rode if it came to it. But I wouldn't want to trust it for anything much. It's been a' sittin' in the chain locker for years I think, and I haven't been tarrin' it or anything. Might not hold a weight without partin'," he replied. "Are ya' thinkin' about hangin' somethin' off it, ma'am?"

"More like using it to keep track of something, Koopmans. Have a look at it and let me know if you think it would be useful."

Jane had been pondering the problem of the stowaway gold and had finally made up her mind to treat the hidden shipment as simply another cargo, albeit an unauthorized one. She had calculated the weight of the coins in each box and determined what the freight charge would be from Matanzas to St. Petersburg. The owners of the coins could simply pay her the rate once she saw how many boxes carried them. Since they had attempted to smuggle the gold without her notice, she doubted very much that presenting a bill to the recipients would produce payment, so she intended to deduct it from the amount she turned over. Once they offloaded the cargo to the warehouse in Russia, she expected she had no more than a day or so before it was discovered that the coins were not in the shipment and the owners would be looking for answers from the captain of the *Destiny*. She intended to be ready for them.

While she waited for Koopmans to return with news of the

rope, she made up a bill of lading for the gold and a receipt showing payment of the shipping fee she would complete once she knew the final tally of the weight. She indicated that delivery was "to the port of St. Petersburg" without further stipulation. She also made a note in the margin of the ship's log for the nineteenth of May that they had unknowingly taken aboard a shipment of gold belonging to Alain, Comte de Bonenfant. If her log ever ended up in court, she could rest easy that it represented the true state of affairs aboard her vessel.

Koopmans ducked back through the saloon door and saluted the captain.

"Aye, ma'am, she'll do so long as you don't ask too much of her," he reported.

"Very good, Mister Koopmans. Now, I intend to hold this shipment back until I have received full payment for it." Jane outlined her plan for the carpenter, who grinned broadly at the cleverness and simplicity of her solution.

"Aye, ma'am, I can have that ready for you on the morrow, if that'll suit," he assured her.

"Very good. I have emptied my trunk and you may take it now. Make sure that your construction is as sturdy as it can be," Jane ordered.

"Aye, aye, ma'am. And if I may say, those Frenchies have met their match" chortled Koopmans as he headed out of the cabin to find his tools.

I very much hope so, thought Jane.

That evening, she asked Dawkins and Galsworthy to join her over a glass of port.

"We'll be landing in St. Petersburg the day after tomorrow if the wind holds. We'll need to keep our wits about us if we are to come out of this with our skins whole, gentlemen. We have been played for fools, and I for one won't stand for it," Jane began in a determined voice as she banged her glass down onto the table. "That bastard Bonenfant and his cronies think they have hoodwinked us from the time we left New York with that imposter aboard. We will now see to it that the tables are fairly turned."

Dawkins gave her a grin as he asked, "And how do you intend to accomplish that, ma'am?"

"It will be a dance, Mister Dawkins, such as you have never seen before," she replied.

Jane refilled her mates' glasses and laid out the details of her plan. They would sail into the river and make straight for the loading docks. There, they would clear the *Destiny's* sugar cargo with the customs office and present the crew's papers and the clean bill of health. Dawkins would make arrangements for warehouse storage while Galsworthy supervised the offloading of the unmarked cases onto the quay. Her business would be with the agent; she needed to find a buyer before the *Jeremiah* hove into view and sent the market spiraling downward.

"We'll station Vaugine below to make sure every bumblebee case is set to the side and left in the hold," she explained. "Dawkins, you'll see to it that the cargo on the quay is moved to the warehouse as quickly as possible. We need to be off the wharf and on the anchor by nightfall."

It took the rest of the bottle of port for her to lay out the remaining details of the plan and rehash its finer points. By the time the bottom was reached, they were in agreement and the rest of the necessary documents had been drawn up. Jane was adamant that the crew receive their share of the gold cargo as set out in their articles. She was also considering charging a premium for "reckless endangerment of the vessel and its crew" to be further divided among the men. She didn't figure the question of its legality would ever see the light of a courtroom.

"We'll need to have the help of the men if we are to make a success of this," Jane said. "They have to know there's something in it for them so they don't feel ill-used that we are letting go of this treasure. I don't want them helping themselves to any portion of it. Every coin is to be accounted for in the bills, and they are to see that we have done right by them. Mister Galsworthy, we'll have an all hands meeting on the deck at the watch change in the morning. Pray see that all the men are there. Mister Dawkins, figure up the crew's portion for each case. We will see in two days' time how much the total will be when we have a full accounting of the number of cases."

After dismissing her officers, Jane wrapped herself in an extra scarf and drew on a pair of woolen mittens. The middle of summer on the Gulf of Finland was beautiful but not warm. As she mounted the ladder to the deck, she cast her eyes to the sky and drew in her breath when she saw one and then many shooting stars arc across the heavens. The clear air made them stand out against the band of shadowy stars of the Milky Way. Jane was enchanted, and called out to Macy at the helm,

"Look up, Macy! It's like fireflies dancing!"

The young sailor put his head back for a moment and stared into the night.

"Aye, ma'am, I always wish for something when I see one," he said as he lowered his gaze once more to the horizon.

"What do you wish for, if you do not mind the question?"

"No, ma'am, it's no secret. Just to come home again to find my family is well. And to kiss my wife."

"Have you been married long?" Jane's eyes didn't leave the night sky.

"Just a year, ma'am. I went to sea again to earn a bit of money so we could buy some land and set ourselves up near my parents' place. Without the whaling money, I know it might take a little longer, but I found I just couldn't stick it on them oil ships."

Jane settled herself with her back to the rail and regarded the young seaman.

"Well, Mister Macy, I hope we do a nice piece of business here in St. Petersburg and that you have your land sooner than you expect." Jane smiled to herself as she thought of the payoff each of the men would receive once they arrived home in New York.

Thursday, July 27   Lat. Obs. 59° 57'N   Long. DR 25° 55'E   Winds steady ENE estimate landfall St. P on the morrow.

As ordered, Galsworthy mustered the men on the deck at the

end of the early watch the next day. With Griggs at the helm and Hitchens assigned to stand lookout at the foremast, the men gathered around Jane where she stood on the hatch cover.

"All right, men, it's time to lay out for you what we have discovered and to ask your assistance in making this passage a success for us all," she began.

The captain related the suspicions they had been harboring of their erstwhile shipmate Fairchild, at which a number of the men nodded. Living in close quarters left little room for secrets on board a sailing vessel and a number of the crew had felt that something was awry with the mysterious Canadian.

"We do not know why yet, but Mister Fairchild hid a load of these in the cargo we loaded in Matanzas."

Jane held up a gold coin. It glinted in the sun and caused a round of gasps among the men.

"We are going to deliver that load to St. Petersburg as seems to be expected of us, but they will pay for our service. We are also taking something extra for the inconvenience, so you should each expect not only a more handsome share than we had thought, but an additional bounty with which to line your pockets. Mister Dawkins will apprise you of the amount once we have calculated the total."

At this news, a rousing cheer went up accompanied by a round of backslapping.

"We will need you to work like dogs after we arrive, repacking an unknown number of cases in the night. I think there may also come a moment when you need to prove that American sailors are men of worth not to be trifled with. The owners of the cargo will most likely not care for my method of delivery. Should they wish to dispute it, I shall rely on you to convince them of their faulty thinking."

A shout went up as she concluded her speech, "Huzzah! Three cheers for the captain!"

Jane stood grinning down on her crew as they raised their hats and cheered. She knew they could be counted on to defend the honor of the *Destiny* in the face of any challenge from the French. If she played her hand well, they would never need to find out how brave they were. But she was glad to have them at her back.

As the men returned to their work, Koopmans approached and gestured toward the companionway. Jane followed him below to survey his handiwork. There in the hold he had built a crate inside of which her trunk was securely fastened. Once filled, the trunk could be closed and the lid now propped against the bulkhead could be nailed into place. It wouldn't keep the water out, but it would keep whatever was inside of it in. Small holes had been drilled in the bottom of the trunk and the wooden crate so that water would run out of it when it was lifted from the riverbed. For that is where it was destined to lie. The gold would be placed in the trunk and sent to the bottom. A length of rope would be tied around the frame and led to the dock, where it would be nailed to the retaining wall just below the waterline at low tide.

Satisfied that her plan had a more than passing chance of success, Jane instructed Dawkins to have the crate brought to the quarterdeck and lashed onto the stern rail. The rest of the day was occupied with turning over the plan in her mind until she was sure that every step had been considered and every eventuality covered. All that remained was to find a good buyer for her sugar load as quickly as possible. She did not relish the thought of tarrying in St. Petersburg after the delivery of her payment demands to the owners of the gold.

XXII

St. Petersburg

St. Petersburg, Russia
July, 1820

The sight that greeted the *Destiny's* crew as she rounded Harmaala Point, headed for St. Petersburg, was astonishing. Out of the low hills arose a city both magnificent and raw. As they sailed up the Neva River to the wharfs, they could see signs of construction all around. Dusty fields surrounded fabulous palaces, and animal pens could be glimpsed from the water. A forbidding medieval fortress dominated the shore on one side of the estuary, and a grand open promenade topped by a fairytale tower faced it across the way. Church steeples soared above red tiled roofs, each church elaborate in its own way.

A commanding building of yellow brick loomed over the wharf with a tall arch large enough for a ship to pass under. As they sailed past the opening and could see that this imposing edifice was a shipyard, Jane shook her head.

"Heavens, if they could see this in Newburgh! We practically build boats in our backyards there. What would they say if they knew the Russians built them in palaces?"

It was approaching noon when the *Destiny* hove to and dropped anchor in the middle of the stream opposite what was marked on Jane's chart as the Customs House. She ordered the skiff launched and climbed into it with Dawkins. Hitchens rowed them the short distance to the broad stone steps that led to street level and looped the painter through an iron ring set into the wall.

"Stay with the boat, Hitchens," Jane commanded. "We'll be back shortly."

A brief walk took them to the door of the Customs House where they were greeted in French by a Russian official clad in an imposing red uniform. Wishing they had Vaugine with them, they muddled through handing over their papers and obtaining clearances for their cargo. The amount of the landing tax made Jane's heart beat a little faster. Their profits were slipping away with every additional duty and fee. She needed to get her sugar into the warehouse immediately and find her agent's office.

As they rowed back to the *Destiny*, Dawkins observed that their unexpected fortune in hiring seaman Vaugine was paying off in many ways.

"I'll take Vaugine with me when I arrange for the warehouse. Thank goodness we have a man who speaks French aboard! Ye' make sure to keep him on your crew, ma'am. He'll be a good man to have in all weathers."

"Aye, Dawkins, I have seen that for myself. Let us see how he fares in New York."

An hour later, the *Destiny* was tied up at the dock. Dawkins set off immediately with Vaugine to wrangle for warehouse space. With any luck, the load would sell quickly and they could eliminate the expense. Meanwhile, Galsworthy had the men open the hatches and set up the boom for use as a crane to transfer the cargo to the dock. In Vaugine's absence, they assigned the carpenter to inspect each box before it was cleared for hoisting from the hold. For her part, Jane made for the offices of Steiglitz & Co., her uncle's agents in New York and abroad.

Arriving in front of the address she had been given by Uncle Josias, she opened the ornate door and stepped into a cool anteroom. Deep carpets on the floor and a vaulted ceiling made the place feel almost church-like. Jane felt she needed to whisper as she approached the young man seated behind a table in front of a closed door.

"Excuse me, sir?" Jane cleared her throat and tried again when the young man continued writing busily and appeared not to have heard her greeting.

"Excuse me? Is this the agent's office?" This in a somewhat louder voice that was greeted by further silence. Well, two could play this game. Jane turned on her heel and marched up to the closed door. Throwing it open, she spoke loudly into the room,

"Excuse me. Captain Jane Thorn of the *Destiny* is arrived to see Mister Mackey. Please let him know I am here."

A woman with her arms full of documents paused long enough to tilt her head to the right corner of the cavernous room.

"You'll find him in there, *mademoiselle*. He will be yelling at someone," she advised and then scurried on her way.

Ignoring the young man from the anteroom, who was now urgently attempting to get her attention by walking backward in front of her and gesturing wildly, Jane marched swiftly through the throng of clerks who populated the busy office and followed the sound of a raised voice until she located its owner.

"It's not on the manifest, I tell you! You can't sell something that doesn't exist, you Russian dolt! *Comprenez-vous?*"

The target of this tirade cowered before a round man in severe clothing that marked him one of the Brethren. At the final shout, the chastened clerk made a short bow and hurried past Jane with his head down. Mister Mackey looked at her and yelled,

"And who in the blazes are you? I don't need any more clerks, lassie, and where is that infernal Whithers? He's supposed to be guarding the door! Whithers!"

Jane crossed her arms and waited until Mackey had stopped yelling long enough to hear her.

"Captain Jane Thorn, Mister Mackey. It is a pleasure to make your acquaintance." Jane stuck her hand out to the surprised agent, who took it seemingly without being aware of what he was doing.

"Thorn? Of the *Destiny*? How in tarnation did you make it here so fast? Do you have a load of sugar? Pray tell me you have sugar! The market has been high these past three months and we've not seen a sugar ship since April. Your uncle didn't tell me Captain Thorn would be a lass. How did you get here so fast, again?" The flood of questions finally petered out and Jane was able to reply.

"I will be happy to tell you of our adventures, Mister Mackey, but that is a matter for another day. At the moment, I need you to sell this. Today, if possible," she said as she placed her silver box of sugar on the table and flipped back the lid. The agent leaned forward and took a pinch between his fingers. His eyes widened as he let the flavor melt into his tongue.

"How much do you have, Captain?"

Jane handed him the contract from the Banks firm. Mackey jumped up and ran to his open door.

"Whithers! Are you still about you fool? Here, take this note to Lewis upstairs. Wait for an answer and bring it right back." Mackey was scribbling furiously on a piece of paper, which he then handed to the hapless clerk. "And make it quick!"

"My dear, I think we have just gotten what you might call a jump on the market. We'll have that sugar sold in a moment; well done!"

Mackey offered her a cup of tea as they awaited the return of the clerk. Jane had just picked up her cup when he entered and handed the note back to Mackey.

"Eureka! They've met our price!" He passed the note to Jane, who was astonished to see a figure a full twenty percent higher than she had anticipated.

"My, there does seem to be a demand, Mister Mackey. Most excellent. In that case, you ought to be able to find a buyer for this at, perhaps, another twenty percent more." Jane handed over her manifest listing the sugar they had shipped on their own behalf.

Mackey threw back his head and laughed. "New York shipping captains! I always tell people to keep their hands on their wallets when one of you is about. You're worse than that Yankee crew out of Boston!"

"I'll take that as a compliment, Mister Mackey. Now, shall we see if the estimable Mister Lewis might be interested in this further tonnage?"

He was, although at only another ten percent advance on the price. Oh well, Jane thought, it had been worth a try. Even at that price they would still make out handsomely on the deal. The firm of Lewis & Willing specialized in the import of sugar to the Russian market and their stores were obviously running low. Jane was satisfied and signed the bill of sale. Before leaving the office, she signed over the contents of the warehouse to the agent while alerting him that the full cargo would not be fully in place until the morning.

"We've got a bit of arranging to do in the hold, but you'll have the balance on the morrow, I promise. The final tally may turn out to be a case or two short, though, so we will adjust the weight once the cargo is ashore."

"I know you're good for it. Your uncle is as straight a trader as I know and I'm sure you follow in his footsteps. Is there anything else I can help you with, captain?"

There was indeed; Jane needed a ballast load of pig iron. If the agent could purchase it for her at her target price or lower, she would be obliged if he could arrange to have it at the dock in the morning.

"You're back out again so soon? My dear, you have barely arrived." The agent lifted his brows in surprise.

"Aye, I want to be gone before the *Jeremiah* catches me sitting at the dock. I showed her my tailfeathers on the way here and I imagine Captain Duncan may feel himself hard done-by that I stole a march on him."

"Bless me, but you are a live one, Captain Thorn! And I am glad to hear that he is on the way while the market is still fresh. He'll do fine this year, so I would not fret myself about passing him in the street, Captain. He won't be in a bad way if he gets here soon."

After completing the order for iron and affixing her signature to the letter of remittance, Jane was ready to head back to her vessel. The amount she had earned thus far on the trip would cover all of the expenses beyond the amount earned with the Banks cargos. The addition of the gold shipment, while a trouble, would put them further into the black before they even picked up their load in Sweden. Jane was proving that a fast vessel with a shallow draft and a daring skipper could take advantage of the winds to make the voyage pay. The bigger ships might run her down if they had a fair wind, but she could shift and turn and find her way with just a hint of a breeze. It took skill and luck, but she had a good measure of both. If only the luck would hold for the rest of the voyage.

At the wharf, the crew had made good progress with the unloading. Dawkins had hired a team of men to transport the cases to their rented warehouse at the end of the block. Nearly half the load was shifted and it looked like the rest would be a matter of a few hours more. Dawkins related his negotiations with the warehouse owner with a great deal of praise for Vaugine.

"Ma'am, he's a born diplomat. I'm not sure exactly what he said to the man, but he had us signed up and squared away quicker than quick. He even found an error in the bill that saved us a pretty penny. I don't think the Russian feller thought our French would be good enough to catch it."

"I am pleased to hear such a marvelous report, Dawkins. We may have more work for him before this episode comes to a close and we leave St. Petersburg behind."

Having seen to the progress of the cargo, Jane set out now for the house of the American consul. The harbormaster had arranged for a horse and carriage to take her to the abode of Abraham Gibson, an old family friend. Consul Gibson was from New York and a frequent guest at her uncle's table over the years.

"He won't want to talk business, Jane," her uncle had warned. "He considers himself a government man and would find it unseemly to mix those duties with making money for himself. Fortunately, he is not in need of the funds as his family is quite well-to-do. But do look him up while you are there, especially if you need something. He will be delighted to see you."

The consul's house on Liteyny Prospekt was a gracious stone building with rows of arched windows and an ornate transom window over the door. Jane had not had time to send a message announcing her arrival, so was prepared to leave her card and come back again should he not be at home.

Her knock brought a liveried servant to the door, and she was ushered into the hall. A moment later, the familiar face of the man known to her as Uncle Abe appeared from the back of the hall, and he rushed to her with his arms open for a warm embrace.

"My goodness, Jinks! To think that you have arrived here! Josias and I had talked of your trying an Atlantic trading voyage, but I had no idea it would be so soon. Have you brought the *Destiny*?"

"Aye, she's a fast boat, and will easily make good on the cost of her purchase and outfitting."

"You're a brave girl and a fine captain, Jinks. Come into the parlor and have tea while you tell me all that has happened since I last saw you," the consul said as he waved her through a door that opened into a room decorated in the heavy tapestries and gilded furniture of imperial Russian style.

It did Jane's heart good to spend the afternoon with friends from home. Mistress Gibson had arrived shortly after Jane and joined them in catching up on old acquaintances and the situation in Russia.

"May I ask what your plans are here in St. Petersburg, my dear?" the consul asked when she had run out of news to relate.

"To leave as quickly as possible, frankly. I would like to make Gothenburg by the end of the month. I've got a big load of bar iron to get aboard there and a pottery shipment from a factory in Falkenberg. We have several weeks of repairs to make and I aim to be westward bound no later than the end of September as we are taking the northern route home, so I must make haste where I can."

"I am glad to hear that, Jinks. There has been unrest here since the war with Napoleon, and Tsar Alexander has set his dogs on anyone he suspects of revolution. Foreigners are always watched and it is too easy to fall foul of the police. While I would welcome your extended visit here in my home, I think you are wise to continue with your current plan."

"Thank you, sir, I will be cautious and keep the men aboard while we are here. Now I must take my leave, and will bring your kind regards to my uncle. It has been lovely to see you both."

Jane hugged the couple after shrugging back into her coat

and hat. This time with the Gibsons had brought up thoughts of family and she was a little misty-eyed as she climbed back into the carriage. The tug of home was feeling more urgent. Jane had made a vow to herself to be home in Newburgh by November and it seemed a long way off.

XXIII

A Night's Work

By the time she had concluded her visit with the consul and made her way back to the waterfront, Jane's crew had transferred the unmarked sugar boxes ashore, the hatches had been closed, and the last of the boxes on the quay were being loaded into the warehouse drays.

"Ah, ma'am, you have returned just in time. We are about to cast off and make for the anchorage," Galsworthy informed her.

"Very good, Mister Galsworthy, I will be below seeing to our special cargo."

Jane stopped in her cabin to see that Dawkins had made a full record of the offloading and disposition of the sugar. She knew he could be trusted but felt it her duty to cast an eye on the records and add a signature approving the notations. All was in order, including the reference to the repacking of the gold shipment that was about to commence. Dawkins would add tallies once they had completed the transfer to the chest and knew how many coins they had aboard.

In the hold, Vaugine and Koopmans had carefully stacked the marked cases along the centerline. Jane quickly counted them and was surprised to see that there were seventeen cases all told. Should they hold the same quantity of coins as the first, there were over three thousand in the shipment. That much gold would keep a nobleman afloat for half a year. A small fortune indeed!

Lying on top of the boxes was a pile of small canvas bags Jane had directed Koopmans to make. These would be filled with coins and put into the sea trunk on deck before it was lowered to the riverbed. Hearing the anchor chain running out, Jane decided it was time to begin their night's work and sent Vaugine to fetch Mister Dawkins so he might supervise the repacking of the sugar while she returned to the deck to find

Galsworthy.

"We are in the thick of it now, Mister Galsworthy, and need to be on our toes. I don't know if the owners of the coins will be able to get at the warehouse tonight, but they are sure to do so tomorrow. We won't have too many watches before they come looking for us. Let us double the lookout and make sure the men have some sort of weapons to hand, even if it is just bollards and pins."

"Aye, aye, ma'am. We'll be ready for 'em if they come," he replied through gritted teeth. Galsworthy's fierce glare would be enough to hold any French conspirators at bay, Jane thought.

"Have the crew join us in the hold so we can assign duty stations, Mister Galsworthy," Jane ordered, and went below.

"Men," she began when all had assembled in the nearly empty cargo space, "we work in darkness tonight. Two of you will stay with Vaugine and Mister Koopmans here to open the cases and count the coins before putting them in bags. Cookie, we will need your buckets again," she nodded to the cook where he stood at the back.

"Two of you will hold lookout on the deck and be ready to shout if any boat looks like she is approaching the *Destiny*. The rest of you will make a chain and hand bags up to Mister Galsworthy, who will pack them in the trunk. Except for the one lantern here in the hold, there is to be no light. And you must be as silent as the grave, men. None must suspect the business we are about tonight." She paused to let them sense the gravity of the moment, then continued, "Right, let us begin."

It took over two hours to open the cases, remove the sugar, pry up the false bottoms and remove the coins before repacking the sugar in the cases. When they were done, there were fifteen full cases of sugar and two empty ones.

"We will add that to the bill, Mister Dawkins. They can repay me for the sugar I bought but which did not come aboard," Jane murmured to the chief. "Let us add up the charges and count out the coins they owe us into the cashbox. And make sure to fill in their receipt of payment."

The men carried the last of the bags to the bottom of the

human chain that led to Mister Galsworthy at the stern, where he was placing the bagged coins carefully in the trunk. Then, while the crew restacked the boxes in preparation for moving the *Destiny* ashore on the morrow, Jane looked through the sheaf of papers they had found in the third box they opened.

"Ahoy, ma'am," Koopmans had whispered. "There's more here than money." He had pried up the second plank of the false bottom in the crate and teased out an oilcloth-wrapped packet with his fingers. Jane took the package from him and opened it sufficiently to note that the papers were in French. That fact did not bring her any surprise. She would have Vaugine translate them for her when they were done in the hold.

Flipping through them now, she saw what appeared to be a letter signed by someone named François Durant. Jane recalled *Monsieur* Sarrazin remarking on the misfortune of the imprisoned French officer. Like many exiles from Napoleon's army, the desperate Durant had joined a revolutionary force bent on overthrow of the Spanish government in Mexico. The royal dragoons had captured him and thrown him into prison in Havana whence he had recently been released. Jane was given to understand that the man had repudiated his revolutionary ideas.

"Mister Koopmans, pray complete the work here and douse the lantern. Hitchens, alert Mister Dawkins that the trunk may be delivered to its new home. Vaugine, in my cabin if you please."

Jane lit the lantern on the mess table and threw the packet of papers onto it. Motioning Vaugine to sit, she said,

"There, Mister Vaugine, see what you make of those. Perhaps they will reveal what this whole sorry business is about."

Picking up the first of the letters, Vaugine began to read as Jane paced the cabin in a fever of impatience. By the time the officers had assembled in her cabin, Vaugine was turning over the last of the papers.

"Well, Dawkins, how do things stand?" she asked as her mates entered and closed the door.

"Aye, ma'am, all is well. The trunk went over with nary a hitch and the rope from it is fast to the aft rail."

"Very good. The next bit of the dance is mine to perform, as I'll not have any of the crew put in jeopardy ashore. Before I go, let us hear what Vaugine has discovered."

"*Oui, ma capitaine,* it is as you feared. This letter is signed by Sarrazin. He says the money comes from the families exiled from Haiti who were refugees for the first time when they left France after Napoleon. They have gathered it to aid in his restoration, and seem to believe there is hope for their cause in Russia. There is another here from a Monsieur Durant, who says to use the money to complete some unfinished business Napoleon had with something called the Kremlin. He does not say what he means, I am sorry," Vaugine related to his grim-faced audience.

"In other words, we have aboard documents that call for some sort of political unrest in Russia. Blast his hide! If we are caught with those, we might have a very difficult time explaining them to the tsar's police. Galsworthy, see that those papers are returned to their wrappings and stow them where they will not be easily found. Thank you, Vaugine, and not a word of this to anyone. Mister Dawkins, take me ashore."

On the deck, Jane hitched up her skirts and clambered quickly down the ladder to the skiff where Dawkins was waiting. He dipped the oars silently in the dark river and carried them to the stern of the *Destiny* where Koopmans untied the rope that led from the trunk and dropped it into Jane's hands. His head disappeared behind the rail as Dawkins pulled for shore.

"Ahoy! *Kto idet?*" The sudden command came out of the darkness ahead of them as they were nearing the bank.

"Patrol boat!" hissed Dawkins. Swiftly, Jane shucked off her captain's coat and threw her hat into the bottom of the skiff. Folding the coat inside out, she tossed it on top of the rope where it crossed the gunwale and pulled the braid from her hair. She then slid onto the bench next to Dawkins and wrapped her arm around his waist.

"Kiss me!" she whispered urgently. Shocked, Dawkins did as she asked and was the picture of a besotted suitor when the imperial guard arrived in a small gunboat.

"*Kto idet?*" the question came again from the officer

standing at the front with his foot balanced on the gunwale.

"Ahoy there! And a fine good evening to you." Dawkins responded as he held Jane tightly to his side. "What can I do for you gentlemen?"

"Americans! Is that your vessel there?" the officer demanded as he held his lantern higher to cast a glow on the scene before him.

"Why yes, sir, it is. We thought to escape it for a few moments for a little, um, privacy. Sir," Dawkins improvised.

A slow smile crossed the man's mouth as he stared down at the boat where Jane was coyly hiding her face from the view of the officer. "Ah, yes, I see how it is. Please make sure that you are back aboard your vessel before we return this way. Good night."

Jane could feel Dawkins' heart beating fast as she held her position until the boat had pulled well away. The chief nearly threw himself backward in his attempt to release her and put some distance between himself and the captain.

"Ma'am, do not ever require of me that I should do something like that again! It is not dignified and is a violation of the trust between master and mate!" Dawkins whispered in shocked anger.

"Oh, pish, Dawk. We saved ourselves from being arrested by the tsar's henchmen, so let us consider the matter well played and forget the details. Come, let us continue."

A few swift strokes of the oars by the perturbed Dawkins brought the boat alongside the wall that held the River Neva in its banks. Jane had timed their arrival to what she guessed was low tide, or as near as they could estimate without a tide table. Picking up the hammer Koopmans had provided them, she drove two nails through the end of the rope, one above the other. She then reached as far as she could under the water, holding on to the edge of the boat as it rocked in the waves, and finished driving the two nails into the wall. The awkward angle nearly tipped her overboard, but the thing was soon accomplished and she then drove a third nail as high as she could reach on the wall directly above the others. The rope was now hidden from all but the most discerning eyes and its location marked in a manner that would only be visible at low tide.

"Is it done, ma'am?" Galsworthy asked in a low voice as he helped them back aboard.

"Aye, that it is. I have but one more step to my figure, and that I shall take tomorrow. Then, we will wait to see who comes calling. Make sure we are back at the dock by early morning, Dawkins. And call me immediately if the watch reports anything more than a gust of wind."

Jane retired to her cabin and pulled a piece of paper and her inkwell toward her as she sat at the desk. Picking up a pen, she paused to consider how to begin, and then bent to her task.

XXIV

The Trap is Set

Jane set off for the agent's office as soon as the *Destiny* tied up at the loading dock in the morning. The hired drays had been waiting for them along with the pig iron ballast, and Dawkins thought they would be back on the anchor within the space of four hours. The captain assured him that she would return well before cast off.

The prior day, Cookie went ashore with Mister Dawkins to arrange for provisions to be delivered. Once the hold was empty and the ballast loaded, the crew would bring the stores aboard under the watchful eye of the cook. Jane had heard a rumor that Cookie wanted to provide the men with fresh eggs and a chicken dinner or two on the way to Gothenburg. She had seen Koopmans building something that looked suspiciously like a cage on the foredeck and knew the change of diet would be welcome.

After giving the agent's address to the driver, Jane settled back in a cab to think over the remainder of her plan for delivering the shipment and collecting full payment. She had baited a trap; it was now just a question of waiting to see whom it would catch. Should there be no mouse brave enough to take the cheese, she would simply send the packet of letters to the river bottom and be on her way. They had kept back the freight fee and crew bonus from the coin hoard, so she was not, financially, owed anything further by the owners of the cargo. But she would like to deliver the papers to their intended recipients lest they wonder where they had gone and seek her out in the future to reclaim them. She also had a second form of payment she intended to collect, but that would have to wait until she arrived in Gothenburg.

In front of the familiar building that housed the agent's firm, Jane climbed down and asked the cab driver to wait. From the anteroom, Jane marched straight for the double doors to the inner office, ignoring the waving arms of the puffed-up Whithers. When he looked to lay his hands on her, she paused and gave him a stony stare that halted him in his tracks. Turning back, she grasped both doorknobs and flung the portal wide.

Mackey was in his office berating an underling, as seemed to be his usual way. Jane waited patiently as he concluded his remarks, and smiled sympathetically at the clerk as he slunk past her.

"Captain Thorn! What a pleasure. Have you got past Whithers again? I do not know why I employ that whelp. But come, have a seat and tell me how I may be of assistance? Is the load all in the warehouse now?" As before, Jane waited for him to run down before answering the most pertinent questions.

"Aye, Mister Mackey, your shipment has been fully delivered. Here is your statement and final bill with the corrected amount. We had slightly less tonnage than expected."

"Good, good. We will get that to Lewis immediately," he said as he reached out a hand for the papers.

"Now, I do have something else that you could help me with Mister Mackey. This packet contains confidential business papers that I wish to leave in your care. A Mister Fairchild will retrieve them before the end of October, if I am not mistaken. I shall of course pay your fee for the keeping of the documents. Do you have a safe into which they might be deposited?"

"Indeed, Captain, I do," Mackey assured her.

"Excellent. Now, there is a stipulation that attaches to the delivery of these documents. I ask that you not write this information down but rather retain it in your head. It is not to be shared with any member of your firm as Mister Fairchild will come to you, and you only, to receive the packet. When he arrives, I request that you ask him the following question. *What was she wearing?* The correct answer is *perfume*, which he must provide before you supply him with the papers. Is that clear, Mister Mackey?"

"Yes, quite, my dear captain. What a remarkable request! But it shall be done," he assured her as he picked up the packet and placed it immediately within his safe and closed the door.

"Good day to you, Captain Thorn. May we see you again next year with as felicitous a load. Shall I give your greetings to Captain Duncan when he arrives?"

Jane laughed. "Yes, pray do, Mister Mackey. Tell him that we look forward to seeing him and his good wife for dinner at my uncle's house in New York. I shall be waiting."

Jane checked the clock in the agent's office and saw that she still had time to complete her final errand. Finding a tattoo den in St. Petersburg had been accomplished with the help of the harbormaster, who knew of a man who was both competent and clean. She directed the cab driver to deliver her there and wait while another small flower was added to her arm. She chose a chamomile after noticing piles of them in the market by the harbor. The daisy-like bloom would look well next to the three-petaled mariposa. As with that first tattoo, she had drawn a design that was elegant but simple. She knew for sure that Mama would have a fainting spell about it, but she was determined to have a reminder of her life as a sea captain once she came ashore.

The afternoon wore away as Jane paced her cabin gnawing at the edges of her plan. Would they come? Would they accept her words as true? What would they do if they did not believe her? She had placed her bet and was simply waiting for the cards to be revealed, but it was difficult to be patient.

Jane and her mates ate dinner with the crew that evening. They felt solidarity with the men as they waited together at anchor for the final steps of the dance they had performed. She had allowed twenty-four more hours for the conspirators to make their appearance, after which they would execute her plan to rid themselves of the letters and sail away. The time was counting down.

Galsworthy set a double watch again as the sun set.

"Keep yer eyes peeled, men, and yer clubs to hand. Dawkins and I have pistols if it comes to that," he exhorted the crew as they gathered on the deck.

Jane had no intention of sleeping as she bid them all good night and went below, but she lay down on her berth fully clothed and closed her eyes to allow her nerves to settle.

She came to rather suddenly, feeling groggy and confused. Her lantern had burned itself out so several hours must have passed. Jane swung her feet to the floor to stand up when she felt something sharp pressed against her neck. She froze as a soft voice spoke in her ear.

"*Non, Capitaine,* you will stay where you are," the voice whispered. "*Vite, vite! Cherchez ici dans le lit.*"

From the sounds they were making, she guessed there were at least two additional men in her cabin, and the man holding her hostage was clearly the ringleader. They seemed to be searching through her things and now dragged her off the berth to tear it apart while the owner of the whispering voice held her firmly by the arm.

"It is not there," she said out loud. "But before I tell you where it is, pray report to me on the welfare of my crew."

The cabin went silent, and then someone uncovered a lantern they had brought aboard with them. Jane was right; there were five men wrapped in dark cloaks crowded into her cabin, each of whom wore a scarf that covered most of his face.

"*Alors, Capitaine,* this is a very dangerous game you are playing," the man holding her arm murmured in her ear. "We have inspected your hold and it is empty. Our boxes in the warehouse no longer contain what we had placed in them. What have you done with the contents, *hein?*" He yanked her arm so hard she cried out as he hissed the question.

"My crew?" she insisted.

"They are tied up in your hold, *mademoiselle.* None of them could acquaint us with the location of our property. We asked." There was no mistaking the menace in his voice. "Now we are asking you."

Alas, Jane thought, her men were clearly no match for the trained swordsmen gathered in her cabin. She had not counted on a company of professional soldiers, and just hoped none of the crew had been hurt while being subdued.

The captain took a deep breath and then jerked away from her captor. She threw her hand up in his face when he went to grab her again and commanded,

"Belay! Stop a moment and think, man. We were loaded and ready to depart at noon today. And yet we have delayed. Why do you suppose that is the case, *monsieur*?" Jane pointed her finger at him and gave him her sternest look. "Ah, I see the situation makes itself clear. Thank you for accepting my invitation. Now let us visit my crew and then we will return here to discuss my terms. Lead on."

It took a moment for the intruders to exchange glances and make up their minds. With a jerk of his head, the leader indicated the other four would wait while he took the captain to see her men. He holstered the sword he still carried in his right hand and reached for Jane's arm again.

"Oh no, sir, you will most decidedly not put your hand on me again." There was no mistaking the captain's order. She picked up her hat and set it on her head, took up the lit lantern, and waved to the man to precede her out the door.

The entry to the cargo hold had been bolted from the outside. Jane unlocked and swung it open to reveal the crew tightly gagged and tied back-to-back lying on the floor. With a swift glance, she saw that they were all accounted for. She held the lantern aloft as she walked around them, and then crouched next to Dawkins where he lay tied to Hitchens.

"Thank you, Mister Dawkins, I believe I will take it from here. Pray join me in my cabin as soon as you are able. We have much to discuss."

She swung around in her crouched position to face the door, then stood up after dropping something into Dawkins' hands.

"All right, let us conclude our business, *monsieur*." She again waved the cloaked man ahead of her and followed him to her cabin, leaving the hold door open.

As Jane set the lantern down on the mess table, she reached under it and pulled loose the packet of letters they had found in the sugar crates, tossed it to the ringleader, and sat down.

"Now, General Lallemand, for I assume you are he to whom those letters are addressed, pray ask your soldiers to wait outside while we conduct our affairs. May I offer you a glass of port?"

Jane reached for the bottle to pour them a drink over which to negotiate a deal. She was amazed at how still her hand was since she was quivering with tension inside. Except for the threat of violence, however, this was just like hammering out a contract with a wily merchant. She fully intended to keep the upper hand, particularly since the winning card was still in her possession.

Lallemand pulled down his scarf once his men had stepped out and closed the door. He did not take up the port, but he did tear eagerly into the letters. He read quickly through a few of the papers and then put the packet on the table.

"And what is your proposal, *Capitaine?*"

Jane was impressed by how quickly the man followed the turns of the game. He acted now as if he were on a casual visit in broad daylight instead of having conducted a clandestine military assault in the dead of night.

"May I first confirm that you are the owner, or perhaps the representative of the owner or owners of the cargo under discussion? I prefer to deal with principals, but I will accept your word as agent if you can assure me that I am in discussion with the correct party." Jane began.

For the first time, the man across from her smiled as he sat down.

"I have been cautioned not to underestimate you Americans, *Capitaine.* Perhaps I did not heed the warning sufficiently. But you have temporarily bested me, so *oui,* I have the authority to treat for the return of our property."

"You mistake me, General. I am not holding your cargo ransom. Although it was not brought aboard in the regular manner, I have undertaken the safe delivery of the freight to what I suppose to have been its final destination. Accordingly, your shipment is securely delivered to St. Petersburg in what I might point out was a rather timely manner." She couldn't help but boast a little.

"We have calculated the cost of the shipment, which has been itemized at the bottom of the bill, as per the gross weight at a rate thirty percent higher than our stated tariffs. Not only did you not apprise us of the cargo, but you put us at risk of being arrested for smuggling since we did not declare it at Elsinore. Further, we have included in our statement of charges an amount to cover the sugar you commandeered and replaced with your own cargo. I have added a small surcharge for the on-board storage of the cargo since we were obliged to hold it for twenty-four hours before delivering it to its final destination. You will also note a fee for labor and materials as we had to create new storage containers for your load."

Jane handed him a paper as she concluded, "Pray look this over and indicate whether or not you agree to the charges."

"And where is the final destination, may I ask?" The astonished general sat up in his chair as Jane calmly described the particulars of the bill he was now holding.

"Yes, well, that detail will be provided once we have settled the matter of payment. Now, the charges?"

"*Oui, oui!* We will pay this bill! Now where is the money?" Lallemand was becoming irate by now and his face was turning red.

"Very good. We have deducted the amount due from the shipment and consider your freight bill paid in full." Jane handed him a receipt for the settlement of the charges, at which she thought the general might explode.

"There remains but the matter of the release of the cargo. I am afraid that I do not have instructions from the owner to turn over the cargo to anyone else, agent or no. Therefore, I will need to consult in person with Count Bonenfant as to its disposition. I will be sending word to him about how to receive instructions as to the whereabouts of the load."

It had taken Jane most of the night before to work out the contents of the letter to be left with Mister Mackey and the message she would send to Count Bonenfant in care of his friend the Marquis. She expected to be laid up in Gothenburg for over a month repairing the jib boom, scraping and painting the bottom, and filling her load. Bonenfant would have plenty of time to find her there.

For his part, the general had come to the end of his fuse

and catapulted from his seat. Drawing his sword as he reached for Jane, he kicked his chair away. Suddenly, Lallemand plummeted to the floor as his feet were swept from underneath him. In a trice, Mister Dawkins was standing on his sword arm with a pistol aimed at Lallemand's head.

Outside the door Dawkins had thrown open, the captain could see the remaining four soldiers trussed up on the floor and the rest of her crew waving various heavy objects about. Dawkin's pistols had finally shown their usefulness, it would appear. She looked down at the general where he was fuming on the floor.

"I think that concludes our business, General Lallemand. We will put you back in your boat, if you would show us where it is, and bid you good night. It appears that it will be light within the hour, and we will be under way as soon as the sun comes up."

The Frenchmen had been divested of their weapons, which had been dropped into the river, and forced to climb down to the boat they had secured at the *Destiny's* stern. Dawkins deemed it best to remove the oars prior to shoving them free and thought the French should at least be grateful they were not still tied up.

"Well, Mister Dawkins, I see you made good use of my knife. It has come in handy for the second time on this most peculiar voyage," Jane remarked as they stood at the rail watching the sun rise over St. Petersburg. Curious as she was about how the band of soldiers had managed to take over her vessel despite their precautions, Jane knew the story would have to wait for another time.

"Are we cleared for departure?"

"Aye, ma'am. We visited the harbormaster yesterday to clear for leaving at first light."

"Well then, let us get under way, Mister Dawkins."

XXV

Passage South

*Monday, July 31   Lat. (chart) 59° 56'N   Long. (chart) 30° 11'E   Winds SE
moderating to E   Passed the Harmaala Point 10:30 am from which I take my
departure.*

"Here's to brave seamen!" Jane lifted her glass and toasted her
crew. She had gathered them on the side deck and had a round
of rum poured once the *Destiny* had rounded Harmaala Point
and they were headed due west to the open Baltic Sea.

The rum, which had been delivered as they were loading the
stores, was a gift from the consul in St. Petersburg. A note for
Jane had been included: *I know you keep a mostly dry ship, my dear,
but pray pour one out for the men and toast the success of the voyage thus
far. Fair winds on your trip home.*

"Cheers for the captain!" the crew replied and raised their
glasses to her.

"We are well away, and I think we have made a good
business of things so far. You have been a stalwart crew and you
have my trust, every last man of you. You also have the gratitude
of Thorn Shipping and this captain. While our intruders gained
temporary command of the *Destiny*, you showed your courage
and things came right in the end. Better men could not be found
and I for one am grateful to be sailing with you!"

Jane paused to set her glass down on the cabin roof, then
continued. "We are making for Gothenburg, where we will pick
up iron and pottery for the trip home. While we are there, we
will put into the shipyard for a month, so you will all have time
ashore to spend your wages. Bless you all. Bottoms up!"

Galsworthy moved among the men and filled their glasses
one more time as the men broke into song, lifting their glasses
on the chorus:

Merrily, merrily, so merry sail we,
No mortal on earth like a sailor at sea,
Heave away, haul away, the ship rolls along,
Give a sailor his grog and there's nothing goes wrong.

"All right, men, back to your stations!" Galsworthy called out as they ended on a shout of *Huzzah!*

Jane picked up her empty glass and handed it to Cookie as she gazed over the rail at the sparkling water rushing past the schooner's beam.

"I meant every word of it Mister Dawkins." She turned to the chief who was standing beside her. "That all could have gone very badly back there. But I feel that I can take risks from time to time if I know that you and Galsworthy and the men are with me."

Dawkins looked at her in alarm and asked, "What else do ye' have in mind, ma'am?"

She looked up at him and answered, "Only what is best for the vessel, and all aboard her. But if trouble comes, it will find us ready."

"Ship ahoy!" Boniface on lookout called from the bow.

"Where away?" Dawkins shouted back.

"Off the starboard bow!" Boniface pointed nearly dead ahead and Jane squinted to see the vessel.

Pulling out her spyglass, she located the ship and traced its spars until she saw the stars and stripes affixed to the topmast. She continued to scan its decks for another minute until she recognized the lines of her.

"Ha! Mister Dawkins, it is Captain Duncan."

Jane headed aft and climbed to the quarterdeck. There, she stood with her arms behind her as she watched the brig draw closer. The vessels glided past each other at a quarter mile distance, and Jane could see the figure of the captain at the *Jeremiah's* stern. Slowly, he lifted his hat in a salute to her. She doffed her own hat to return the gesture, holding it to her chest and watching the *Jeremiah* as it sailed on for St. Petersburg. She knew it was a reflection of an unseemly emotion, but Jane allowed herself the tiniest bit of a smile.

Wednesday, August 2 Lat. Obs. 59° 55'N Long. DR 25° 30'E gale winds ENE, making good time, vessel holding her own.

The late summer weather on the Baltic brought long sunny days with temperatures warm enough that the crew worked without their jackets. Jane stowed her heavy cocked beaver hat and donned her flat-brimmed straw cap to keep the sun at bay. Taking advantage of the fine days, she ordered the torn sails brought out and repaired. The storm off Hatteras had shredded one of the foresails and they had torn the main in April trying to make Cape Elizabeth in front of a gale. With a dry deck and calm seas, they could now be spread out and sewn.

The further south they sailed the more Jane began to watch the skies. She knew there were frequent storms on this land-bound sea, and they had been lucky to miss them so far. She figured their luck had to change at some point; three days out of St. Petersburg proved to be that point.

The morning had been eerily calm at the forenoon watch change. The light winds overnight had dropped to a whisper by dawn and the sea had barely a riffle. The *Destiny* had slowed to less than a knot, but Jane refused to add more canvas. The barometer was falling and she was sure they were in for a blow. At noon, she ordered the decks cleared and everything loose battened down. With double-reefed sails, *Destiny* waited through the afternoon for the weather to move in.

The first gust hit as Jane sat down to evening mess with Dawkins. She had picked up her fork to eat when the schooner heeled over so quickly that her plate flew into Dawkins' lap. By the time she had her oilskins on and had climbed to the quarterdeck, the wind was blowing the tops off the waves, filling the air with spray so thick they could not see more than a few hundred yards.

"Come to starboard, Mister Macy," she called to the

helmsman. "Two points!" The beam-on wind was knocking the *Destiny* down and making her hard to handle. With no load but the ballast below, the schooner was riding high in the water and exposing most of her flanks to the punishing blow.

"Two points to starboard, Captain!" Macy called as he turned the wheel.

The storm raged through the evening and into the night, making it hard to sleep or eat. Each gust sent the vessel rocking to leeward and then back to windward in a rhythm set to bring seasickness on the entire crew as they worked the lines on deck, awash in cold seawater, or tried to get some rest tied into their berths. Jane ordered sails set and changed to combat the violent motion, and watched her charts carefully as they threaded the ninety-mile wide passage between Gotland to the west and the mainland to the east. She had the sounding lead put overboard as often as they could; it was hard to get an accurate measure as the *Destiny* rose and fell on the breaking seas, but Jane knew there were shoals on both sides. Her latitude sighting at noon put them off Herrvik with a dead reckoning longitude that said they had twenty-five miles of open water between them and the rocky shore. If they could hold their south by southwest course without being blown too far to leeward, they should easily clear the eastern landmass. But Jane would not rest easy until she could get another sighting. She hoped for clear skies in the morning.

The winds had not abated when the middle watch came on and the captain went below to catch what sleep she could. Unless the storm increased in strength, the *Destiny* would ride out the gale under her current sails, rolling and dipping her rails in the water, but keeping her crew and cargo secure. As she wedged her bolsters in the berth to keep her steady, Jane could feel the hum of the keel and water pounding on the hull as her schooner plowed its way through the roiling sea bound for Elsinore.

Thursday, August 3   Lat. Obs. 59° 20'N   Long. DR 21° 51'E Winds E storm early, Middle part rain, pleasant late, people employed washing deck and clothes.

Jane mounted to the quarterdeck with the morning watch in time to see a sliver of golden light to the east. The storm clouds were breaking up, and the breeze that greeted the dawn carried a scent of land. Dawkins posted double lookouts amidships to both port and starboard while they pushed on at over ten knots to the south. By midmorning they had several land birds in the rigging, but no hint of shore on either side.

Galsworthy called all hands on deck with sand and stones and set them to scrubbing the *Destiny's* planks. The end of the storm brought two hours of rain under calmer winds and the fresh water bath left the deck sparkling. The crew set out buckets before the storm hit, and many of them took advantage of the returning sun to wash and dry their clothes. Accordingly, it was a ragtag bunch of half-dressed sailors Jane saw from the quarterdeck that day, and she thought they looked rather like a band of pirates.

Tuesday, August 8   Lat. Obs. 55° 23'N   Long. DR 12° 50'E   Winds ESE Making for Falsterbo anchorage.

The weather held for the next week as they cut north through the narrow strait between Sweden and Denmark. They saw dozens of American flagged ships headed east to the Baltic or travelling north or south between the European ports and Dawkins was once again reduced to noting "Many ships to port and starboard" in the log.

In the early evening of the eighth of August, they anchored off Falsterbo to wait for the dawn. Jane ordered the lanterns hung from the spars. With the increase of traffic in the sound, she did not dare keep the *Destiny* moving forward blindly in the dark. Once they were back under way with the current behind them, Jane thought they would make the toll station in two or three hours, and decided to give the crew a few hours of rest before they embarked on the final leg up the coast to Gothenburg.

"Dawkins, let's serve out the rest of that excellent rum to the men. And bring a couple of glasses to the mess for you and Mister Galsworthy. I have been considering our arrival in Gothenburg and would like to share my thoughts with you," the captain said.

Galsworthy and Dawkins had stopped at the galley to warm their rum and add an egg from Cookie's prized hens together with a dollop of the last of the cream they had brought from St. Petersburg and a spoonful of the muscovado sugar Cookie had commandeered for his use. They were now settled in the saloon with their feet propped on the stove and an air of contentment.

Jane poured herself a glass of port and sat down at the table.

"Gentlemen, I mean to take a holiday," she announced after a few minutes.

Her mates could not have looked more shocked if she had poked them with a hot fire iron. Dawkins sat up and let his feet fall to the floor.

"Is aught amiss with ye, Captain?" he asked. "Ye haven't got some sort of illness have ye?"

"No Dawkins, I am in perfectly good health, but we shall be six weeks in Gothenburg making repairs and taking on the load. While I might take rooms in town and enjoy city life, I find myself wanting to walk in the hills and smell the trees. I shall make arrangements for a walking holiday and will return in plenty of time to meet Count Bonenfant before we go. Indeed, I think it wise that I not be easy to locate until just prior to our departure. I would not want his friends to pay me a visit earlier than I am ready to receive them."

Her chief and the carpenter would supervise the work on the *Destiny* while the vessel was ashore. Her mates would not expect her to be in attendance while the repairs were done, so she thought she would take some time to explore the country she had but sampled as she sailed its rocky coast and made the brief visit to Varberg. She relished the idea of time alone with her thoughts as she prepared to see dear Endeavor on her return home in the autumn. A good tramp through the countryside would clear her lungs of saltwater and allow her to stretch her legs too.

"Well, ma'am, you are probably right on that score. We shall hold off any Frenchies that come looking for you, but I can't answer for my actions if I see that Fairchild, or whatever his name is," Galsworthy declared. "We owe them a second round for taking us unawares last time. Those clever devils won't sneak up the anchor chain again without us knowing about it!"

Jane refrained from smiling as she heard the disgust in his voice. He and the crew had not taken it well that the French general and his men had been able to make their way aboard and subdue the watch with no one the wiser. It had been a simple matter for them to round up the rest of the crew one by one, even catching the drop on Mister Dawkins before he could grab his pistols from under his pillow as he lay resting. Brave as they were, her crew of ten seamen was no match for five well-armed soldiers.

"Thank you, Galsworthy. But do refrain from coming to blows with any French soldiers you might encounter. I need your services for many years to come," Jane said as she stood up to retire to her berth. "Good night, good friends."

XXVI

Gothenburg Arrival

Gothenburg, Sweden
August, 1820

Jane had grown up on the Hudson River, where the shoals and currents taught her respect for the power of wind and water. She learned to keep off the rocks of the Hudson Highlands and, later, the New England shore as she had seen at close quarters the damage that could be done when a captain misjudged how quickly his vessel could tack. Accordingly, Jane thought herself an excellent sailor, but the rocky coast of the western archipelago of Sweden challenged even her skills. Where the chart showed several fathoms of water, there might appear a rocky outcropping that lifted a scant foot above the waves. As the *Destiny* sailed up the coast, Jane learned to keep well away from these jagged rocks since they tended to be surrounded by dozens more just below the surface. The first time she encountered one, she had stood at the rail with her heart in her throat as they glided past a field of underwater pillars, each with a collar of seaweed and a sharp edge that would tear a hole in the *Destiny's* side at the slightest scrape.

As they approached the inlet to Gothenburg, Jane gave up trying to thread between the dangerous rocks and ordered the helmsman offshore. She waited until she spotted a vessel flying the Swedish colors, then followed her into the mouth of the harbor where the *Destiny* picked up a pilot who directed them to the docks below the fortress at the mouth of the Göta älv. There, they tied up alongside a dozen or more enormous ships that dwarfed the *Destiny*, each flying the burgee of its owner. It was a glorious sight, and a testament to the success the Swedish merchants had achieved with their trading voyages to the east over the last century.

After checking the lines were well secured, Jane ordered the schooner made shipshape with all gear on deck stowed and the cabins and forecastle put to rights in preparation for hauling the *Destiny* to the repair yards. The vessel had held up well through the strains of the past few months, but she was showing wear that could lead to failure in a storm. Koopmans was to supervise the work at the yard, where the jib boom would be repaired and the bottom scraped and painted. Jane also intended to have the spars inspected, along with the rigging, before they set out on their passage across the North Atlantic toward home. At the yard, the sails would be taken ashore and reinforced at the seams, while a troublesome leak in the deck was located and repaired. Meanwhile, the rest of the crew would be billeted on land for several weeks, where they were bound to spend their wages in the waterfront taverns.

"Ahoy *Destiny*," came a voice from below.

Sticking her head over the side, Jane saw a tall man in an American captain's uniform grinning up at her. He held his hat under his arm and shaded his eyes from the sun as he searched the deck for the master.

"Captain Thaddeus Harrison of the *Friheten*, miss. Is the captain aboard?"

Dawkins looked around from where he was sorting dock lines to see Jane's response. He knew the steely gaze she bestowed on those who questioned her identity and authority. Dressed as she was in her skirt and linen blouse, with the sleeves rolled up for work and her hair pulling loose from its braid, Dawkins thought the visitor could be forgiven for not recognizing her position.

Jane set the cup of coffee she had been sipping for the last hour on top of the deckhouse. She reached over and pulled her greatcoat off the wheel where she had thrown it together with her hat. Smoothing back her hair, she slipped into the coat, then jammed the hat on her head as she turned once more to the rail.

"Captain Thorn, sir. Good day to you."

Harrison's face tried out several expressions before settling on a curious smile. He put his hat on his head and touched the brim to salute her.

"Ah, beg your pardon miss, captain, I was not aware that…" Harrison began. The stony stare on Jane's face caused him to lose his tongue and he finished by shrugging his shoulders.

"Would you care to come aboard, Captain Harrison? I believe I could offer you a glass of port in my cabin if you are so inclined," she asked the flustered man.

Jane stood above and watched as the visitor climbed the Jacob's ladder that hung from the larboard rail. At nearly six feet tall with a head of dark curls and a well-pressed uniform, the captain made a favorable impression. He appeared to be not much older than Jane herself.

"Good afternoon to you, Captain." Harrison removed his hat with a slight bow. "I thought to pay a visit to the master who hung at my heels on the way into harbor and compliment him, er, *her* on his, *her* caution. I have seen many an unwary navigator put a vessel on these rocks. They are most unforgiving." Harrison pointed east up the river as he continued, "Right over there is a tremendous hidden shoal that sank the *Götheborg* last century even though she had a pilot aboard; she still lies at the bottom. Yours was a wise choice, if I may say so, miss. Ma'am. Sir." He finally gave up and shrugged his shoulders helplessly again.

Jane was about to reply when a group of men carrying despatch cases scurried down the pier past the *Destiny's* nose, and were gone in an instant.

"My goodness! I hope that is not a fire in their ship they are escaping."

Captain Harrison laughed as he explained, "Nay, that was my supercargo and his men. If they don't present the accounting to the owners today, he will be fined for every hour he delays. Fortunately, he has good news to share as we did well on this voyage, and the goods presently in the hold should fetch a fine price at the auction tomorrow."

"Pray, Captain Harrison, join me below," Jane said as she led the way aft. She was charmed in spite of herself, and looked forward to finding out more about this American captain and his Swedish ship.

Once they had seated themselves in her cabin with a glass of port and their hats on the table, Jane took a good look at the visitor. Now that she could see him clearly, it was obvious he was a few years older than she first thought, perhaps thirty-five or so. He was impeccably turned out and had the refinement of a gentleman.

"I am intrigued, Captain Harrison, at the nature of your command. How does it happen that you are in the employment of a Swedish ship owner?"

"It did not start out that way... do I call you miss or ma'am?"

"I am Miss Jane Thorn, but you may call me Captain. Or ma'am," she replied. How odd it was to think of herself that way. Jane never considered herself 'Miss' anything. In general, she lived in the world of men without the usual trappings and duties of women. She certainly did not care for the idea that she was defined by the lack or presence of a husband, and so preferred the neutral "Captain" as a form of address. Her men called her ma'am, though, since they could hardly call her "sir."

"Well then, Captain, surely you know of the difficulty we had with the British impounding our ships during the war?" Harrison began as he leaned back and made himself comfortable in the upholstered chair that took up one corner of the saloon. "Many of the owners found it expedient to form partnerships with investors in other countries and change the flag. Such is the case with the *Friheten*. I used to sail on her as the *Arabella* out of Boston, but old Fosdick, her owner, was afraid she would be taken as a war prize. So he went into partnership with a fellow here named Olof Wijk. Wijk owns enough of the vessel that she can fly the Swedish flag, but Fosdick keeps control. She had a Swedish captain during the war, but I was given her command again five years ago."

"Ah, yes, I remember my uncle telling me that some of his business acquaintances moved their residence to one of the Caribbean islands when it looked like things were heating up with the British again. St. Barthélmy, was it not?"

"Aye, many Swedes run their operations out of there. I was based on the island for a year, but I do not care for hurricanes, ma'am. Last year I heard they lost over forty ships in the September storms. I'll take my chances with the archipelago." He nodded as Jane offered to refill his glass.

They worked their way through another round of port, talking of the shipping trade with the Far East, before Captain Harrison finally stood to take his leave. He held out his hand to bid Jane farewell, holding hers a moment before dropping it with a slight shake of his head.

"It has been a pleasure to make your acquaintance, Captain Thorn. I shall be returning ashore to wait out the winter on the morrow. Should you find yourself at leisure while you are here, I would be delighted to show you something of my adopted home."

"That would be most lovely, Captain Harrison." Most lovely? She shuddered inwardly to hear herself talking like a mincing miss.

"Very good. Shall I call round in two days?" Harrison seemed quite determined to have her firm promise.

"Yes, I should have finished my business by then and would be ready to see the sights. Thank you, Captain." Jane showed her guest to the companionway stairs and followed him on deck. She watched as he climbed down the ladder to the dock, and returned his wave when he lifted his hand in farewell.

Being careful to school her face and appear indifferent, she turned to Dawkins and Galsworthy at the galley door where they stood watching her.

"All well, mates?"

"All well, ma'am," Dawkins answered. "We will be ready to see the shipyard man in the morning."

"Very good. Perhaps you would join me below so we may discuss the work to be done and the arrangements for the men."

The following two days were so busy that Jane had scant opportunity to think about her promised outing with Captain Harrison. The first day had been filled with visits to the agent, the very same Olof Wijk who was part owner of the *Friheten*, and the various shipyards and chandlers. Dawkins and Galsworthy were busy ashore finding rooms for the crew and arranging for a tow to the repair docks.

Before returning to the *Destiny* after the day's errands, Jane stopped to post a letter addressed to Count Bonenfant at the home of his friend the marquis in Varberg. She had labored hard at this letter over the past week. Jane wished to retain her dignity while making it clear that it was urgent that she see him in Gothenburg. She wanted to deliver her response to his insulting note in person as well as provide instructions for retrieving the gold shipment in St. Petersburg; she did not dare trust the details of that in a message that could be intercepted. The final version was, she felt, both pointed and clear about the consequences of his choosing not to come.

Monsieur le Comte~

Your personal presence is requested on the twentieth of September at eight o'clock in the morning in Gothenburg, where you will find the schooner Destiny in port. Further details regarding your recent shipment with our firm will be provided to you at that time. Should you find yourself unable to attend on this date, we caution you that your cargo may become unavailable, and the value of it will become forfeit.

> *Very truly yours,*
> *Capt. Jane Thorn*

She penned the note on the firm's letterhead and sealed it with her official stamp. Now it was just a question of waiting for September to see if he would show up.

On her second day ashore, Jane made arrangements for a lengthy sojourn on the west coast of Sweden. She wanted to see the colorful houses she had spied from the water up close, and to explore a few of the little fishing villages with their intriguing churches. The trip would take her by steamer up the coast to the bathing resort at Marstrand and then to the town of Lysekil, where she would disembark. Travelling by coach, she would arrive at her final destination, the small village of Hagatorp on the shores of Kärnsjön lake, where she thought to take a room in the guesthouse and spend her days hiking the forests. She hoped to make her way without being able to speak Swedish, intending to rely on her sense of adventure and the good will of the inhabitants.

Having completed her plans, Jane returned to the *Destiny* to find Captain Harrison standing on the dock.

"Good afternoon to you, Captain," he called out when he saw her approaching. "I hope I have not mistaken the day!"

"Good day to you, Mister Harrison. Not at all, I merely had business to conduct. I hope I have not kept you long?"

"I took the liberty of inviting myself aboard to await your return, but I must confess that your mates are a rather frightening pair. They looked as if they would eat me alive should I cross them. I suspect they are very loyal to you, ma'am," he observed with a grin. "I eventually decided it might be more comfortable for all concerned for me to wait here on the dock."

"Perhaps you would like to call back in a quarter of an hour? I shall be ready to join you then," she suggested.

"Aye, ma'am, that would suit. I shall return shortly."

Jane climbed back aboard and made her way to the saloon. There, she found her mates looking over the list of items for the shipyard, which she spent a few minutes reviewing before retiring to her cabin to change her clothing. Once dressed in one of the simple frocks Pru had made for her, she returned to the saloon to inform her officers that she would be out to dinner and would return later in the evening.

"Very good, ma'am," they replied and returned to their accounting.

Captain Harrison had returned to the dock and was waiting with a small bouquet of flowers in hand when she climbed down the ladder. He handed them to her, then tucked her hand into his elbow and smiled down at Jane as they began to walk.

"I must say, ma'am, it will be a pleasure and an honor to escort you this evening. It has been a great long while since I have had the benefit of such lovely company."

"The pleasure, Captain Harrison, is equally mine."

XXVII

An Evening Out

To Jane's surprise, Captain Harrison turned left at the end of the pier, toward the water instead of the shore. He looked down at her with a smile and said,

"I thought you might like to see the *Friheten* up close. We will begin offloading the cargo tomorrow, but things are calm this evening in case you would find a visit of interest?"

"I would be delighted, Captain. I have seen many large merchantmen at the docks in my travels but have never been invited aboard one before."

"Well then, we shall have to remedy that. Welcome to the *Friheten!*" They arrived at the side of one of the giant ships and he waved his arm in an elegant bow toward the gangplank that stretched from the merchantman's side.

Jane paused to take in the ship's elaborate mermaid figurehead and ornately carved bow, then turned to look up at the towering stern of the enormous vessel. The brilliantly colored ship had each of its three upper decks painted in alternating bands of blue and gold, with the gallery windows outlined in red and the gun port covers picked out in navy blue. The East Indiaman was an imposing ship even with the cannons hidden behind their doors and the sails tightly furled on the spars. Jane froze as she realized that she had seen this ship even before following it into the harbor.

"May I ask where you are bringing cargo from, Captain Harrison?"

"From New Orleans, on this trip. We have a load of cotton and tobacco that sent us into quarantine for three weeks at Känsö. We are grateful to be arriving home at long last."

"Ah, I know Känsö well. We were laid up there ourselves last month. You must have arrived shortly after us, although I did not notice you there among the many ships. Pray tell, Captain, did you happen to make landfall in Cuba during your voyage?" Jane was sure she knew the answer.

Harrison swung toward her in surprise. "I did, ma'am. Well, that is to say I put in at Matanzas to retrieve a passenger, but how in blazes did you deduce that?"

"There is no mystery there, Captain Harrison; I saw you. It would appear that we have much to talk about, but perhaps we might delay that conversation until we have taken the promised tour of your vessel?" Jane suggested as she moved toward the gangplank and grabbed the rail to steady her as climbed the steep ramp.

Their visit began at the lowest deck, where the hold was filled to bursting with baled cotton and sheaves of bundled tobacco. Every inch of the space was packed, and the cargo gave off a strong odor of sulphur that made Jane's eyes water.

"I fear the quarantine officials were rather enthusiastic in their application of cleansing smoke to the cotton. We shall have to air it out before bringing it to the buyer's warehouse. I cannot for the life of me understand their methods, but we must make the best of things, I suppose," Harrison lifted his right shoulder in a small shrug.

"Aye, I am right glad that we were not forced to offload during our own quarantine. They merely wished to see that the men were healthy and let us go after what was at the time an interminable five days, but which I have come to understand was generously short," Jane remarked.

"Indeed, you were most fortunate. Since you mentioned seeing us in Matanzas, shall I assume that your load consisted of sugar bound for the Baltic?"

"Aye, that it did. And we beat the merchantmen from Havana to St. Petersburg to make our own market. So the voyage was most successful," she grinned. "We used wood to secure the load instead of cotton dunnage and so escaped the enforced cargo quarantine."

Harrison laughed as he remarked "It is a smart owner who hires a clever captain, ma'am!"

They continued their tour with the crew quarters and the gun deck. The sight of the cannons made Jane uneasy, but she knew that large merchant ships were prime targets of the Caribbean and Barbary Coast pirates. The ships had to be ready to defend themselves if the presence of the guns was not enough to scare off any would-be attackers. Jane was not sure if she would be willing to sail in such a vessel as she would be reluctant to loose the guns on her fellow man, pirate or no.

The tour concluded on the quarterdeck, where a number of crates had been piled in preparation for offloading.

"The supercargo's trade goods," Captain Harrison explained. "He has brought back primitive carvings from the West Indies. I believe he hopes they will be popular among the society ladies who wish to collect exotic objects for their drawing rooms in order to impress their friends."

"And did you bring back trade goods for your own reckoning?" Jane looked up at Harrison.

"Aye, that I did, and I aim to display the wares for you now. Pray, join me in my cabin," he held open the door for Jane to pass through. As she entered the ornately decorated quarters, Jane threw up her hands and cried out,

"Mister Pfyfe's furniture! How wonderful to see it here!"

Pushed up against every inch of exposed bulkhead was a collection of gleaming mahogany tables, desks, footstools, chairs, bookshelves, and bureaus. Every nook and corner of the space held a piece that was a testament to the fine skills of the artisan.

"Aye, the pieces are beautiful. I came upon this lot at an auction I attended as I was waiting for the cotton to be loaded. I cleared out my quarters and bought the entirety of what was on offer. It looks well in here, does it not?"

"It does," Jane's eyes moved longingly over every piece, "although I think there might be rather much of it, if I may say so. You hardly have room to turn around much less entertain guests. But it is most decidedly handsome. My uncle called in the decorators for his house in New York this past year, and they filled it with the latest offerings from Mister Pfyfe's workshop. My aunt was most taken with the intricate lines and inlay. Will you be filling your own house in a like manner?"

"No, ma'am, *these* are my trade goods!" Captain Harrison replied with a grin.

"How clever of you, then! My very best wishes in finding a buyer who appreciates American furniture, Captain Harrison."

"Ah, but you see, I have been most exceedingly clever, dear captain. I sold it to the supercargo before we left port in New Orleans. It has merely been on loan to me for the duration of the voyage," he waved her to a seat at the gold accented maple table in the center of the crowded space. "He will return for it tomorrow, so pray enjoy it this evening, for I fear we shall never see it again."

Captain Harrison and Jane shared a laugh as he poured out two glasses of spiced rum.

"A toast to trade goods and clever captains," he saluted.

"Huzzah!" she replied and tipped back her glass. "Captain Harrison, I must say that this has already been the most pleasurable evening I have had in a great while, if you do not mind my being so bold."

"Not at all, and I do wish that you might call me Thaddeus as if we were old friends."

"Aye, Thaddeus, I believe that I shall. And I am Jane to you, now that we have agreed to be friends. Here, let us shake on the matter." Jane held out her hand and they shook hands most solemnly, then threw back their heads and laughed again.

As Jane set her glass upon the table, she leaned toward her new friend on the other side.

"Now, tell me of your visit to Cuba, if you will. I suspect we may have an acquaintance in common."

"Indeed?" Harrison raised his eyebrows. "It was a strange business, I own. We left New Orleans with instructions to put in to Havana, where we were to pick up a small load along with a single passenger. When we arrived and made to enter the harbor, we were intercepted by a man in a small boat who spoke with the supercargo. It seems we had been given new orders to pick up just the passenger, who was awaiting us in Matanzas. We were to sail in under cover of the evening and board the man without question or interference, and to leave at first tide in the morning. I was given to understand that he was a French nobleman on his way home. I cannot say, for I did not see him again for the entire voyage except when he left the ship after we entered quarantine. He was taken off by one of the officials and we did not encounter him again."

"Did you perchance get the name of the nobleman in question, Thaddeus," Jane wondered.

"Aye, he was one of the Bonenfant clan. Alain, I believe was his Christian name."

"Just so," Jane said with a satisfied smile as she related her own tale of the perfidious Count Bonenfant, naturally omitting some of the more personal details. "I do happen to have discovered the purpose of the man and his associates, but I am afraid that I am not at liberty to share them with you at this time, for the affair is not yet concluded. Perhaps, however, I will be free to do so in the future."

"Well, to the future then, which I will consider to be a promise from you, dear Jane, that there will be one." Harrison lifted his glass to her, and they toasted one more time for new friends.

As Jane prepared for bed that evening, she reflected that they had never managed to bestir themselves from Thaddeus' ship. Instead, they had spent several hours in warm discussion interrupted only by the serving of the meal Thaddeus had sent for from the galley. After dinner, they had adjourned to the afterdeck and sat on the rail to continue their contemplation of the best route from Gothenburg to the ports of the Eastern Seaboard. Jane was sure that the *Destiny* could make a swift passage in five or six weeks via the northern route. Thaddeus, who had made the voyage seven times, counseled waiting until the end of September to set out as the hurricanes that spun up from the warm waters of the Caribbean could wreak havoc even across the upper reaches of the Atlantic in the earlier part of the month.

She felt a great sense of satisfaction and pleasure at the congenial evening spent in the company of a seasoned colleague. Their interchange had been both enlightening and fruitful now that Jane knew how Bonenfant had gotten himself to Varberg ahead of her. She and Captain Harrison had parted on warm terms, and she had promised to visit him again upon her return to Gothenburg after her sojourn in the country.

It was good to have a friend, Jane thought as she blew out her lantern and pulled up her quilt. She had shared her concerns and aired her questions without fear of jeopardizing her standing, as would not have been the case had she done the same with Dawkins and Galsworthy. She looked forward a great deal to seeing the captain again.

XXVIII

A New Friend

Hagatorp, Sweden
August, 1820

Before leaving Gothenburg, Jane had outfitted herself with a rugged knapsack and a pair of walking shoes. With some clothes in the bag and her straw hat on her head, she considered herself well attired for her holiday.

"Is that to last ye the entire month, ma'am?" Dawkins asked with a skeptical frown at the small satchel.

"Indeed it is, Mister Dawkins," she smiled lifting her bag. "I aim to be walking in nature most days, and the trees do not give a fig for a pretty gown or a handsome bonnet."

"Aye, ma'am, ye' have the rights of that. Well, we will be pleased to see ye on your return," he said as he handed her a slip of paper. "Here is the address of my lodgings. We will send word to your hotel in Hagatorp should we have need of ye, but we hope ye' will have a restful journey with no need to fret yourself about anything here. *Bon voyage*, ma'am, as the French say."

"Ah yes, speaking of the French," Jane stopped as she was about to leave the saloon, "I nearly forgot my instructions for you in my haste to be on my way. Should Count Bonenfant present himself before the twentieth of September, pray ask him to return on the arranged date and time and no sooner. Inform him that I am not available until that time."

"Very good, ma'am," Dawkins replied as he tipped his hat in farewell.

Setting forth, Jane stopped at the dock office to ask for directions to the post office and the steamboat wharf. The *Destiny* had been moved up the river by tugboat and was now tied up near the shipyard pier on the riverbank near the center of the city. It was a short walk to the Postkontoret, where she sent off her letter to Bonenfant, and thence to the departure dock.

Jane stood on the deck of the steamship *Elisabeth* and craned her head back to watch the black smoke that belched from the tall pipe amidships. Below the deck she could feel the working of the enormous steam engine that drove the paddlewheel on the starboard side of the vessel. The clank of the drive wheel and whistle of the escaping steam made the passage interesting but hardly relaxing.

Watching the shore, she reckoned they were travelling at about four knots. This was hardly a swift pace, but the vessel moved in a straight line toward its destination at a steady speed. Once the captain ordered the sails raised, they would pick up an extra few knots, but they would not need to tack and wear to keep the sails filled. As they made harbor at their first stop in Marstrand nine hours later, Jane pondered that she was aboard a vessel that would supplant the *Destiny* and her ilk before too many more years had passed. For now, the need to transport enormous quantities of fuel made these steam powered ships fit only for coastal passenger service and trade. But she was sure the engineers would devise better ways of feeding the boilers, and more efficient uses of the steam, and soon the sailing fleet would give way to these wonders of modern invention. She was eager to hear her uncle's opinion of the new vessels, and wondered if Thorn Shipping might find its future in the steam trade.

Jane went ashore for dinner in Marstrand that evening so that she could walk among the beautiful wooden houses perched on the rocky cliffs. Bathing houses lined the shore and the imposing Karlsten fortress towered over the town. Jane thought she might stay overnight on her way back so that she could hike the hill and explore the fort.

Jane slept well in her cozy berth aboard the *Elisabeth* that night, lying abed in the morning as she heard the steam engine come alive and felt the vessel move away from the dock. It was an unaccustomed pleasure to leave the direction of the crew and navigation to others, and Jane turned over to face the bulkhead and fell back asleep.

The steamboat arrived at Lysekil in the late afternoon and Jane positioned herself by the wheelhouse to watch as the captain and his helmsman steered the boat through the channel and into the passenger dock. Noticing her interest, the captain waved her in and offered her a closer vantage point. When she introduced herself as the captain of the *Destiny*, he expressed delight that she should be interested in his vessel, and offered her a tour of the engine room once the passengers had disembarked. It was an offer she was pleased to accept, and she took careful note of the disposition of the crew, the handling of the coal, and the management of the engine. She asked the captain so many questions he finally threw up his hands and laughed that she would need to acquire such a vessel herself in due course so that she might understand it all. Thanking him for his generosity, and thinking he was most likely correct, Jane took her leave of the captain and went ashore in a thoughtful mood.

Once ashore in Lysekil, Jane took up her knapsack and walked briskly through town to the guesthouse where she had been advised to take a room for the three days she would need to wait for an eastbound coach. She would spend her time among the fishing docks, she decided, inspecting the gaff-rigged dories the men used to catch the cod she saw hanging from wooden poles on the wharf. She had also seen a church steeple rising above the houses in the harbor, which she planned to investigate, and was intent on doing some shopping. All in all, Jane thought it would be a most satisfactory start to her holiday.

Two days later, Jane was walking back from the chandler's workshop when the steamboat from Gothenburg pulled in to the pier. She waved to her friend the captain and then stopped in astonishment as she recognized the brown curly head and straight back of the man crossing the gangplank to the shore.

"Thaddeus! My heavens, what has brought you to Lysekil?" she called out as she ran to greet him.

"Why you, my dear, of course," he replied as he wrapped her in a warm hug.

Jane pulled back to look up at him, "Have you come all this way to find me, then? What in goodness' name for?"

"Ah, I had hoped it might be welcome news to you that I have arrived. Have I misjudged our friendship, dear Jane? For if so, I will return with the ship this very evening," he replied soberly.

"Dear Thaddeus, it pleases me no end to see you here, of that you can be assured. How long do you intend to stay?"

"In that, I shall be guided by you, Jane. I can return on the morrow after having the pleasure of your company at dinner this evening. But I have also arranged to be absent from the city for two weeks if you would care for my company on your rambles," he replied hopefully.

"Nothing would please me more, dear friend. What fun we shall have together! And it is no mean thing that you speak the language, for I confess myself somewhat at a loss from time to time. Just this morning I attempted to purchase a roll for my lunch in the bakery and came away with a dozen poppyseed biscuits," she laughed.

Jane felt a rush of joy at the thought of having a good friend with her on her explorations, and she relished the thought of spending more hours conversing with the captain.

Arm in arm, they wandered to Jane's hostelry, where Thaddeus took a room for the night. They made arrangements with the coach firm for an additional passenger to Hagatorp, after which they spent a pleasant few hours in conversation over dinner. As she slid between the sheets that night, Jane found herself smiling over the prospect of more such evenings to come.

The coach ride to the small village of Hagatorp the next day took more than three hours over rutted dirt roads. By the time they arrived at the tiny hamlet nestled on the shores of a deep blue lake, the passengers were well shaken and somewhat unsteady on their feet as they descended from the conveyance.

"My goodness," Jane said in a weary voice, "I shall need to find my land legs again after that voyage."

"Aye, the rocking and bouncing was worse than my last trip round the Horn," Thaddeus agreed. "Come, let us make our way to our lodgings and find a place to rest that is not moving."

The next ten days passed quickly as Jane and her companion explored the surrounding countryside. The unspoiled vistas they chanced upon, and the charming small farmhouses that dotted the countryside, reminded Jane, sometimes painfully, of her own home.

"Do you miss your family?" Jane asked Thaddeus one afternoon when she was feeling particularly wistful.

"I must confess, I do not," he said. "My parents are gone these many years, and I have but a sister who resides in Virginia. She is busy with her husband and children, and I do not see her more than every few years when I am able to travel to her. We are not close, and I often have difficulty finding subjects on which to converse with her. I do not comprehend the life of a farmer, and her husband is much preoccupied with the state of his pigpen and cowshed. These things do not, I fear, interest me."

Jane laughed as she agreed that agricultural pursuits were far from her own thoughts as well.

"And yet, do we not suffer from a similar affliction?" she observed. "How many of our acquaintances have been bored to tears by our own wearisome tales of life on the water? It can hardly seem amusing to those who do not live their lives in the pursuit of trade aboard sailing ships."

"Nay, you surely have the right of it," he agreed. "It would take someone who shared the life to truly understand the lure of the sea," he added meaningfully as he looked down at her where she walked at his side.

Jane was unsettled as she realized the meaning in his words, and his thoughts became obvious to her. "It would indeed," she said. "I have often wondered how I might find someone to share my life when I expect to find myself far from home for many years to come. But come, let us speak of happier subjects than the state of my spinsterhood on this lovely afternoon."

Having diverted Thaddeus from his clear intent, she grabbed his hand and began to run toward the pond she had spotted in the distance.

"Come along, let us see if we can catch a fish for our supper!

Fru Nilsson will be so pleased if we bring her something to cook."

On Thaddeus' last morning in Hagatorp, Jane walked him to the village to board the coach that would return him to Lysekil. Thaddeus had made her a gift of drawing paper and charcoal pencils purchased at the village shop, and she was determined to have something respectable to show him when she returned to Gothenburg. At the moment, however, she was feeling somewhat sad as she contemplated his leave-taking and her solitude in the coming days.

As the coach drew into sight, Thaddeus turned to face her and took her hands in his. He began to speak, but then stopped as if he had changed his mind. Finally, he drew breath and said, "Dear Jane, this has been the most marvelous two weeks of my life. I look forward to seeing you upon your return to the city. Shall we set a date when I will come to you at your hotel?"

"Aye, dear friend, that it has been. Allow me to send word to you when I arrive, as I am not certain of my plans yet, but rest assured, I am also eager to renew our friendship when I return."

With that, they gave each other a warm embrace and Thaddeus climbed the step to enter the coach. Jane stood and waved for as long as she could see it, then walked slowly back to the guesthouse deep in thought.

XXIX

Headed Home

Gothenburg, Sweden
August, 1820

The following days were a time of reflection for Jane. The days, weeks, and months since leaving home had been both exciting and, she knew in her heart, lonely almost beyond bearing. She cherished the company of her mates and crew, but the necessary distance of the captain meant that she had no bosom friend to tell her secrets to, no dearest companion with whom to share confidences, no helpmeet to carry part of the burden. This first long voyage had taught her that her heart yearned for the warmth and support of a mate in life, and perhaps even children should the time come. She must choose wisely, but she now knew that she would choose.

How was she to answer the question she was sure dear Thaddeus was going to ask? As her time in Hagatorp drew to a close, she forced herself to face the truth of her feelings in that regard. Captain Harrison's congenial character, handsome face, and obvious ardor had drawn her along farther than her actual feelings extended. She treasured their conversations and the way they laughed together. But his was the face of a comrade, not a lover, and it was time to tell him so. She considered what would be the kindest course of action, and finally resolved to write to him. Should he then still choose to see her before the *Destiny* set sail for New York, he would harbor no untoward hopes. Jane sat down that evening and set pen to paper to make her heart known to the man she hoped to call *friend*.

Dear Friend,

It has been a pleasure to learn to call you such. I have greatly valued your acquaintance, first as a fellow though more experienced master, and later as a cherished companion.

Our connexion, Thaddeus, is exceedingly important to me, yet my fond recollections of our rambles are now clouded by the thought that I may have unthinkingly offered hurt. I fear my pleasure in your company may have created the impression that my feelings were of a warmer nature than is the case. If I have been mistaken in your intentions, please forgive the imaginings of a silly woman. I fervently desire to depend on and deepen our friendship whether in such ports as we may frequent together, or at the distances to which our voyages may lead us.

It would give me great pleasure to see you in Gothenburg upon my return. I would understand, however, should you choose to let our farewell in Hagatorp be the final good-bye. I shall send a note when I return from my journey, and rest assured that I remain, Dear Thaddeus, your Friend,

Jane

On Friday, the eighth of September, Jane took her leave of Herr and Fru Nilsson. They hugged her as she bid them farewell and handed her a packet of food to sustain her on the trip to Lysekil. They had seen how sad and thoughtful she had been after Captain Harrison's departure, and had gone to extra lengths to cheer her with delicious meals and summer flowers at the table and in her room. She would miss the lovely couple, and promised to write from America to let them know she had arrived home.

The coach trip to Lysekil passed more quickly than she remembered and Jane was soon boarding the steamer for Gothenburg. She had lost the desire to extend her holiday and was anxious to rejoin her crew as they outfitted and loaded the *Destiny* for the inbound voyage west across the Atlantic. She planned now to take rooms at a hotel in the city and send for Dawkins and Galsworthy as soon as she arrived. She would let Captain Harrison know where she was lodging in case he wished to visit her before she left.

The steamboat brought Jane to the wharf on the evening of the tenth of September, a mere ten days prior to their scheduled departure on the twentieth. She left notes with the hotel clerk to be delivered to her mates and Captain Harrison, then promptly went to bed and slept until late the following day.

She was awakened by someone pounding on her door and a gruff voice calling out, "Captain, ma'am, are ye' decent?"

Jane smiled as she realized how much she had missed her officers and the loyal affection that accompanied their respect for her as their captain.

"Damn it, man, give me a moment to gather my wits, will you?" she called out. Slipping her shawl on over her night-rail and pushing her hair into a hasty knot, Jane shuffled toward the door. When she yanked it open, she found Dawkins with his fist raised, about to pound the planks again, and Galsworthy leaning against the wall across the way.

"All right, gentlemen, pray enter and set yourselves down while I ring for some breakfast. Have you two eaten yet today?"

Galsworthy exchanged a look with Dawkins, then cleared his throat. "Ma'am, it is gone noon and we have both breakfasted and dined. Shall we return when ye' have fully gathered those wits? Ma'am?" Galsworthy grinned as he knew his captain would forgive the saucy tone of the remark.

"Set where you are, sir, and hold your tongue 'til I am dressed and have at least a cup of coffee down my gullet."

An hour later, Jane and her mates arrived at the shipyard to view the repairs to her vessel. Koopmans saw them arrive and headed them off as Dawkins turned to walk to the pier where he had left the schooner the day before.

"Good day Captain. Sirs. Good to see you back, Captain Thorn. Yes indeed, it is good to see you looking so well," Koopmans said as he stretched out his hand to Jane. She shook it heartily and replied,

"A fine day it is, Koopmans. Now, where is my vessel?"

"We've moved her ma'am, to the loading wharf below what they call Stigberget," he said as he pointed to the southwest. The iron is ready for us to load; that fella Wijk has been true to his word and it is all there just waiting."

"Excellent, Mister Koopmans. Now tell me about the repairs while we walk to her berth."

Jane kept a brisk pace as her officers and the carpenter hurried to keep up. She was anxious to see her vessel after so many weeks, and the promenade along the waterfront seemed interminable. Finally, she saw the *Destiny's* spars among a forest of masts and her heart leaped. Here was both her home, and the ship that would take her home. Tears welled in her eyes as Koopmans concluded his recounting of the past month's work.

"Thank you, Mister Koopmans. You have done a fine bit of work. We shall all be grateful to you when we arrive home in one piece. Have you arranged for the settlement of the shipyard bill with the agent?"

And so she rejoined her vessel, her crew, and her captain's life. She would be content to leave for home once the cargo was aboard and a few final details attended to, including the coming interview with Bonenfant, if the blackguard showed his face at the appointed time.

XXX

Friends and Foes

Gothenburg, Sweden
September, 1820

"Has the pottery shipment arrived from Falkenberg, Mister Dawkins?"

Jane and her chief mate were at her hotel going over the shipping documents for the homeward voyage and attempting to assess how much spare room they would have in the hold. They were four days from their scheduled departure and it was time to work out the final details of the voyage.

"Aye, it was a day later than expected, ma'am, but it is all here. We stowed it in the lockers where it is safe from damage by the iron bars."

"Very good. It appears that we shall have several hundred cubic feet of space above the iron, but we are reaching our tonnage limit if your calculations are correct," Jane said.

"Aye again, ma'am. I am mindful of securing the load, as it does not fill the hold. I am thinking to have Koopmans devise a way to bolster it," Dawkins replied. "Perhaps we might lay in cross bars and wedge it against the beams."

The Destiny's hull was sharp built, and the cargo needed to be stowed low to keep her from becoming crank, and to make it easy to carry more sail to advantage. In heavy seas, however, the extra headroom above the load could allow it to shift and result in the schooner being unable to right itself should the cargo slide to one side during a roll. Accordingly, Jane was most diligent about inspecting the way the hold had been packed before leaving the wharf, particularly when the load included heavy items the crew would be unable to handle if a problem arose.

"Good, see to it, Mister Dawkins. I also think I have an idea for the extra space; when I visited the chandler in Lysekil while waiting for my coach, I discovered that the Swedes produce excellent sailcloth at a price far below what we have become accustomed to at home. I am thinking to buy as much as we can to put into the hold for use on our own fleet. What say you to that?"

"An excellent plan, ma'am, and one that I am sure Captain Josias would approve as well."

"Aye, thank you, Dawkins. Tell me, has Cookie seen to the stores yet?"

And so the morning wore away as the captain and her chief reviewed every repair that had been carried out on the *Destiny,* calculated loads and tonnage, planned the sailcloth purchase and delivery, and reviewed the accounting of the stores and fresh water. Finally, Jane showed Dawkins her navigation plan for the western passage.

"We are but five or six weeks out if we take the line we followed east from Nova Scotia. We are still early enough in the year that we should not see any ice in the water, but we can swing to the south if need be. What say you?" Jane asked.

Dawkins ran his finger over the chart and furrowed his brow. "Ye'll be bringing us back against the westerlies, ma'am. We may find ourselves changing course and sails every few hours if we are to make westing. Your schooner is not at her best sailing to weather, Captain."

"Aye, Dawkins, and well I know it. But if we tell Koopmans now, he can adjust the spars and rigging to give us our best chance of sailing close hauled. And we will save at least a week or more over the southern route. I intend to be safe in port before the storms of November build across the northern reaches."

"I hear tell that Captain Duncan has arrived at the river mouth and is taking on stores. Perhaps we might make company with him on the way home if he is bound on the same route," Dawkins suggested.

"A very good thought, Mister Dawkins. I will seek him out this afternoon. Can you tell me where I might find a conveyance?"

It took Jane but a short time to locate a water taxi tied to the steps at Östra Hamngatan. A quick negotiation for the fare, and Jane was on her way down the river to the docks where the *Destiny* had first tied up on arrival in Gothenburg. As Dawkins had relayed, the *Jeremiah* was indeed moored in the river mouth with lighters plying back and forth loaded with barrels of water and other supplies. The waterman pulled up at the *Jeremiah's* side and Jane shouted to the watch.

"Ahoy the *Jeremiah*! Captain Thorn of the *Destiny* to see Captain Duncan. Permission to come aboard?"

"Belay, ma'am, while I fetch the master," came the response.

A moment later, the head of the burly captain appeared at the rail and he stared down at Jane with a deep scowl.

"Ye've a large set of balls, Captain, to come a'courting after keeping me in the dark in Elsinore. Last I saw your vessel, she was passing to starboard after stealing a march on me to the sugar docks in St. Petersburg." As he concluded, Captain Duncan crossed his arms and his frown grew even grimmer.

"Ah, Captain Duncan, I was just priming the pump, sir. Getting the audience warmed up for the main act, if you will," Jane replied with a large grin.

Duncan threw back his head and laughed. "Aye, ye've bested me at my own game, miss! Come aboard and tell me how ye' managed to escape that quarantine hell so damned quick."

Jane and the captain repaired to his spacious quarters where he treated her to a glass of port and a half hour of lively discussion of the various routes home. In the end, he agreed that the northern route would give them the best chance of making good time, and they arranged to sail in convoy. It meant that Jane might be delayed a few days should the winds drive the square-rigged brig back to the east, but she knew there was safety in numbers and she was no longer in competition with the *Jeremiah* for a market as Duncan's ship was loaded with Russian pig iron.

As she was climbing back down the side of the ship to the waiting water taxi, Duncan sighted the brigantine *Gazelle* passing the headland and preparing to signal for the river pilot.

"Ahoy, Captain Thorn! Captain Chaffee on the *Gazelle* will be making for New York as soon as she can load her provisions. Let us see if she will join us on our little adventure, shall we? I shall seek out her master as soon as they are settled. It sounds a right festive voyage, does it not?" Duncan shouted to her.

"Aye, that it does! We will bring the *Destiny* downriver on the morning of the twentieth at low tide and pick up a mooring. Will the *Jeremiah* be prepared to depart on the afternoon high water?"

"That she will, Captain Thorn. Good day to you."

When Jane returned to her hotel that evening, the clerk handed her a note from Captain Harrison. He had come by in the afternoon with the hope of seeing her, and would return in the morning. Jane was glad that he desired to speak with her, and hoped they might come to some understanding that would lead to an enduring friendship.

The sun was up when Jane awoke the next morning, but the early Nordic dawns were behind them now as the autumn chill arrived. She was finishing her breakfast in the dining room when the waiter brought her a note. Signed by Thaddeus, it asked if she would join him in the hotel parlor for coffee. Jane set it down on the table and took a deep breath, willing herself not to cry. How she wished that she could return the affections of the dear man, but her heart told her that it would be as lonely to live a lie as to live alone.

Straightening, she stood up and gathered her shawl from the back of the chair. As she entered the parlor a moment later, she saw Thaddeus stand and reach out his hand to her. She lost her battle with her tears and they streamed silently down her face as she stood helpless in the doorway.

Thaddeus came to her and enveloped her in his arms, holding her head to his chest as he stroked her hair.

"Dear Jane, how it pains me to see you so sad. And to think I am the cause of it," he murmured in her ear.

"Nay, dear Thaddeus," Jane extricated herself from his embrace, "I make myself sad. You have been nothing but the kindest of friends and I am undeserving of your forgiveness," she now openly sobbed.

"Perhaps I am not entirely blameless in the matter, my dear. I am older, and am supposed to be wiser for it. I fear in this case I have betrayed my age by not employing its wisdom. It was foolish of me to forget your position and see you only as the captivating woman you are. For this, I need to beg your forgiveness, dearest Jane," he said as he extended her a handkerchief

"I am so grateful you have come to see me, Thaddeus. I could not bear to sail home without knowing that we might still be friends." She accepted the handkerchief but still sniffled.

"Not see you? And miss retrieving the drawing you promised? It never crossed my mind! Now, buck up and fetch me my reward, dear friend. I shall wait here."

Jane knew he was giving her an excuse to return to her room and pull herself together. As ever, she was grateful for the simple decency of the man. When she returned with the charcoal rendering of the Nilsson guesthouse with the proprietors posed in front, he seemed genuinely pleased and admiring of her skill.

"It is a fine drawing, Jane. You have an excellent eye and a sure hand. Should you wish to send me other drawings as a token of our friendship, they would be well received, and would have pride of place in my home," he promised. "Now, let us drink our coffee before it is entirely cold and you shall tell me of your plans for your passage to the west."

Her final night in Gothenburg, Jane packed her few belongings into her knapsack and looked wistfully at the walking shoes that had taken her so many happy miles. She could not say that she regretted her time with the kind captain, but she did regret that she had not examined her own feelings before allowing him to read more into them than she truly felt. She vowed to herself that she would be more careful in the future, knowing that sometimes her intentions were not always known to others, and least of all to herself.

In keeping with her port visits in Matanzas and St. Petersburg, Jane had visited an inking den in the afternoon and added a delicate twinflower to her growing bouquet. She had seen thousands of the small, pink flowers growing in pairs on the forest floor during her walks in Hagatorp. It would remind her of her time in Sweden and of the friend she had found there.

On the morning of the twentieth, Jane set out for the wharf while it was still dark. She wanted to be well aboard before Bonenfant would appear at the watch change. All the better if she could catch her crew still asleep and give them a proper captain's dressing down, she smiled to herself. Alas, her mates were well ahead of her. As she turned the corner of the pier she saw a lantern hoisted on the *Destiny's* deck and heard the chief cry out,

"All hands! Sideboys form up. Pipe the captain aboard!"

She grinned as she stepped over the rail of her vessel to the sound of the bosun's whistle for the very first time in her career. By the light of the lamp, she saw her entire crew in formation at attention with their hands holding the corners of their caps in salute. She was moved by their display of respect, and returned the salute as if it were an ordinary thing.

"Thank you, Mister Dawkins. Carry on," she said as she turned to the quarterdeck stairs to descend to her cabin. In a few minutes, she heard the sound of the morning watch taking up their duties and Cookie bellowing that fresh coffee was to be had in the galley. It was good to be home.

Jane occupied herself over the next hour by putting her cabin to rights for the voyage and stowing her belongings. As was her way, she pulled out the charts and reviewed her course one final time. At seven bells, she heard the river pilot board and went above to greet him. She arranged to have him taken out of view to the galley, to be plied with coffee until she was ready to depart shortly after eight bells and the watch change. The tug captain was requested to wait at the bow for the pilot's signal, then she gave her final instructions to Dawkins before retiring to the saloon to await her expected guest.

"Keep him moving when he appears, Dawkins. Bring him right below and then cast off with as little noise as you can. I want to be well out in the river before he knows that aught is amiss."

"Aye, aye, Captain," he said, and disappeared back to the deck.

Jane returned to her cabin to fetch the final letter that would put an end to this troublesome matter, then cleared the saloon of all the chairs save her own. She sat down at the table in the remaining chair and waited to play the final card in her hand.

The clock had just gone eight when she heard a commotion on deck and then the sound of running feet approaching the saloon. She stood as the door was wrenched open and she was treated to the sight of Count Bonenfant holding a sword in front of him as her two mates brandished clubs.

"Back, you two dogs, or I will see that your captain pays the price for her arrogance and thievery," he snarled.

"Mister Dawkins, please remove the count's sword before I find it necessary to blow a hole clean through his hide." Jane was amazed at how steady her voice sounded as she delivered this threat. She lifted Dawkins' pistol from where it lay on the table in front of her and leveled it at the count's head.

Bonenfant could be seen to be weighing his options once again before choosing to hand his sword to the grinning Dawkins.

"Ye' can have it back when we put you overboard, ye' wharf rat," Dawkins said as he shoved Bonenfant through the door and closed it behind him.

Jane reseated herself and looked up at the count. She waited as he looked around the saloon for another chair. He turned to her with a sneer.

"I suppose you think yourself clever, don't you, captain,"

"Not particularly Count Bonenfant, but clearly cleverer than you," Jane replied.

"Where is my property? Tell me now or I shall sink your vessel and all aboard her," he threatened.

"Let us not be too hasty, shall we? We have a few matters to discuss before I deliver the gold to you. Rest assured that you will be in a position to retrieve it shortly. However, first is the matter of the note you had delivered to me at the house of your friend the marquis. I was truly flummoxed and unable to grasp the intent of the message you sought to deliver. Perhaps you could enlighten me now, sir," Jane said with a tilt of her head and a quizzical expression.

Bonenfant stared at her as he realized that a further insult at this juncture was unlikely to bring about the delivery of the missing coins into his waiting hands.

"Perhaps I was mistaken, ma'am. I simply wished to avoid any misunderstandings about the nature of our liaison."

"And what, pray tell, do you suppose to be its nature, Count Bonenfant?" Jane asked pleasantly. She paused while he considered his answer and then continued. "If you suppose it to be that you have abused my good nature for your own ends without regard for the welfare of my vessel and crew, and are thereby in my debt, you suppose correctly."

For the first time since arriving in her quarters, Bonenfant allowed his shoulders to slump as his eyes fell to the floor.

"What will you have of me, ma'am?"

As before, Jane was not fooled by the performance.

"Nothing, Count Bonenfant. Absolutely nothing. You and your petty schemes are as nothing in this world, and I wish for you that history will forget your name as we leave behind the insignificant aims and trappings of your corrupt aristocracy. And now, I will bid you adieu with this final instruction. In this envelope is the information you seek. Retrieval of the coins will require your presence in St. Petersburg, a place you have gone to great lengths to avoid. There is no escaping the journey should you wish to regain the gold, sir. I wish you Godspeed."

As Bonenfant reached out to snatch the envelope from her, he called out, *"Allons-y! À moi! Vite!"*

Jane smiled and opened her cabin door to point up the aft companionway where the hills of Gothenburg could be seen slipping quickly astern. "Your friends, sir, are a mile behind us. We will set you down as soon as we arrive at the fort and you may make your way back to them."

In consternation, Bonenfant gaped at the receding harbor, then lunged toward Jane with the clear intent to do her harm. He was pulled up short by Jane's knife, once again held in front of his face, and the steely look in the captain's eyes.

"No sir, that will not do. Dawkins!" she called to her mate where he waited in the passage. "Here is your pistol. Please feel free to use it should our guest prove troublesome before we send him overboard."

As she turned away, Jane could see the anger on Bonenfant's face, and guessed that he would not take easily to being bested by her yet again. Well, she thought, she was simply playing the game and had clearly won. He would just have to live with that.

Leaving Dawkins to mind Bonenfant, Jane returned to the deck to watch their progress down the river. As they reached the lower harbor, the pilot shouted to the captain of the tug that was pulling the *Destiny* downstream. The tug cast loose and steamed back to fetch the pilot, who scrambled quickly down the ladder into the boat, and pulled away. Captain Thorn promptly ordered the skiff lowered and Bonenfant rowed ashore.

"Macy, dump him on the first pier you come to, then row out to the *Jeremiah*. Tell Captain Duncan we will heave to off the coast. He may join us there with the *Gazelle* and return my boat and crewman. Go!"

As soon as the skiff was away, the remaining crew raised sail and set a course for a point a mile beyond the rocky islands that dotted the river mouth. There, they hove to and waited for the *Jeremiah* and the *Gazelle* to join them. The pair did not tarry long as they needed merely to slip their moorings. With no anchors to weigh, they were under sail within moments of receiving Macy's message.

Once she had her skiff and seaman Macy safely back aboard, the captain ordered Dawkins to trim the canvas and proceed north by northwest. Lifting her spyglass, she turned aft to watch the brigs release their own sails. As they fluttered and filled, she felt relieved to see the convoy finally headed home.

XXXI

Bound for New York

Wednesday, September 20   Lat. (chart) 57° 41'N   Long. (chart) 11° 48'E from which I take my departure. Sailed from Gothenburg at 10am. At 9 pm passed the Skagen light. Wind generally from South to SW.

Dawkins joined Jane on the quarterdeck to help guide her through the changes in course and tack required to keep the line as they passed out of the Kattegat and into the North Sea. The chief had sailed in convoy across the Atlantic several times, and Jane was glad to have his advice as she directed Griggs at the helm.

As soon as they were out of danger of grounding on the rocky shore, Dawkins mustered the crew on the afterdeck for the captain's customary remarks.

"Aye, men, we are on our way home!" Jane had barely begun before the men were cheering and waving their hats. She smiled as she continued, "We aim to round Sandy Hook in early November, so we have a way to go. But you are all coming home with much to show for your hard work these past months, even those of you who emptied your pockets in the bars of Gothenburg."

The men eyed each other as Jane paused, and wondered how much she had heard of the goings on while she was on holiday and away from the crew. It was not really her place to chide them on their doings ashore, but they found themselves wanting her respect. More than one of the men hoped the captain would never hear of some of the high times they had enjoyed in low places.

"Every last one of you has shown himself to be a stalwart fellow and I take it upon myself to offer each of you a place in the Thorn fleet once we have returned. You won't get better wages or a squarer deal, so think on it while we sail home!"

A final cheer went up as the captain raised her hat to the men and led them in three "Huzzahs".

Saturday, September 23   Lat. Obs. 59° 42'N   Long. DR 1° 36'W   Passed Fair Isle today. Wind from SW. Whale sighting.

The captain felt she had been neglecting the training of the two ship's boys under her care and meant to remedy that on the passage home. Each day at noon, she ordered them onto the quarterdeck with her and Dawkins so they could try their hand at taking the sighting. Hitchens was a fast learner and could already do the calculations as fast as the chief mate. He had been filling the role of ordinary seaman since Vaugine had come aboard in Cuba, and Galsworthy was well pleased with his progress. He was a serious lad who applied himself to a task, and Jane knew he would do well in the merchant service if he decided to make it his livelihood.

He and Boniface had joined Jane in the saloon after the midday meal to practice their penmanship by copying the ship's log. They were sighing and fidgeting as they worked, making it clear to all observers that they were well bored with the work and ready to leave off in favor of more active pursuits. When the lookout shouted "Thar she blows!" they threw down their pens and sprinted for the foredeck before Jane could open her mouth to chide them.

The crew had crowded onto the starboard rail when Jane came forward to see what the commotion was about. She took a step backward as she looked over the side and saw a large whale and her calf surface just a few feet from the *Destiny*. Her hand flew to her throat as the pair breached and then breached again right near the hull. They blew noisily out of their spouts as they surfaced the second time, and the stench was enough to drive everyone back from the rail.

"Macy," she called. "You are experienced in the pursuit of whales. What sort is that?"

"It is a Fin whale, ma'am, and she won't bother us none. She just wants to keep her calf breathing and is paying more attention to the babe than to us," he replied. "I guess they come down from the north sometimes, from where the whaling ships harry them."

The pair lazed in the water near the *Destiny* for another twenty minutes or so before diving and disappearing for good. The site of the two animals up close had been awe-inspiring and Jane was most eager for the next time they might see one of the impressive creatures. She had never seen anything larger than a dolphin as she traded up and down the east coast, in part because the New Bedford and Nantucket whalermen had been ruthlessly efficient at hunting the beasts and there were few left in those waters.

Wednesday, September 27 Lat. DR 60° 15'N Long. DR 6° 00'W Thick weather from the 24 to the 26 September. The wind from WSW to WNW. Hard gales and very heavy sea. Brigs laboring much, making much water. Making and taking in sail and wearing ship on occasion. Just holding their own.

The last week of September brought storms and heavy seas to the north Atlantic. There were no reports of hurricanes yet this season when they left Gothenburg, and Jane wondered if they were feeling the effects of the first autumn storm.

Maintaining the convoy line was becoming increasingly difficult as the square-rigged brigs were blown backward despite their captains' best efforts to make westing. The fore-and-aft rig of the schooner allowed the *Destiny* to meet headwinds close hauled and proceed on their designated course, but she was forced to heave to for several days and wait for the winds to shift so the brigs could once again make headway. The delay was costly as it meant additional days of crew provisions and wages. Jane decided it was time to consider leaving the group and striking out on their own.

"What say you, Mr. Dawkins? Are we better off making our way as best we can? Or shall we hang back in hopes the wind will cooperate?" She had called her mates into the saloon to talk over the situation as they rode out the weather and made little progress to the west.

"Aye, we are fighting the westerlies, but the luck seems particularly bad this voyage for those brigs, ma'am. Mayhap we wait another day to see if the winds swing round."

As night fell with no change in the conditions, Jane ordered the sheets loosened and a second reef taken in the sails to slow the schooner further and give them more sea room in the dark. Captain Duncan ordered lanterns hung at the stern of the *Jeremiah* while Jane instructed the crew hang their own lamps from the bowsprit and taffrail. In the distance, they could see bow lights from the *Gazelle*, and so the convoy rode out the night.

Sunday, October 1   Lat. Obs. 59° 27'N   Long. DR 16° 12'W   First part wind from West, middle calm, latter wind squalls SSW, left convoy at noon, agreed positioning with Gazelle + Jeremiah

The first break in the relentless westerly winds came on Sunday the first of October. Jane calculated that the convoy was making less than three knots on average toward their destination. She knew the *Destiny* could improve on that speed. It was time to strike out on their own. When the winds dropped in the last part of the morning, she signaled the other two captains for a parlay while they sat becalmed. The helmsmen brought the vessels within two cables of each other and the boats were put out to windward.

"Aye, Jane Thorn, if my guess is right, thou are about to leave us sluggards behind, eh?" Captain Chaffee asked as soon as the captains had convened in the Destiny's saloon.

"I regret to say I think we can make better progress against this headwind, sir." Jane agreed.

"You are no doubt right. Unless our luck improves we may be going backward a bit more before we reach harbor. But get there we will, and you will stand us a round in New York when we finally make land!" Captain Duncan agreed with a laugh.

"Ah, I can do better than that, gentlemen." Jane reached under the table, where she had tucked the last two bottles of her favorite port, and handed one to each captain. "Think of me kindly when you partake, sirs!"

Captain Duncan waved his bottle toward the other brig master, "I told you she was a straight-up gal. Those Thorns know what is important in life, I said, did I not? Thank 'ee, ma'am, and we will drink to your health every time we find ourselves headed in the wrong direction!"

"And I anticipate extending an invitation to dinner with Uncle Josias when you arrive. Bless you and your crews and look for me at the journey's end."

The three captains shook hands and the brig captains were rowed back to their vessels.

On board the *Destiny*, Jane gave orders to make what headway they could to the south, away from the wind shadow of the brigs. As soon as they began to pick up speed, Jane turned and waved to the *Jeremiah* and the *Gazelle*. She smiled when she saw each of the captains standing at the rail with a raised glass in his hand.

Monday, October 23   Lat. Obs. 41° 17'N   Long. DR 67° 39'W   First part strong breezes from NNE to NE middle moderate latter part moderate wind from E and ESE Thick rainy weather

It had been four days since the *Destiny* dropped below the latitude of Nova Scotia, and the winds had sheered around to follow them from the east and north. She picked up speed and was making good time toward home; Jane was optimistic they would reach port by the end of the month. The weather had turned cold and the crew hunkered around the wood-burning stoves in the forecastle and saloon when not on watch. Jane strove to stand alternately with the larboard and starboard watch so that her men would know she was willing to face the same hardships; Galsworthy let her know that the crew noticed.

It had been squally all day but the sun finally broke through as the afternoon watch came on duty. Jane asked her chief to muster all hands on the afterdeck, then climbed the quarterdeck stairs to address her men.

"All right, crew, we have rounded Nova Scotia and are on the down hill run toward home. If the winds keep up, we should see port by the end of the month. So what do you say? An extra day's wages for every twenty-four hours before the thirty first of October that we arrive!"

Even a well-trimmed vessel could be made to eke out more speed if the men were motivated. At the end of a five-month journey, things aboard had settled into a routine. Jane hoped to spur the men to extra effort to keep the sails trimmed and the heading as close to the course as possible to push the *Destiny* just a tiny bit faster. It seemed as if the schooner was as eager to be home as her crew; she responded with a leap forward when the hands ran to the sheets to adjust her sails and wring another knot of speed out of her.

In the evening, Jane asked Galsworthy to send Vaugine to her when he came off watch. She heard a knock on the saloon door just as she was finishing her evening meal, and bade him enter.

"Good evening, Vaugine, pray join me by the warmth," she waved the man into the room.

Doffing his cap, the tall seaman ducked his head and entered.

"Mister Vaugine, have you given thought to what the future holds once we arrive in New York?" she asked once he had settled himself near the stove.

"Aye, ma'am, that I have. I saw many ships from America in St. Petersburg, where the language of business would seem to be French. I thought I might make myself useful to the merchants of New York in writing correspondence and the like."

"May I take it that you are minded never to go to sea again?" Poor Vaugine had spent three days in his bunk again on the way home after they left Gothenburg. By the time he ceased purging and could stand, he looked emaciated and wan. While he went about his duties with a willing and cheerful attitude, it was obvious the man was suffering.

"Aye, ma'am, that is my intent," Vaugine responded with a decided tone.

"Aye, I thought so. Well, your fate is your own, and you will make enough on this voyage to pay off the note. So you are free to do as you please. May I recommend you to my uncle to take you into his business? We are looking to expand our trade to the Baltic States and it seems you would be of great help to us there."

Vaugine smiled, "I would be most pleased, ma'am, and am honored to have your trust. Thank you for your kind words." With that, he stood and bowed, then saluted as he left the cabin.

Jane knew her uncle would like the man, and he was always in need of good clerks, especially now that their business was growing rapidly. The Erie Canal was due to open in a few years and the firm intended to expand their Hudson River trade west as soon as the canal-way was ready. They had already formed a consortium with a riverboat company in Albany to forward trade goods on the barges, leaving the question of whether it was time to invest in steam.

Before settling into her berth that night, Jane took out pen and paper to compose a brief note to Endeavor. She hoped to send it upriver as soon as they arrived at the Thorn company wharf, and to follow it herself within a day.

Jane had done much thinking over the prior weeks as she watched the miles slip away under the schooner's keel. Increasingly as the months passed, she found her thoughts turning to Endeavor, anxious to share with him all of the sights and sounds of her adventure. She had collected a small trove of treasures for him – things she knew would make him laugh, or send him off to his books to investigate. Each time, she had thought, "for my friend" as she tucked the item away. She had pulled them all out yesterday to arrange them and make notes for the dear soul. He would want to know everything she could tell him about the objects, and the drawings she had made of things she could not bring with her such as the volantes of Cuba.

As she worked, she found herself thinking, "for my love" and knew that she had in some manner settled things in her mind. Her only fear was that Endeavor had come to a change of heart during her absence, and was now occupied elsewhere. She would simply have to trust that their bond was deep enough to have endured the separation.

Dearest E,

If this letter has been put into your hand prior to my delivering myself to you, know that I am following closely behind. The Destiny has brought us safely home, and my steps will turn northward as soon as my business in town is accomplished.

Your wandering friend who has wandered back to you,

I remain, yours truly,
Jane

Monday, October 30   Lat. DR.   40° 22'N   Long. DR 73° 37'W   First part calm Middle and latter strong breezes from E thick rainy weather. Pilot will board in early morn.

Jane stood on the quarterdeck straining to see ahead into the mist. The winds had died over the last three days and the *Destiny* was making slow progress toward port. Dead reckoning placed them a scant fifteen miles from the channel up the East River, but the lookout was unable to see more than a few dozen feet in any direction.

"All right, Mister Dawkins, let us heave to here and put up the lanterns. Get the watch onto ringing the fog bell and drop an anchor."

"Aye, aye, ma'am. I thought I spied a skiff inbound afore this fog thickened up, so we may have a pilot aboard before long."

"Well, we shall have to wait until morning to try for shore. We will never make it before dusk and I don't like my chances in the dark even with the pilot and the tugs."

No sooner had she finished speaking than they heard the bump of a boat on the larboard beam and the cry, "Ahoy the *Destiny*! Mister Soames of the Sandy Hook Pilots. Permission to come aboard?"

"My goodness, Mister Soames, permission granted," Jane called back. "How in blazes did you find us, may I ask?" she watched the shivering pilot as he climbed over the rail.

"Aye, ma'am. I saw you scootin' in along the beach and I thought to be the one to welcome you home since I saw you off last spring. How fare ye' all, if I may inquire?"

"Come below, Mister Soames, for some hot coffee and a warm up by the stove, and I shall tell you," she said as she led the way aft. As they entered the saloon, Soames stripped off his oilskin coat and rubbed his hands by the heat. Cookie delivered two mugs of steaming brew a few minutes later, and the pilot took a large swig before settling back in his chair with a sigh.

"I hope we shan't be a disappointment, Mister Soames, but we will wait out the night at anchor and try for port in the morning. May I ask you to return then?"

"Aye, ma'am, there's no one aiming to take their vessels in tonight, so I am free to set awhile and hear of your adventures."

Soames listened and sipped his coffee while Jane related a few stories of their voyage, leaving out the saga of Bonenfant and the hidden gold. Best to tell uncle Josias that story herself before the tale was spread on the waterfront and beyond. An hour later, Soames deemed himself warm and dry enough to head back to shore. He agreed to post a note to her uncle, send off the letter to Endeavor, and return at the start of the forenoon watch to bring the *Destiny* home.

After Soames left, Jane returned to her cabin to find Dawkins hard at work with the cargo manifests and crew papers. As soon as they arrived, Jane would clear the crew and shipment for landing while Dawkins arranged for the cargo to be offloaded into her uncle's warehouse. She would report with the logbook and papers from the journey to the business office immediately afterward to give an accounting of the voyage and the crew. Then, she would be free to head upriver to Newburgh and the friends and family waiting there. It was enormously frustrating to be sitting at anchor so close to home.

XXXII

Home

New York, New York
End of October, 1820

Dawn broke with a clear sky and light winds from the east on the final day of October. All hands were on deck busily preparing to land and everyone was in a jolly mood. Jane had followed through on her promise of an extra day's wages for having arrived at the mouth of the bay on the thirtieth. The trip from Gothenburg had taken forty-one days, which Jane knew was an excellent time. The crew was healthy, the cargo intact, and the *Destiny* newly repaired. The captain felt that she had done well for the company, especially with the substantial profit they made prior to arrival. It would be up to her uncle's brokers to make the most of the iron and pottery in her hold, but she knew the trip had been a success, and she felt a great sense of relief to have carried it off.

Jane stood at the bow watching the pilot return as Hitchens ran the house flag up the starboard shroud. The white burgee sporting blue stripes top and bottom and a red letter "T" in the center flapped gaily in the light breeze as Soames came aboard and they prepared to weigh anchor.

Soon, they had cleared Sandy Hook and the tugs were waiting to pull them the final mile up the river and home. As when they had left five months earlier, the river was teeming with vessels, and the docks were lined with every type of ship imaginable. New York was the busiest of the American ports, becoming busier each year, and Jane was glad to be back among the bustle and sights of the city. She stood on the quarterdeck behind the pilot and watched the shore slide by until they spotted the Thorn wharf ahead. At the end of the dock, a familiar figure stood and waved, then ran to meet the Destiny as her lines were taken ashore.

"Jinks. Jinks. You have returned! Welcome home, dear girl." Josias shouted from the dock as the schooner glided the last few feet. As soon as the side touched, Jane jumped down and threw her arms around her uncle, momentarily ignoring the harbormaster and customs officials who were waiting to receive them. She lingered in his embrace a moment, then pulled back smiling broadly.

"Aye, here I am, uncle, and all is well. I shall not tarry long, and will join you as soon as I have visited with these gentlemen."

With an approving nod, Josias gave her a final pat on the arm and made his way back to the head of the pier to await the captain. There, he stood and watched proudly as she conducted the firm's business with the government representatives, then mustered her crew for a final send-off and a few words of farewell before Dawkins handed them their pay packets and sent them ashore. When she finally turned to meet him, she had in tow a crewmember that could only be Vaugine, the man she had picked up in Cuba. Curious to meet him, Josias stuck out his hand in greeting.

"Good day to you, my man. You must be Vaugine," he said. "I am Captain Josias Thorn."

Vaugine responded with a deep bow and then a salute. "*Bonjour, Capitaine* Thorn. It is a pleasure to make your acquaintance, sir."

"I shall tell you more once we are arrived at the office, but I have assured Vaugine that he would be welcome at Thorn Shipping. Shall I have him report round in the morning, uncle?" Jane asked.

"Aye, you will be most welcome, Mister Vaugine. Now, Jinks," he said, turning to his niece, "let us walk together while you tell me all that has happened!"

Jane spent the remainder of the day conferring with the firm's accountants and brokers and arranging for the disposition of the cargo. Josias assured her he had sent word ahead to Newburgh that she had arrived safely and would be home on the morrow.

The long day drew to a close and Jane stepped into the

family coach with her uncle for the journey to the house on Beekman Street in the early evening. There, her aunt Margaret and the children surrounded her with happy cries of welcome, dragging her into the parlor to be fussed over before sitting down to eat. She was still finding her land legs, so staggered a bit as she went in to dinner, much to the amusement of her nieces and nephew. She had brought them presents from Russia, and they were happily distracted tearing open the wrapping to exclaim over the dolls and carved animals she had purchased at the market near the dock.

After the children had been sent to bed, she relaxed with her aunt and uncle in front of the drawing room fire. It felt good to once again sit on a chair that did not rock on a floor did not rise and fall below her. Coming ashore had been an adjustment each time they landed on their voyage. She was not accustomed to weeks of seafaring at a time, and found the change from land to sea and back to land disconcerting. She knew she would find her legs soon enough. In the meantime, she would just hang on to things for a while when she walked.

"So my dear," her aunt asked, "how does it suit you, this life at sea?"

Jane pondered her reply for a moment. "The life suits me just fine, Aunt Meg, and I feel that I likewise suit the life. Were it not for having to leave you all behind, I would set out again tomorrow. But the leaving is hard, and I do not relish having to do it again. However, the coming home is all the sweeter for it!"

"Yes, that is true enough, Jane. Every time Josias left, I was sure my heart would break. But the reunion on his return was always, shall we say, very warm," her aunt replied with an unconscious upward gaze to where their four children could be heard noisily preparing for bed.

"Ah, you make me blush, my dear," her uncle said with a laugh. "But aye, Jinks, it is a lonely time at sea and one longs for home although the life is grand."

"And will you want to set off again so soon?" Aunt Meg asked. "I am sure Josias could find another customer rather easily once word of the profits this trip has made is spread around."

"Well, that will be a question for another day, I am afraid!" Jane replied. "For now, I need to excuse myself and lay my head on a soft pillow in a bed that does not sway beneath me. And when I awake in the morning, I fully mean to use every drop of hot water your maids can fetch for my bath."

With a lingering embrace, Jane made her exit and climbed the stairs, anxious for tomorrow, and the trip home to Newburgh.

In the morning, Jane spent a luxurious half hour in the bath before dressing in one of her sensible gowns. She pulled her greatcoat on over her simple lawn shift and wrapped a warm muffler around her throat to ward off the chill of the first of November. She bid good-bye to her family, pushed her hat on her head, and set off for the steamboat dock. She would be home by the early afternoon, and each minute seemed an hour as she thought of those who would be awaiting her at journey's end.

The steam whistle blew as the boat turned for the dock in Newburgh, announcing its arrival. From where she stood at the bow, Jane could see her father and sister, along with her sister's family, waving madly from the top of the pier. Searching further, she finally spied Endeavor where he stood with an armful of flowers at the end of the gangplank. As soon as it was pushed aboard, Jane ran across it and threw herself into the tall man's arms.

As he pulled back to wipe away the tears she had not known were there, he held the flowers up for her to view. "Thou can see," he said, "I find myself resorting to all manner of pagan practices in thy honor, dearest Jane."

Epilogue

St. Petersburg
October 5, 1820

The clerks at Stieglitz & Co. had mostly gone home for the evening, leaving Whithers to mind the anteroom and run any errands required by the two agents working within. Few clients came to the office late in the day, so he pulled out the daily paper from the bottom drawer of the desk and was resting with his feet propped on a stool when the front door opened.

A rather rough-looking individual dressed in seaman's garb with a watch cap pulled low over his eyes sauntered into the room with the sailor's typical rolling gait.

"Fairchild, here to see Agent Mackey," the man growled.

Dropping his feet to the floor, Whithers stood up and said, "Wait right here, sir, while I find out if he will see you."

He had no more than turned his back to open the door to the inner room when he felt the seaman reach past him to push his way through. After the verbal drubbing the clerk received from the principal about Captain Thorn's high-handed entrances a couple of months ago, Whithers was taking no chances with letting any further visitors past his desk unannounced.

"Oh no you don't, sir!" he yelled and stepped quickly in front of the man.

Before Whithers could blink an eye, Fairchild had landed a solid blow to his jaw, knocking the young man senseless as he fell backward onto the floor. The seaman yanked open the door and followed the sound of the only voice in the room to an office marked Mister Mackey at the back. Within, he saw the agent in friendly conversation with a man seated across from him smoking a cigar. They were obviously enjoying a moment of leisure as Fairchild stepped into the office.

"Are you Mackey?" he demanded of the man behind the desk.

"And who, may I ask, are you? And where is Whithers? Damn it, has he let you past him? I don't know why I even pay that boy! Whithers!" Mackey shouted.

"Your clerk got in my way, sir, and I left him on the floor. Now, I mean to conduct my business with you in private if you please," Fairchild said in a more moderate tone and eyed the gentleman seated in the chair to his left.

"What is your name, sir, and what business have you with me?" Mackey glared back at him.

"Fairchild."

"Ah. Lewis, we shall continue this interesting topic at another point as I do, in fact, have business with this person," Mackey said as he ushered his prior visitor to the door then closed it behind him.

"Mister Fairchild, please have a seat," he said, and waved to the newly vacated chair.

"I am content standing. Now pray hand over the letter which I understand you have in safekeeping for me."

"Suit yourself, man. Yes, I will deliver the document to you, but there was a stipulation placed on my relinquishing it. Namely, you are to answer a simple question, and it is this: What was she wearing?"

"How the blazes should I know that?" Fairchild yelled. "If I remember correctly, the answer is 'nothing'!" He had at this point abandoned all pretense of dignity and was fixated on acquiring the letter and departing as swiftly as possible.

"No, sir, that is most decidedly not the answer, and I will have to ask you to leave the premises if you continue in this insulting manner," Mackey stated firmly.

Fairchild paused to think for a moment, then threw back his head and laughed.

"Aye, the minx, I know what she was getting at. The answer is 'perfume', sir. And now may I have the letter please," Fairchild stretched out his hand.

Mackey retrieved the paper from his safe and was frankly relieved to be finally quit of the thing. He suspected there might be something amiss with the transaction, and the appearance of the fellow before him confirmed his suspicions. Nevertheless, he couldn't help but offer his advice in the interest of saving the man some trouble.

"Perhaps you would be better off reading that here, and burning it before departing," he suggested.

"I know my own business, sir," Fairchild sneered, and left as hastily as he had arrived.

Shaking his head, Mackey reflected he was pleased to be quit of this matter. There had been something unsettling about the whole thing. He went in search of Whithers and was soon focused on attempting to revive him.

St. Petersburgische Gazette, October 7, 1820:

A disturbance was reported in the dock area yesterday evening. The harbor watch of His Majesty's police apprehended several individuals engaged in suspicious activity and have taken them into custody. No further information is available at this time.

Author's Note

1820 was an interesting time in history in Europe and the Americas. The newly independent United States had fought a second round with Great Britain to secure their interests at home and on the seas, France was in turmoil as Napoleon Bonaparte had left behind a band of supporters who had still not given up the idea of an imperial restoration. The Age of Sail was slowly coming to a close as steamships began plying coastal waters and shipbuilders were pioneering cheaper, safer, and swifter steam-powered designs.

How much of Jane's world is based in historical fact? Nearly all of it. The retreating Bonaparte really had a plan to blow up the Kremlin. And one of his field marshals was elected king of Sweden. All of the shipwrecks are real, unfortunately, as is the description of trade and merchant activities in the West Indies and the Baltic, including the quarantine. The *Destiny's* travels are based on the real-life journeys of several vessels from the early 19th century, including the log entries and events such as the finding of the oil cask.

Most importantly, how accurate is the idea of a young woman filling the role of shipmaster in 1820? Perhaps not as unlikely as you may think. While the vast majority of captains were men, there were plenty of women who went to sea as crew and, occasionally, officers, not always in men's clothing. Emilie Flygare Carlén, born in 1807 in western Sweden to a merchant captain, was running her own vessel in the cargo trade by her late teens, for example. So Jane is an unusual character, but not an impossible one.

Thanks for purchasing and reading *Destiny's Gold*, I hope you enjoyed it.

A lot of people don't realize that the best way to help an author is to leave a review. So, if you had fun accompanying Jane and her crew on their voyage, please return to the site you purchased this book from and say a few words. It doesn't have to be long, just saying what you thought is fine and much appreciated. It also helps other readers make an informed decision about their purchases.

I love hearing from readers and authors alike, so if you'd like to stay in touch and be the first to know about forthcoming books and what I am up to, please visit me at:

www.pamelagrimmauthor.com/

www.facebook.com/pamelagrimmauthor

Printed in Great Britain
by Amazon

29664719R00128